Armistead Maupin was born in Washington, D.C. in 1944 but grew up in Raleigh, North Carolina. A graduate of the University of North Carolina, he served as a naval officer in Vietnam before moving to California in 1971 as a reporter for the Associated Press. In 1976 he launched his daily newspaper serial, *Tales of the City*, in the *San Francisco Chronicle*. The first fiction to appear in an American daily for decades, *Tales* grew into an international sensation when compiled and rewritten as novels. Maupin's six-volume *Tales of the City* sequence – *Tales of the City*, *More Tales of the City*, *Further Tales of the City*, *Babycakes*, *Significant Others* and *Sure of You* – are now multi-million bestsellers published in eleven languages. The first two of these novels were adapted as a pair of widely acclaimed television mini-series: the third, *Further Tales of the City*, is currently in production. Maupin's 1992 novel, *Maybe the Moon*, chronicling the adventures of the world's shortest woman, was a number one bestseller. As a librettist he collaborated in 1999 with composer Jake Heggie on *Anna Madrigal Remembers* for mezzo-soprano Frederica von Stade and Chanticleer, the classical choral ensemble. Maupin's latest novel is *The Night Listener*. He lives in San Francisco, California.

Official Author Web Site:
www.ArmisteadMaupin.com

D0239115

Also by Armistead Maupin

TALES OF THE CITY
MORE TALES OF THE CITY
FURTHER TALES OF THE CITY
BABYCAKES
SIGNIFICANT OTHERS
MAYBE THE MOON
THE NIGHT LISTENER

and published by Black Swan

Sure of You

Armistead Maupin

BLACK SWAN

SURE OF YOU
A BLACK SWAN BOOK : 0 552 99881 8

Originally published in Great Britain
by Chatto & Windus Ltd

PRINTING HISTORY
Chatto edition published 1990
Black Swan edition published 1991

13 15 17 19 20 18 16 14

This book is set in 11/12½pt Mallard
by Colset Private Limited, Singapore.

Black Swan Books are published by Transworld Publishers,
61–63 Uxbridge Road, London W5 5SA,
a division of The Random House Group Ltd,
in Australia by Random House Australia (Pty) Ltd,
20 Alfred Street, Milsons Point, Sydney, NSW 2061, Australia,
in New Zealand by Random House New Zealand Ltd,
18 Poland Road, Glenfield, Auckland 10, New Zealand
and in South Africa by Random House (Pty) Ltd,
Endulini, 5a Jubilee Road, Parktown 2193, South Africa.

Printed and bound in Great Britain by
Cox & Wyman Ltd, Reading, Berkshire.

For Ian McKellen

Piglet sidled up to Pooh from behind.
'Pooh!' he whispered.
'Yes, Piglet?'
'Nothing,' said Piglet, taking Pooh's paw.
'I just wanted to be sure of you.'

A. A. MILNE
The House at Pooh Corner

Pretty Is

There was something different about his wife's face, Brian Hawkins had decided. Something around the mouth, maybe. It was there at the corners, where her real mood always showed, even at a moment like this, when she certainly couldn't want it to show. He tilted his head until his eyes were even with hers, then withdrew a little, like someone appraising a portrait.

God, she was pretty! She gave depth to pretty, investing it with seriousness and intent. But something was eating at her, nibbling away from inside, while she sat there smiling, nodding, speaking softly of pet bereavement.

'And Fluffy is . . . ?'

'A Pomeranian,' replied this morning's guest, a big, blowsy matron straight out of Laurel and Hardy.

'And when did she . . . pass away?'

The pause was masterful, he thought. Mary Ann's gentle little search for the euphemism was either admirably kind or savagely funny, depending on the sophistication of the viewer.

'Three months ago,' said the matron. 'Almost four.'

Poor old cow, he thought. Headed straight for the slaughterhouse.

'So you decided to have her . . . ?'

'Freeze-dried,' said the woman.

'Freeze-dried,' said Mary Ann.

There was nervous tittering in the studio audience. Nervous because Mary Ann had yet to abandon her respectful, funereal face. Be nice to this lady, it said. She's a human being like anyone else. As usual, it was hugely effective. Mary Ann was never caught with blood on her hands.

His partner, Michael, walked into the nursery office, dropped his work gloves on the counter, draped an arm across Brian's shoulders. 'Who's she got today?'

'Watch,' said Brian, turning up the sound. The woman was opening a wooden carrying case, shaped like a doghouse. 'She's my child,' she was saying, 'my precious little baby. She's never been just a dog to me.'

Michael frowned at the set. 'Whatthefuck.'

The camera moved in for a tight shot as Mary Ann silenced the gigglers with another glance. The woman plunged her chubby hands into the box and produced her precious Fluffy, fluffy as ever.

'It's not moving,' said Michael.

'It's dead,' Brian told him. 'Freeze-dried.'

While Michael hooted, the woman arranged the rigid beast on her lap, patting its snowy fur into place. To Brian she seemed horribly vulnerable. Her lip trembled noticeably as her eyes darted back and forth between the audience and her inquisitor.

'There are some people,' said Mary Ann, even more gently than before, 'who might find this . . . unusual.'

'Yes.' The woman nodded. 'But she keeps me company. I can always pet her.' She demonstrated this feature half-heartedly, then gave Mary Ann a look of excruciating innocence. 'Would you like to try it?'

Mary Ann shot the quickest of takes to the audience. The camera, as usual, was ready for her. As the studio reverberated with laughter, Brian reached out and slapped the set off with his palm.

'Hey,' said Michael. 'That was good stuff.'

'She was set up,' said Brian.

'C'mon. You don't go on TV with a freeze-dried dog and not expect a little teasing.'

'Did you see her face, man? She wasn't expecting that.'

'Hey, fellas,' said a customer in the doorway.

'Oh,' blurted Michael. 'Find what you need?'

'Yeah. If someone could help me load them . . .'

Brian jumped to his feet. 'Hey . . . fix you right up.'

The woman strode – no, slinked – through several aisles of shrubbery, making her selections. Brian followed her, feeling a boner growing in his overalls, then lugged the cans back to the office, where he tallied her bill and clipped the cans.

'Will that be all?'

She handed him her Visa card. 'That'll do it.' Her hair was brick red and sleek as sealskin. Something watching from behind her molten eyes made him think she might be shopping for more than shrubbery.

Fumbling, he ran her card through the machine.

'You been here long?' she asked.

'Uh . . . me or the nursery?'

Her mouth flickered. 'You.'

'I've been here three years, I guess.'

She tapped her long fingers on the countertop. 'I used to come here when it was called something else.'

'God's Green Earth.'

'Oh, yeah.' She smiled. 'I like Plant Parenthood better.'

'Yeah, so do I.'

He removed the slip and handed it to her with a pen. She signed it with a flourish, then ripped the carbons into neat little squares, smirking at him all the while. 'Not that I don't trust that face,' she said.

He felt himself reddening. *You fucking dork. How long has it been, anyway?*

'Think I could tax those muscles?'

'What? Oh . . . sure.'

'My car's down the street.'

11

He gestured toward the cans. 'Is this all?' Of course this is all, asshole. You just rang up the purchase, didn't you?

'That's it.' She wet her lips with a cat's precision, touching only the corners with the tip of her tongue.

He had grabbed two of the cans when Polly came bolting into the office. 'Need a hand with those?'

'That's OK,' he said.

'You sure?'

'Yeah.'

His employee sauntered around the shrubs as if to size up the situation for herself. 'You can't do three.'

'Says who?'

Polly gave him a half-lidded smile and a courtly little sweep of the hand, as if to say: She's all yours, greedy. Polly was young enough to be his daughter, but she could be pretty damn intuitive when it came to sex.

The woman looked at Brian, then at Polly, then at Brian again.

'OK,' he told Polly. 'Gimme a hand.'

Flashing a freckled grin, Polly hefted two of the cans and strode out of the office. 'Where to?'

'Over there,' the woman told her. 'The Land Rover.'

Polly led the way down the sidewalk, her tank top wet at the breastbone, her silky biceps made wooden by her cargo. Behind her strode the redhead, pale and cool as marble, her ass looking awesome in a knee-length white sweater. Brian brought up the rear, lugging his lone plant and feeling, against his better instincts, less a man for it.

'This is nice of you,' said the woman.

'No problem,' said Polly.

'You bet,' Brian put in idiotically. 'Part of the service.'

They stuffed the cans into the back of the Land Rover, Polly pondering the placement a lot longer than usual. 'That oughta hold you,' she said at last, whacking one of the cans.

'Thanks.' The redhead smiled at Polly, then slipped behind the wheel and pulled the door shut.

'Remember,' Brian said, dropping his voice conspiratorially. 'Keep 'em real wet. I know we've got a drought on, but they'll die if you don't.'

'I'll do it at night,' she said, looking at both of them, 'when the neighbors aren't looking.'

He laughed. 'There you go.'

'Thanks again.' She turned on the ignition.

'Nice car,' said Polly.

The redhead nodded. 'She's all right.' She pulled away from the curb, flashing her palm in a sort of parting salute. Brian and Polly watched until the car had disappeared around the corner.

'She's been here before,' Polly told him as they walked back to the nursery.

'Oh, yeah?'

She nodded, scratching a fleck of dirt off her cheek. 'I'd have those panty hose off so fast . . .'

Brian smirked at her sideways.

'You would too,' she said.

'Nah.'

'C'mon.'

'In a pinch, maybe.'

Polly chuckled.

'You think she likes girls?' he asked.

She shrugged. 'Maybe. Maybe not.'

'I thought she might be one of yours.'

'Why?'

He thought about this for a moment. 'She called her car 'she,' for one thing.'

'Huh?' Polly screwed up her face.

'Her car. She referred to it as a she.'

'And you think that's some kinda . . . what? secret lesbo code?'

He shrugged.

'I call my car Dwayne,' she said.

13

He smiled, picturing Polly behind the wheel of her vintage Mustang.

'You're something,' she said. 'You check 'em all out, don't you?'

'Look who's talking,' he said. 'I thought you found your main woman last month.'

'Who?'

'Whoever. That one you met at Rawhide II.'

Polly rolled her eyes.

'Done with her, huh?'

No answer.

Brian chuckled.

'What?'

'How long did that last, anyway?'

With her ragged haircut and guilty grin, Polly looked like something out of Norman Rockwell: a truant school-kid, maybe, caught red-handed at the fishing hole.

'You know,' he told her, 'you're worse than any man I know.'

'That's because' – she moved alongside him and bumped him with her lean little butt – 'I'm *better* than any man you know.'

Polly's teasing aside, he was hardly the rogue he used to be. He hadn't strayed from home for over three years now, ever since Geordie Davies got sick. Diagnosed several weeks before Rock Hudson's announcement, Geordie had lasted almost two years longer than the movie star, finally succumbing offstage, at her sister's house, somewhere in Oklahoma.

He had offered to care for her himself – with Mary Ann's knowledge – but she had dismissed the idea with a laugh. They had been playmates, not lovers, she'd told him. 'Don't make us into something we weren't. We had a good time, pilgrim. Your services are no longer required.'

When his test came back negative, his relief had been

14

so profound that he embarked on a regime of feverish domesticity. Now he rented movies and baked brownies and stayed at home with his daughter, even on the nights when Mary Ann had 'important' parties to attend. He had lost his stomach altogether for the sycophants and socialites who revolved around his famous wife.

If something had been lost between him and Mary Ann, it was nothing dramatic, nothing he could pinpoint with certainty. Their sex life still flourished (though it slacked off dramatically during ratings periods), and over the years they had grown increasingly adept at avoiding arguments.

Sometimes, though, he wondered if they weren't *too* careful in each other's presence, too formal and solicitous and artificially jolly. As if their domestic arrangement were no more than that: an arrangement, which demanded courtesy in the absence of the real thing.

Or maybe, as she often suggested, he was just over-analyzing again.

He was back in the office, updating the work schedule on the computer, when Michael's beeper sounded. He tracked the shrill plastic disk to the pocket of his partner's cardigan, clicked it off, and took it out into the greenhouse, where he found Michael on his knees, potting succulents.

'Oh, thanks,' he said, pocketing the pillbox. 'Sorry 'bout that.'

'Hey.' Brian shrugged, embarrassed by the apology. He had long ago accepted the beeper as a fixture in both their lives, but it was Michael for whom it really tolled. Every four hours. 'You need some water?' he asked.

Michael had already returned to his potting. 'I'll take 'em in a minute.'

As a rule, he realized, Michael refused to jump to the beeper's commands. It was his way of keeping the poisonous drug in its place.

15

'So,' asked Michael, 'which one of you got her?'

Brian pretended not to know what he meant.

'You know.' Michael jerked his head toward the door. 'Jessica Rabbit out there.'

'Who said there was a contest?'

'That's funny. I could have sworn I smelled testosterone.'

'Must've been Polly,' said Brian.

Michael laughed and plunged the trowel into the soil. 'I'll tell her you said that.'

Brian turned and headed for the door. 'Take your pills,' he said.

'Yes, Mother.'

Chuckling, he headed out into the sunshine.

Her Day

Back in the dressing room, a vein pounding brutally in her temple, Mary Ann Singleton stretched out on the sofa and kicked off her shoes with a sigh. No sooner had she done so than someone rapped tentatively on the door.

'Yes?' she called colorlessly, already certain it was Raymond, the squirrely new assistant they'd assigned her while Bonnie, her regular, was off houseboating in the Delta with her boyfriend.

Just what she needed right now. Another greenhorn who didn't know squat about television.

'Mary Ann?'

'Yeah, Raymond, come in.'

The door eased open and Raymond eased in. He was wearing a thigh-length black Yamamoto shirt that was meant to be stylish but only served to exaggerate his dorkiness. 'If this is a bad time . . .'

'No,' she said, managing a thin smile. 'Sit down, it's fine.'

He took the stool in front of the makeup table and fidgeted with the notes on his clipboard. 'Interesting show.'

She groaned.

'Where did they find her?'

'Are you kidding? They find us. Have you seen the lineup this week? It looks like talent night at Napa.'

He nodded solemnly, obviously not getting it.

17

'It's a mental hospital,' she explained. 'Up north.'

'Oh.'

'You're not from here, are you?'

'Well . . . I am now, but I'm originally from the Midwest.'

After a moment's consideration, she decided not to tell him she was from Cleveland. This was a professional relationship, after all, and she didn't want things to get too chummy. Why give him something he could use against her later?

'So,' she said, 'what have you got for me?'

Gravely and with great deliberation, Raymond perused his clipboard. It might have contained a list of fatalities from an airlines disaster. 'First off,' he said, 'Channel Two wants you for the Jerry Lewis telethon next year.'

'Meaning what? That I have to go to Oakland for it?'

He shrugged. 'I guess.'

'OK, tell 'em I'll do it, but I don't wanna be paired off with that imbecile cohost they gave me this year. Or anybody else, for that matter. And make sure it's at a decent hour, like not after midnight or something.'

'Gotcha.' He was scribbling furiously.

'Did you know they actually like him in France?'

'Who?'

'Jerry Lewis.'

'Oh. Yeah. I'd heard.'

'That is the sickest thing,' she said. 'Isn't it?'

Raymond merely widened his eyes and shrugged.

'Don't tell me you like him,' she said.

'Well . . . I know he's been sort of a joke for a long time, but there's an increasing number of American cineastes who find his early work . . . well, at least comparable to, say, Tati.'

She didn't know what that was and didn't care. 'He uses too much Brylcreem, Raymond. Give me a big break.'

18

His tiny eyes locked on the clipboard again. Apparently he found her uncool for not knowing that Jerry Lewis was cool again – among film nerds, at any rate. If she'd told him she was from Cleveland, he'd be using that against her now. You just couldn't be too careful.

'What else?' she asked.

He didn't look up. 'Some professor at City College wants you to address his television class.'

'Sorry. Can't do it.'

'OK.'

'When is it? Never mind, can't do it. What else?'

'Uh . . . one of your studio regulars wants you to autograph a picture.'

'Talk to Julie. We have a whole stack of them, presigned.'

'I know, but he wants something personal.' He handed her the clipboard with a glossy. 'I brought you an unsigned one. He said anything personal would do.'

'Some people,' she said, grabbing a felt-tip. 'What's his name?'

'Cliff. He says he's watched you for years.'

After a moment's consideration, she wrote: *Cliff – Thanks for the Memories – Mary Ann*. 'If he wants more than that,' she told Raymond, returning the clipboard, 'he's shit outa luck. Is that it?'

'That's it.' He turned up his hands.

'Great. Fabulous. Get lost.' She gave him a lame smile to show that she was kidding. 'I'm about to do our PMS show a week ahead of schedule.'

'Oh . . .' It took him a while to get it. 'Can I get you a Nuprin or something?'

'No, thanks, Raymond. That's OK.'

He edged toward the door, then stopped. 'Oh, sorry – there was a phone call during the show. A guy named Andrews from New York.'

'Andrews?'

19

He retrieved a pink phone memo slip from the pocket of his Yamamoto. 'Burke Andrews,' he read.

'Oh, *Andrew*. Burke Andrew.'

'Yeah. I guess so. Sorry.' He set the slip on the makeup table. 'I'll leave it here.'

A thousand possibilities whirred past her like a Rolodex. 'Is it a New York number?'

Raymond shook his head. 'Local,' he said, sliding out the door. 'Looks like a hotel.'

Had it really been eleven years?

He'd moved to New York in 1977 after the Cathedral Cannibals fuss, and she hadn't heard from him since, unless you counted the Kodak Christmas card, circa 1983, of him, his grinny, overdressed wife, and their two little jennifer-jasons – strawberry blonds like their father – hanging cedar garlands somewhere in Connecticut. It had stung a little, that card, even though, or maybe even because, she was already married to Brian.

She had met Burke on the Love Boat, as irony would have it, drawn instantly to his affable collie face, his courtliness, his incredible thighs. Michael Tolliver, who'd been there at the time, maintained later that it was Burke's amnesia she'd fallen for: the tempting clean slate of his mind. His memory had returned, however, in a matter of months, and he'd moved to New York almost immediately. He'd asked her to come with him, of course, but she'd been too enraptured with her new life in San Francisco to seriously consider leaving.

From then on her interest in him had been strictly professional. She had followed his increasingly prestigious byline through a succession of glamorous magazines – *New York*, where he'd started out, *Esquire*, a media column in *Manhattan, inc.* – and through television, where he'd recently been making waves on the production end of the business.

She had often wondered why he'd never made an effort to get in touch with her. Their brief romance aside, they had a certain media visibility in common, if nothing else. True, she wasn't a national figure in the purest sense, but she'd been profiled on *Entertainment Tonight*, and no visitor to San Francisco could have failed to notice her face on television or, for that matter, on billboards on the sides of buses.

Oh, well. She had a funny feeling he was about to make up for it. He was staying at the Stanford Court, it turned out. The operator put her through to his room.

'Yeah,' he said briskly, answering immediately.

'Burke?'

'Yeah.'

'It's Mary Ann. Singleton.'

'Well, hello! Hey, sorry – I thought you were room service. They keep botching my order and calling back. How are you? Boy, it's great to hear your voice!'

'Well,' she said lamely, 'same here.'

'It's been a long time.'

'Sure has.'

A conspicuous silence and then: 'I . . . uh . . . I've got kind of a problem. I was wondering if you might be able to help me.'

Her first thought, which she promptly discarded, was that his amnesia had come back. 'Sure,' she said earnestly. 'I'll do what I can.' It was nice knowing that she could still be of use to him.

'I have this monkey,' he said.

'Excuse me?'

'I have this monkey. Actually, she was more like a friend than a monkey. And she died this morning, and I was wondering if you could arrange to have her freeze-dried for me.'

Catching on at last, she collected herself and said: 'You shithead.'

21

He chortled like a fifth grader who'd just dropped a salamander down her dress.

'God,' she said. 'I was actually picturing you with a dead monkey.'

He laughed again. 'I've done worse.'

'I know,' she said ruefully. 'I remember.'

She was embarrassed now, but for reasons more troubling than his dumb joke. Of all the shows he might have seen, why did it have to be today's? If he'd come a week earlier he might have caught her interview with Kitty Dukakis or, barring that, her top-rated show on crib death. What was he laughing at, anyway? Freeze-dried dogs or the way that she had made her name on television?

'How the hell are you?' he asked.

'Terrific. What brings you to town?'

'Well . . .' He seemed to hesitate. 'Business mostly.'

'A story or something?' She hoped like hell it wasn't AIDS. She'd grown weary of explaining the plague to visiting newsmen, most of whom came here expecting to find the smoldering ruins of Sodom.

'It's kind of complicated,' he told her.

'OK,' she replied, meaning: Forget I asked.

'I'd like to tell you about it, though. Are you free for lunch tomorrow?'

'Uh . . . hang on a sec, would you?' She put him on hold and waited for a good half minute before speaking to him again. 'Yeah, Burke, tomorrow's fine.'

'Great.'

'Where do you wanna meet?'

'Well,' he said, 'you pick the spot, and we'll put it on my gold card.'

'Only if you can deduct it.'

'Of course,' he said.

She thought for a moment. 'There's a new place downtown. Sort of a tenderloin dive that's been upscaled.'

'OK.' He sounded skeptical.

'It's kind of hot right now. Lots of media people.'

'Let's do it. I think I can trust you.'

She wasn't quite sure how to take that, so she let it go. 'It's called D'orothea's,' she said. 'It's on Jones at Sutter.'

'Got it. Jones and Sutter. D'orothea's. What time?'

'One o'clock?'

'Great. Can't wait.'

'Me too,' she said. 'Bye-bye.'

She hung up, then stretched out on her chaise again, discovering to her amazement that her headache was gone.

The rest of the afternoon was consumed by staff conferences and a typically silly birthday party for one of the station's veteran cameramen. Just before three, somewhat later than usual, she left the building hurriedly and drove to her daughter's school in Pacific Heights.

Presidio Hill was a pricey 'alternative' institution, which placed special emphasis on creative development and one-on-one guidance. At five, Shawna was the youngest kid in Ann's Class (that was what they called it, never kindergarten), and her classmates included, among others, the daughter of a famous rock star and the son of a celebrity interviewer for *Playboy* magazine.

The adults were 'strongly urged' to participate in school functions, so the rock star's girlfriend could be found at Presidio Hill on alternate Wednesdays making pigs-in-a-blanket for the children. Mary Ann herself had been drafted once or twice for these duties, though she deeply resented the intimidation involved. For five grand a year they could damn well hire their own wienie roasters.

When she arrived at the rustic redwood building, the usual after-school mayhem was in progress. Voyagers, Audis, and latter-day hippie vans were double, even triple, parked on Washington Street, while clumps of grownups gossiped among themselves and clucked over the artwork of their off-spring.

She scanned the crowd for Shawna. This was never a simple task, since Brian dressed and delivered the kid, and you never knew what she might be wearing. Lately, egged on by the school's policy of creative dressing, Shawna had delivered one lurid fashion statement after another. Like yesterday, when she came home wearing high-top Reeboks with a tutu and tights.

'Mom,' called a reedy voice among many. It was Shawna, bounding toward the car in her flouncy red dress with the big Minnie Mouse polka dots. Mary Ann approved of that one, so she relaxed a little until she caught sight of the rest: the pearls, the lipstick, the turquoise eye shadow.

'Hi, Puppy,' she yelled back, wondering whether Brian, a teacher, or Shawna herself was responsible for this latest atrocity. She flung open the car door and watched nervously as her daughter left the curb. Next to her, against the sidewalk, a Yellow Cab was parked, driver at the wheel. A little girl was climbing into the passenger side. Somehow this smacked of parental neglect, and Mary Ann watched the scene with something approaching indignation.

'That's her dad,' said Shawna, hopping on to the seat.

'Who?'

'Duh! That guy right there! The cabdriver.' The child was getting more smartass by the day. Mary Ann gave her a menacing look. When she glanced at the cabbie again, he beamed back at her knowingly, parent to parent, and she couldn't help being impressed. How many airport runs would it take, anyway, to pay for this glorified baby-sitting service?

'His name is George,' said Shawna.

'How'd you know that?'

'Solange told me.'

24

'Solange calls him George? Instead of Daddy, you mean?'

Shawna rolled her eyes. 'Lots of kids do that.'

'Well, not this one. Fasten your seat belt, Puppy.' Her daughter complied, making a breathless production of it. Then she said: 'I call you Mary Ann.'

This was clearly a gauntlet flung at her feet; she opted to kick it aside. 'Right,' she said, pulling out into the street.

'I do.'

'Mmm.'

'I called you that today at circle time.'

Mary Ann shot her a glance. 'You talked about me at circle time?' Why should this make her feel so uncomfortable? Did she really think Shawna was going to bad-mouth her in front of the other kids?

'We talked about TV,' the child explained.

'Oh, you did?' Now she felt foolish. Shawna must have told the other kids about her famous mom.

'Nicholas says TV is bad for you.'

'Well, too much TV, maybe. Puppy, did you talk about Mommy during . . . ?'

'Put on a tape,' said Shawna.

'Shawna . . .'

'Well, I wanna listen to something.'

'You can in a minute. Don't be so impatient.'

The child cocked her head goofily and did her impression of Pee-wee Herman. 'I know you are, but what am I?'

'Nice. Very funny.'

Another tilt of the head. 'I know you are, but what am I?'

Mary Ann glowered at her. 'I got it the first time, OK?'

After a moody pause, Shawna said: 'Guess what?'

'What?'

'We had quesadillas today.'

25

'Oh, yeah? I like those, don't you?'

'Yeah. Nicholas's father made them, and Nicholas had cheddar cheese, and I had modern jack.'

Modern jack. She would save that one for Brian. He loved it when Shawna said 'aminal' for 'animal' or otherwise flubbed a word charmingly.

'Sounds yummy,' she told the child, reaching across to pop open the glove compartment. 'Find a tape you like. I think there's some Phil Collins in there.'

'Yuck!'

'OK, Miss Picky.'

Shawna gave her an indignant look. 'I'm not Miss Piggy.'

'I said *picky*, silly.' She smiled. 'Go on. Find what you want.'

After foraging for a while, Shawna settled on Billy Joel. This was one taste they shared, so they sang along together at the top of their lungs, thoroughly pleased with themselves.

> *ALL YOUR LIFE IS TIME MAGAZINE*
> *I READ IT, TOO. WHAT DOES IT MEAN?*

'I like that part,' said Shawna, shouting over the music.

'Me too.'

> *BUT HERE YOU ARE WITH YOUR FAITH AND YOUR*
> *   PETER PAN ADVICE.*
> *YOU HAVE NO SCARS ON YOUR FACE*
> *AND YOU CANNOT HANDLE PRESSURE.*
> *PRESSURE . . . PRESSURE . . . ONE – TWO – THREE –*
> *   FOUR*
> *PRESSURE*

Mary Ann gazed over at the child's animated face, the tiny hands rapping rhythmically on the dashboard. Ordinarily she welcomed this little sing-along, since it

26

strengthened her tenuous bond with Shawna, but today, because of that damned makeup, something entirely different was happening. All she could think of was Connie Bradshaw.

She'd noticed the resemblance before, of course, but this time it was overwhelming, almost creepy, like a drag queen doing Marilyn just a little too well. She turned the volume down and spoke to Shawna calmly. 'Puppy, did you have dress-up at circle time today?'

Shawna seemed to falter before saying: 'No.'

'Then, why did . . . ?'

'Turn it back up. This is the best part.'

'In a minute.'

I'M SURE YOU'LL HAVE SOME COSMIC RASH-SHUH-NAL . . .

'Puppy!'

'That's my name, don't wear it out.'

Mary Ann switched off the tape player. 'Young lady!' It was time to play mother now – that is, to impersonate her own mother thirty years earlier. 'I want you to listen when I'm talking to you.'

Shawna folded her arms and waited.

'Is that my makeup you're wearing?'

'No.'

'Where did you get it, then?'

'It's mine,' said Shawna. 'Daddy bought it for me.'

'It's for kids,' Brian told her calmly after dinner that evening. Shawna was in the bedroom, out of earshot, watching television.

'You've got to be kidding.'

He shook his head, smiling dopily.

'Brian, that is just the sickest!'

'I know, but she's a big fan of Jem, and I figured it couldn't hurt just this once.'

27

'Jim?'

'Jem. This rock star in a cartoon. Saturday morning.'

'Oh.'

'They make a whole line of cosmetics and stuff.' He wasn't in the least disturbed, she realized. 'It's just dress-up.'

'Yeah, but if she makes a habit of it . . .'

'We won't let her.'

'It just looks so tarty.'

He chuckled. 'OK. No more makeup.'

His cavalier tone annoyed her. 'I just don't want her running around looking like some kiddie-porn centerfold.' Projecting morbidly, she imagined Shawna's daylight abduction, then envisioned her photograph – lipstick, eye shadow, and all – emblazoned on milk cartons across the country.

Brian rose from the table, taking their plates with him. 'To tell you the truth,' he said, 'I thought she kinda looked like Connie.'

She thought it best not to comment.

'Didn't you? With all that makeup?'

'That isn't very nice,' she said.

'Why not?' said Brian. 'She was her mother.'

He seemed to be goading her for some reason, so she made a point of staying calm. 'Maybe so,' she said, 'but I don't think we're trying for the total look.'

'You noticed it, though?'

'A little, maybe.'

'A lot,' he said, 'I thought.'

She followed him into the kitchen and told him about Shawna and her modern jack. When they had both finished laughing, she said: 'Guess who I heard from today?' She'd already decided it was best to be breezy about it. Any other approach might freight it with too much importance.

'Who?'

28

'Burke Andrew.'

He opened the dishwasher. 'No kidding?'

'Yeah. He called this morning after the show.'

'Well. Long time no hear.'

She tried to read his face, but he turned away and busied himself with the loading of the dishes. 'He's in town, apparently,' she said.

'Apparently?'

'Well, I mean, he is. We're having lunch tomorrow at D'orothea's.'

It shouldn't have made her feel funny to say this, but it did. There was no reason on earth she should have included Brian in the lunch. He and Burke, after all, had never been friends, even though they'd lived for a while under the same roof. Brian had been too busy trolling for stewardesses to waste any excess energy on male bonding.

'Great,' he said. 'Say hello for me.' She monitored this instruction for irony and couldn't find a trace. Burke might not be an issue at all, though she never could tell for sure with Brian. He had a maddening way of being hip one moment and rampantly jealous the next.

'He's here on business, I think. Sounds like he wants to dish a little television dirt.'

'Ah.' He closed the dishwasher door. 'Should be good.'

'We'll see.' She didn't want to come off as too enthusiastic.

Fiddling with the dishwasher controls, Brian said: 'Does he know you're famous?'

She couldn't tell if he was being snide, so she took the question straight. 'He's seen the show, apparently.'

He seemed to ponder something for a moment, then asked: 'The one today?'

She had no intention of resurrecting those furry little bodies again. 'I don't know,' she lied. 'He didn't say.'

Brian nodded.

29

'Why?' she asked.

He shrugged. 'Just wondered.'

She started to ask if he'd watched the show, but a well-oiled defense mechanism told her to leave it alone. He'd seen it, all right, and he hadn't approved. Why give him another chance to tell her so?

Life with Harry

When Charlie Rubin died in early 1987, Michael Tolliver and Thack Sweeney had inherited his dog. They had known Harry a good deal longer than that, of course, caring for him intermittently during Charlie's third bout with pneumocystis and later boarding him at their house when it became apparent that Charlie wouldn't leave the hospital again. While Charlie was still alive, Harry had been addressed as K-Y, but Michael had found it more and more humiliating to walk through the Castro calling out the name of a well-known lubricant.

The name change, however, was only partially effective, since he couldn't go to the bank or mail a package at P.O. Plus without discovering someone who had known Harry in his former life. With no warning at all, the dog would pounce ecstatically on a perfect stranger – strange to Michael, at any rate – and this person would invariably exclaim 'K-Y!' in a voice that could be heard halfway to Daly City.

Michael and Thack doted on the dog to a degree that was almost embarrassing. Neither one of them had ever planned on owning a poodle – they regarded themselves as golden retriever types – but Harry had banished their prejudices (poodlephobia, to use Thack's term) on his first visit to the house. For one thing, Charlie had always avoided those stupid poodle haircuts, keeping the dog's coat raggedly natural. With his round brown face and button nose, Harry seemed more like a living teddy bear than like a classic Fifi dog.

Or so they assured themselves.

They had lived on the hill above the Castro for over two years now. Michael's decade-long residency at 28 Barbary Lane had come to an end when he and Thack recognized their coupledom and decided to buy a place of their own. Thack, who'd been a preservationist back in Charleston, was far more keen on their home-to-be than Michael, who on first sighting the For Sale sign had regarded the place as a hopeless eyesore.

Faced with green asbestos shingles and walled with concrete block, the house had seemed nothing more than a hideous jumble of boxes, like three tiny houses nailed together at odd angles. Thack, however, had seen something quite different, hurdling the wall in a frenzy of discovery to pry away a couple of loose shingles near the foundation.

Moments later, flushed with excitement, he had announced his findings: underneath all that eisenhowering lay three original 'earthquake shacks,' refugee housing built for the victims of the great disaster of 1906. There had been thousands of them in the parks, he said, all rowed up like barracks; afterward people had hauled them off on drays for use as private homes.

In negotiation with the realtor, of course, they kept quiet about the house's architectural significance (much in the way the realtor had about the bum plumbing and the army ants bivouacking below the deck). They moved in on Memorial Day, 1986, christening the place with a Chinese meal, a Duraflame log, and impromptu sex in their Jockey shorts.

For the next two years they had set about obliterating the details that offended them most. Much of this was accomplished with white paint and Michael's creative planting, though Thack made good on his promise to bare

32

the ancient wood in both the kitchen and the bedroom. When, after a season or two of rain, their new cedar shingles took on the obligatory patina of old pewter, the householders glowed with parental appreciation.

Yet to come were a new bathroom and wood-frame windows to replace the aluminum, but Michael and Thack were pressed for money at the moment and had decided to wait. Still, when roaming flea markets and garage sales, they thought nothing of splurging on an Indian blanket or a Fiesta pitcher or a mica-shaded floor lamp for the bedroom. Without ever stating it, they both seemed to realize the same thing:

If there was nesting to be done, it had better be done now.

A record hot spell had finally broken. Beyond their deck (which faced west into the sunset), the long-awaited fog tumbled into the valley like white lava. Michael stood at the rail and watched as it erased the spindly red television tower, until only its three topmost masts were left, sailing above Twin Peaks like the Flying Dutchman. He filled his lungs, held it, let it go, and breathed in again.

His potted succulents were looking parched, so he uncoiled the hose and gave them a thorough drenching, taking as always a certain vicarious pleasure in their relief. When he was through, he aimed the cooling stream into a neighbor's yard, where the scorched and curling fronds of a tree fern testified to its need. The fern, in fact, was the last patch of green in sight down there; even the luxuriant weeds of the past spring had turned to straw in the drought.

'Hey,' said Thack, coming on to the deck from the kitchen. 'We're rationing, remember?'

'I know.' Michael turned the nozzle to mist and gave the fern a final, guilty shower to wash away the dust.

'They're gonna fine us.'

33

He turned off the water and began to coil the hose. 'I didn't take a shower this morning.'

'So what?'

'So the tree fern gets my water. It evens out.'

His lover turned and headed back to the kitchen. 'Since it's not even our tree fern . . .'

'I know. OK.' He followed him through the sliding glass door.

Thack opened the oven and knelt to study a bubbling casserole, pungent with shrimp and herbs. 'Mrs Bandoni says the new owners are gonna level the place.'

'Figures,' said Michael, sitting at the kitchen table. He could see the tree fern from here, see the empty house with its streaky windows and cardboard boxes, the fading beefcake pinup taped to the refrigerator door. The sight of the place always made him shiver a little, like a deserted hamster cage with the straw still in it.

'The foundation's bad,' said Thack. 'Whoever bought it will have to start from scratch.'

The previous owner had been an architect or draftsman of some sort. A wiry little guy with a silvery crew cut and a fondness for jeans and sweatshirts. In the months before his death, Michael could see him at his table, hunched over his blueprints, removing his glasses, rubbing his rabbity eyes. Since his house fronted on another street, they had hardly ever spoken, except to yell neighborly things about the weather or the state of their respective gardens.

He'd been a bachelor, Michael knew, but one who seemed comfortable in his solitude. His illness only became apparent, in fact, when visitors started showing up at his house. There were older folks mostly, people who might have been relatives, arriving with fresh linens and covered dishes, sometimes in groups of three or four. Once, when the man's primroses were still in bloom, Michael looked down to see a uniformed nurse sneaking a cigarette in the garden.

34

'I hope,' said Thack, 'it's not some hideous stucco-on-plywood job.'

Michael frowned at him, lost for a moment.

'The new house,' said Thack.

'Oh. Oh, yeah. Who knows? Probably.'

Thack closed the oven door. 'Go ahead and water the damn thing, if it bothers you that much.'

'No,' said Michael. 'You're right.'

His lover stood up, wiping his hands on his Levi's. 'Your mother called, by the way. She left a message on the machine.'

Michael grunted. 'About the weather, right?'

'C'mon.'

'Well, that's usually what she says, isn't it? "How's the weather out there?" '

'That's because she's afraid of you.'

'*Afraid* of me?'

'Yeah, as a matter of fact.' Thack took two Fiesta platters from the cupboard and set them on the counter. 'You treat her like shit, Michael.'

'*I* treat *her* like shit? When have you ever heard me say anything that could . . . ?'

'It's not what you say, it's how. The color just drains out of your voice. I can always tell when she's on the other end. You don't talk that way to anybody else.'

He wondered what had brought this on. 'Have you been talking to her or something?'

'No.' Thack sounded faintly defensive. 'Not lately.'

'You talked to her at work. You told me so.'

'Last week,' Thack answered, searching in a drawer. 'Are the napkins in the wash?'

Michael thought for a moment. 'Yeah.'

His lover tore off two sections of paper towel and folded them lengthwise.

'She never calls me at work,' said Michael.

'Well, maybe she would, if you wouldn't be so hard on

35

the old gal. She's trying her damnedest to hook up, Michael. She really is.'

He didn't want to discuss this. If the 'old gal' had made overtures of reconciliation, they hadn't come until last year, when his father had died suddenly of a heart attack. Like most country women in the South, she required a man's guidance at any cost, even if that meant making up with her hell-bound gay son in California.

'She misses you,' said Thack. 'I can tell you that.'

'Right. That's why she calls you.'

Thack dumped a handful of butter lettuce into the salad spinner. Slowly, maddeningly, a smile surfaced on his face. 'Sounds to me like you're jealous.'

'Oh, please!'

In point of fact, Thack and his mother had become cloyingly chummy in recent months, swapping homilies and weather reports like a pair of Baptist housewives in a sewing circle. This from the woman who had never spoken to his first lover – not even when she knew he was dying.

It was her grief, after all, that had finally made the difference, her loss that had sent her to the telephone, desperate for company. If he was jealous, he was jealous for Jon, who had asked for her blessing and never received it. But how could he ever say that to Thack?

'She's against everything you stand for,' Michael said finally. 'You have nothing in common at all.'

Thack began to spin the lettuce. 'Except you,' he said.

At dinner they talked about Thack's day. He'd worked at the Heritage Foundation for almost a year now, organizing tours of historic houses. Lately, more to his taste, he'd been testifying before the Board of Permit Appeals, pleading the case of endangered buildings.

'They're dragging their asses again. It really pisses me off.'

'What is it this time?' Michael asked.

'Oh . . . an Italianate villa off Clement. Fuck off, Harry. I'm not through.'

The dog sat at Thack's feet, head cocked for maximum effect, licking his little brown lips.

'It's the shrimp,' said Michael.

'Well, he can wait.'

Michael gave the dog a stern look. 'You heard him, didn't you?'

Harry skulked off, but only as far as the doorway, where he waited stoically, rigid as a temple lion.

'We're gonna lose it,' said Thack. 'I can tell already.'

'Oh . . . the villa. That's too bad.'

'It's near the nursery, you know. I stopped by around noon to see if you wanted to have lunch.'

Michael nodded. 'Brian told me. I was out delivering Mrs Stonecypher's bamboo.'

'Delivering?' Thack frowned. 'I thought you had employees for that.'

'I do, but . . . she likes me and she spends a lot of money. I make an exception in her case.'

'I see.' Thack nodded. 'You were whoring.'

Michael smiled at him. Rich people were beyond redemption in Thack's view of the world – just another corrupt facet of the white, male, sexist, homophobic, corporate power structure. Even poor old Mrs Stonecypher, with her bad hats and wobbly teeth.

'Sorry I missed you,' he said. 'You should call first next time.'

Thack shrugged. 'I didn't know. It's no big deal. I had lunch with Brian.'

Michael shuddered to think what his partner and his lover found to talk about when he wasn't there. 'Where'd you eat?'

'Some new place downtown. Sort of Mexican nouvelle.'

'The Corona,' said Michael. 'We went there last week.'

'It's nice.'

'What did you have?'

'The grilled seafood salad.'

'Oh, yeah,' said Michael. 'Brian had that last time.'

Thack poked at his shrimp for a moment, then said: 'I feel so sorry for that poor bastard.'

'Brian? Why?'

'Oh . . . just the way she treats him.'

Michael looked at him for a moment. 'What did he tell you?'

'Not much, but it's easy enough to deduce.'

'Well, stop deducing. You have no way of knowing what goes on between them.'

Thack smiled at him slyly. 'There in the strange twilight world of the heterosexual.'

'That's not what I meant.'

Thack chuckled.

'Have they had a fight or something?'

'I don't think they're together enough for that. She's always out somewhere.'

'She's a public figure,' said Michael, resenting the way Thack always sided with Brian. 'She can't help it if people want her to do things.'

'But she loves it.'

'Well, what if she does? She should enjoy it. She's worked hard enough for it.'

'I'm just telling what he said.'

'He can be a real slug, you know. He's a helluva sweet guy, but . . .'

'What does that mean – slug?'

'He gets stuck in ruts. He likes ruts. That's why he likes the nursery so much. It doesn't challenge him any more than he wants it to. He can just coast along . . .'

'I thought you said . . .'

'I don't mean he isn't doing a good job. I just meant he isn't as ambitious as she is. I can see how it might be kind of a drag for her.'

'I thought you guys got along great.'

'We do. Stop changing the subject.'

38

'Which is?'

'The fact that . . .' He stopped, not really sure what the subject was.

Realizing this, Thack smiled. 'Did you see her show today? Dead dogs.'

'Yes.'

'Was that lower than Geraldo or what?'

'I thought it was funny, actually. Besides, she can't help what her producers decide . . .'

'I know. She can't help anything.'

Michael gave him a sullen look and let the subject drop. In the long run, Thack was too much of a newcomer to fully grasp the nature of Mary Ann's personality. You had to have known her years ago to understand the way she was today.

Somehow, in spite of the immense changes in their lives, Michael continued to see them all as perennial singles – he and Brian and Mary Ann – still chasing their overblown dreams, still licking their wounds back at Barbary Lane.

But he had been gone for two years; Mary Ann and Brian, even longer. His employee, Polly Berendt, occupied his old digs on the second floor, and the rest of the house was inhabited by people whose names he hardly knew. Except for Mrs Madrigal, of course, who seemed constant as the ivy.

He had seen the landlady just that morning, poking among the fruit stands at a sidewalk market in Chinatown. She had hugged him exuberantly and invited him and Thack to dinner the next day. He had felt a twinge of guilt, realizing how long he'd neglected her.

He mentioned this to Thack, who shared his concern.

'We'll take her some sherry,' he said.

Now they lay on the sofa – Michael's back against Thack's chest, Harry at their feet – watching *Kramer vs Kramer* after dinner. It was a network broadcast, and the censors had doctored the scene in which Dustin Hoffman and his young son are heard, one after the other, taking their morning pee.

'Can you believe that?' Thack fumed. 'They cut out the sound of the pee! Those fuckers!'

Michael smiled sleepily. 'Must not be in keeping with Family Values.'

'Damn, that pisses me off!'

He chuckled. 'So to speak.'

'Well, dammit, that was a sweet scene. You can't even tell what's happening now. It's not funny any more.'

'You're right,' said Michael.

'Fuckin' Reagan.'

'Well . . . he's almost gone.'

'Yeah, and his asshole buddy will be running things.'

'Maybe not.'

'You watch. Things are gonna get worse before they get better.'

Thack gestured toward the TV. 'You wanna watch this?'

'Nah.'

'Where's the clicker?'

Michael ran his hand between the corduroy cushions until he found the remote control, one of three at their command. (He had no idea what the other ones did.) Poking it, he watched the screen crackle into black, then turned over and laid his head against Thack's chest. He sighed at the fit they made, the sheer inevitability of this moment in their day.

Thack stroked Michael's hair and said: 'I picked up more vacuum cleaner bags.'

'Good.' He patted Thack's leg.

'I'm not sure they're the *right* ones. I got confused about our model.'

'Fuck it.'

Thack chuckled. 'You know what I've been thinking?'

'What?'

40

'We should just go to an ACT-UP meeting. I mean, just stop by to see what it's like.'

Somehow, Michael had been expecting this. Thack's advocacy had been bubbling like a broth all week, close to overflowing. If it hadn't taken this form, it would have almost certainly taken another. An irate letter to the *Chronicle*, maybe, or a shouting match with a Muni driver.

When Michael didn't react, Thack added: 'Don't you feel like kicking some butt?'

He tried to keep it light. 'Can't we just hug it for a while?'

Thack was not amused. 'I have to do something,' he said.

'About what?'

'Everything. AZT, for one thing. How much do we pay for that shit? And Jesse Fucking Helms is gonna fix it so poor people can't even get it. And you know what those sorry bastards think? Serves 'em right, anyway. Shouldn't've been butt-fucking in the first place.'

'I know,' said Michael, patting Thack's leg.

'I can't believe how cold-blooded people have gotten.'

Michael agreed with him, but he found his lover's anger exhausting. Now, more than ever, he needed time for the other emotions as well. So what if the world was fucked? There were ways to get around that, if you didn't make yourself a total slave to rage.

'Thack . . .'

'What?'

'Well . . . I don't understand why you're mad all the time.'

His lover paused, then pecked Michael on the temple. 'I don't understand why you're not.'

Harry heard the kiss and scrambled frantically over their intertwined legs, whimpering like a spurned lover. 'Uh-oh,' said Thack. 'Kiss Patrol.'

They parted enough to admit the dog, then scratched

41

him in tandem, Thack attacking the lower back, Michael attending to his head. Harry invariably left the room when they were having sex, but simple affection was too much for him to miss.

'This jealousy isn't healthy,' said Michael.

'He's all right.' Thack kissed the dog's neck. 'Aren't you?'

Harry gave a breathy har-har in reply.

'He smells gross,' said Michael.

'Is that right, Harry? Do you smell gross?'

'I'll wash him tomorrow.'

Thack leaned closer to the dog's ear. 'Hear that, Harry? Better head for the hills.'

Soon enough, Harry did retire to the bedroom, leaving his masters to snooze on the sofa. Michael drifted off to a rising chorus of foghorns and the occasional screech of tires down in the Castro. At eleven o'clock he was jolted awake by his beeper, prickly as a needle in the darkness.

A Practicing New Yorker

For several years now the Tenderloin had been on a surprising upswing. Where formerly had been wino dives and inflatable plastic lady shops now bloomed chocolatiers and restaurants with arugula on the menu. Easily the most stylish of the new eateries was D'orothea's Grille, a postmodern fantasia with trompe l'oeil marble walls and booth dividers that looked like giant Tinker Toys.

As Mary Ann entered, her eyes made a clandestine dash to the wall behind the maître d's stand. There a row of caricatures alerted newcomers to the restaurant's more illustrious customers. Her face was still there, of course – why had she worried that it wasn't? – sandwiched comfortably as ever between the renderings of Danielle Steel and Ambassador Shirley Temple Black.

The maître d' looked up and smiled. 'There you are.'

'Hi, Mickey. I'm expecting a guy . . .'

'He's already here.'

'Ah. Great.'

The maître d' leaned forward conspiratorially. 'I put him at the banquette in the back. There's a table available in the front room, but Prue's there with Father Paddy, and I thought' – and here he winked – 'it might be a little quieter back in Siberia.'

She rewarded him with a rakish chuckle. 'You're way ahead of me, Mickey.'

'We try,' he said, and smiled wickedly.

Grateful for this promise of privacy, she fled to the back, while Prue and the priest yammered away obliviously. When she reached the furthermost banquette, Burke Andrew leapt to his feet and hugged her awkwardly across the table.

'Hey,' he said. 'You look great.'

'Thanks. Look who's talking.'

He let his head wobble bashfully. She caught a glimpse of the troubled youth who had left her for a career in New York. Most of that person was gone now, with only the broad shoulders and great hair (strawberry blond and receding heroically) remaining to trigger her memories. His earnest collie face, once such a blank slate, had developed crags in becoming places.

He sank to the banquette and studied her for a moment, shaking his head slowly. 'Ten years. Damn.'

'Eleven,' she said, sitting down.

'Shit.'

She laughed.

'And you're a star now,' he said. 'They've got your picture on the wall and everything.'

She thought it best not to know what he meant. 'Huh?'

'Over there. Next to Shirley Temple.'

A quick, dismissive glance at the caricature. 'Oh, yeah.'

'Don't you like it?'

She shrugged. 'It's OK, I guess.' After a beat, she added: 'Shirley hates hers.'

One of his gingery eyebrows leapt noticeably. 'She's a friend?'

She nodded. 'She lives here, you know.'

OK, maybe 'friend' was stretching it, but Shirley had been on the show once, and Mary Ann had chatted with her extensively at the French Impressionist exhibit at the De Young. Anyway, she was certain the ambassador wouldn't approve of that pouty-faced portrait with the

44

dashiki and the cigarette. Mary Ann had told D'or as much when they hung the damned thing.

Burke's eyes roamed the room. 'I like this.'

She nodded. 'It's kind of a media joint.'

'Yeah. So you said.'

At the moment, she realized, the wattage of the lunching luminaries was embarrassingly dim, so she made do with the material at hand. 'That showy blonde,' she muttered, nodding toward the front room, 'is Prue Giroux.'

He had obviously never heard of her.

'She was in *Us* last month. She took some orphans to Beijing on a peace mission.'

Still no reaction.

'She's a socialite, actually. Kind of a publicity hound.'

He nodded. 'How 'bout the priest?'

'Father Paddy Starr. He has a show at my station. *Honest to God*.'

'Honest to God, he has a show? Or that's the name of it?'

'That's the name of it.'

He smirked.

She smirked back, feeling a little queasy about it. She hated how rubey all this sounded. Burke, after all, was a practicing New Yorker, and the breed had a nasty way of regarding San Francisco as one giant bed-and-breakfast inn – cute but really of no consequence. She made herself a curt mental note not to gossip about the locals.

'How's Betsy?' she asked, changing the subject.

'Brenda.'

'Oh. Sorry. I knew it was B.' She mugged and rolled her head from side to side. 'Burke and Brenda, B and B.'

'She's doing fine. Got her hands full with the kids, of course.'

Wouldn't she just, thought Mary Ann.

'She wanted to come with me this time, but Burke junior came down with flu, and Brenda didn't trust the house-keeper to manage without her.'

45

'God, I know what you mean!' She seized his wrist lightly. 'We have this Vietnamese woman. She's really dear, but she can't, for the life of her, tell the difference between Raid and Pledge!'

His laughter seemed a little strained, and she worried that the remark had come off as racist.

'Of course,' she added, releasing his wrist, 'I can only speak one language myself, so . . . anyway, her family had a rough time over there, so we figured it was worth a little extra trouble.'

'You have a kid or two of your own, don't you?'

'One. How'd you know?'

His smirk came back to life. 'I saw you with her on *Entertainment Tonight*.'

'Oh . . . you saw that?' It was good to know, anyway, that he'd seen her on national TV. At least now she knew he didn't think of her as completely local. Even if that *ET* segment had been about local talk-show hosts.

'She's a cute little girl,' he said.

For an unsettling instant she flashed on Shawna's tarty makeup of the day before. 'Well, she's a lot bigger now, of course. That was over three years ago.'

'Really?'

'Yeah.'

'I bet she looks more like you than ever.'

She smiled at him benignly, hoping he wouldn't make a big deal out of this. 'She's not my biological daughter, actually. We adopted her.'

'Oh. Yeah.' He did his bashful wobble again. 'I guess I knew that.'

'I don't see how you could, really.'

'Well, maybe not.'

'Her mother was a friend of mine. Or someone I knew, anyway. She died a few days after Shawna was born. She left a note asking me and Brian to take care of her.'

'How wonderful.'

'Yeah.'

46

'That's a great story. She's a lucky little girl.'

She shrugged. 'Brian was a little more crazy about the idea than I was.'

This unraveled him noticeably. 'Still . . . you must . . . I mean, I'm sure it took some getting used to, but . . .'

She smiled to put him out of his misery. 'I'm learning,' she said. 'It's not terrible. It's OK, actually. Most of the time.'

'How old is she?'

'Oh . . . five or six.'

It took him forever to realize she was joking. 'C'mon,' he said finally.

'She'll be six next April.'

'OK. There.' He nodded to fill the dead air. 'And . . . Brian?'

'He's forty-four,' she answered, though she found the question a little weird.

'No.' He laughed. 'I meant, who is he?'

'Oh, I thought you knew. Brian Hawkins.'

It didn't register.

'He was upstairs at Mrs Madrigal's.'

Now he was nodding, slowly. 'The guy who lived on the roof?'

'Right. That's him.'

'Well, I'll be damned!'

His apparent amazement unsettled her. 'You remember him, huh?'

'I remember how much you hated him.'

'Excuse me?' She gave him the sourest look she could muster.

'Sorry,' he said. 'I mean . . . you know, disapproved of him . . .'

She was about to take him on, when the waiter appeared. 'You folks had a chance to look at the menu yet?'

'I'll take the grilled tuna,' Mary Ann told him crisply. 'And some orange-flavored Calistoga.'

47

Burke cast a cursory glance at the menu, then flapped it shut. 'Sounds great.'

'Same thing?' asked the waiter.

'Same thing.'

'You got it.' The waiter spun on his heels and left.

'OK,' said Burke. 'Let me start over, if I can.'

'Let's just leave it.'

'No. That sounded terrible.'

'I knew what you meant, though. He was a real womanizer then.'

'I liked him, though, I thought he was nice.'

She realigned her silverware against the salmon tablecloth. 'He is nice. He puts up with a lot, believe me.'

He smiled gently. 'C'mon.'

She shrugged. 'He does. It isn't easy being married to Mary Ann Singleton.'

He blinked at her for a moment, then asked: 'When did you start seeing him?'

'Oh . . . a year or so after you left.' Make that a week, she told herself. No, make if four days. She remembered all too well the weepy night she had headed up to Brian's room with a joint of Maui Wowie and a bottle of rotgut Chianti. He'd been dating Mona Ramsey at the time, but he'd been ready and willing to offer consolation.

How odd it was to sit here now with the man who had caused her all that pain and feel nothing but a sort of pleasant sense of shared history. She could scarcely remember their passion, much less reconstitute it for a moment's titillation.

'How's Mrs Madrigal?' he asked.

'She's OK, I guess. I saw her down at Molinari's a month or so ago.' She smiled and shook her head. 'Just as dear and loony as ever.'

Burke smiled back.

'Brian and I moved out of the house after we got Shawna. It had a certain funky charm, I guess, but it wasn't much of a place to raise a kid.'

'What about Michael and . . . Jon, was it?'

She nodded solemnly. 'Jon died of AIDS in '82.'

'Damn.'

'I know.'

'Is Michael OK?'

Another nod. 'He's got the virus, but so far he's been fine.'

'Good. Thank God.'

'He has a new boyfriend,' she told him. 'They bought a house in the Castro.'

'What does Michael do now?'

'He runs a nursery out on Clement.'

'No kidding?'

'Yeah. He and Brian run it together, actually.'

He seemed to like this idea. 'All in the family, huh?'

'Yeah.'

He nodded slowly, absorbing their lost decade with a look of sanguine acceptance. 'You look great,' he said finally.

Fine, she thought, but isn't this where we came in?

This particular waiter knew she didn't like a chatty presentation, so their tuna arrived without fanfare. Burke took a few bites and said: 'I'm producing now. For Teleplex. Did you know that?'

'Sure,' she said. 'Doesn't everybody?'

He chuckled. 'No way.'

'Well, I do.'

He focused on his plate as he composed his words. 'I'm developing a new morning talk show. Out of New York. We think there's a real market for something more home-oriented and . . . more intelligent than what's currently being offered.'

'You got that right. People have had it with this tabloid shit. There's bound to be a backlash.'

'I think so,' he said, still addressing his tuna. 'I think we can *make* it happen, in fact. We've got the backing, frankly, and some very real interest from the networks. What we need now is the right host. Someone who knows how to chat with, say, Gore Vidal and yet still be lively in a kitchen segment.'

Mary Ann's fork froze in mid-descent. *Don't*, she warned herself, jump to any hasty conclusions. Maybe he just wants your advice. Maybe he . . .

'What do you think?' His eyes met hers at last.

'About what?'

'Doing it.'

She set the fork down and waited for a count of three. 'Me?'

'Yes.'

'As host?'

'Yes.'

It took all the discipline at her command to conceal her excitement. 'Burke . . . I'm tremendously flattered . . .'

'But?'

'Well, for starters, I have my own show.'

'Right. Local.'

Stung, she composed herself, then said coolly: 'This is one of the most sought-after markets in the country.'

He gave her a patient smile. 'I know you know the difference.'

'Well, maybe so, but . . .'

'And I think you'll find the money is a whole lot better.'

'That isn't the point,' she said calmly.

'Well, what is? Tell me what I have to do?'

He was practically begging. God, how she loved this. 'I have a home here, Burke, a family.'

'And they wouldn't want to move?'

'That's part of it, yes.'

'OK.' He made a little gesture of concession with his hands. 'What's the other part?'

'When have you even seen me, anyway? I mean, the show.'

'Lots of times. On my way through the city. I've never

seen you when you weren't brilliant.' He gave her an engaging little smile. 'We can even keep the name, if you want. I like the sound of "Mary Ann in the Morning." '

She was thinking more along the lines of just plain 'Mary Ann.'

'Look,' he added, 'if it's gonna be no, fine. But I want to make damn sure you know exactly what's being offered here.'

'I think I do,' she said.

'Then what can I tell you?'

'Well . . . what you think I can offer, for one thing.'

He gave her a disbelieving look. 'C'mon.'

'I mean it.'

'OK.' He thought for a moment. 'You're not an automaton. You listen to people. You react. You laugh when you feel like laughing, and you say what's on your mind. And you've got this great . . . Cleveland thing going.'

She drew back as if he'd hit her with a mackerel. '*Cleveland thing?*'

He grinned maddeningly. 'Maybe that was the wrong way to put it . . .'

'I've spent *years* making sure Cleveland was gone forever.'

He shook his head. 'Didn't work.'

'Well, thanks a helluva lot.'

'And you're lucky it didn't. That naïveté is the best thing you've got going for you. Look, c'mon . . . where would Carson be without Nebraska?'

With a private shiver, she realized that she could be on Carson in a matter of months, chatting chummily about her meteoric rise to fame.

'So how was it?' asked a throaty female voice, taking Mary Ann by surprise.

'D'or . . . hi. Yummy, as usual. Burke, this is our hostess, D'orothea Wilson.' She looked especially elegant today, Mary Ann thought, in a mauve silk blouse and gabardine slacks.

51

'This is great,' said Burke, indicating the remains of his tuna. 'Especially the peanut butter sauce.'

D'or nodded. 'I've been making that one at home for years.' She looked at Mary Ann and smiled wryly. 'DeDe and the kids are sorta pissed that I went public with it.'

'Is she here today?'

D'or shook her head. 'Not till two.'

'Well, tell her I said hi, OK? It's been a while since we've talked.'

'You bet,' said D'or, and she sailed off to the front room on her proprietorial rounds.

'She's a beauty,' said Burke.

'Yeah. She used to be a model. She and her lover escaped from Jonestown just before everybody . . . you know, drank the Kool-Aid. They hid out in Cuba for three years.'

'My God.'

She enjoyed his amazement. 'Yeah. I broke the story, actually.'

'On your show?'

'No. Earlier. When I was still hosting the afternoon movie. Back in '81. It's how I got my start.'

'They made you a reporter so you could break it?'

'No.'

'Then . . . ?'

She shrugged and gave him an enigmatic smile. 'I just broke it during the afternoon movie.'

'Uh-huh' was all he could manage.

'It was just a local thing. I doubt if you would've heard about it in New York.'

He caught the irony and narrowed his eyes at her. 'When did you get to be so dangerous?'

'Who, me?' she replied. 'Little ol' me from Cleveland?'

52

Some Rather Exciting News

The velvety fog which arrived that evening had sketched a halo around the streetlight at the foot of the Barbary steps. Thack stopped beneath it and muttered, 'Shit.'

'What?' said Michael.

'We forgot to get sherry.'

Michael's guilt flared up again. After several months' absence, he hated showing up at Mrs Madrigal's house without some reassuring talisman of his affection. Gazing up the impossible slope of Leavenworth, he mused aloud. 'There's a mom and pop up at the top there.'

'Forget it,' said his lover. 'We can send her some flowers tomorrow.'

'Will you help me remember?'

'Of course,' said Thack.

When they reached the eucalyptus grove at the top of the steps, a cat shot past them on the path, flashing its tail like a broadsword. Michael called to it seductively, but the creature merely spat at them and bounded off into the mist.

'Carpetbagger,' he yelled after it.

Thack gave him a funny look.

'He's from there,' Michael explained, gesturing toward the new condo complex at the head of the lane. It was pale green and postmodern, with security gates and sunken garbage cans and buzzers you could hear for miles. Most of the eucalyptus grove had been sacrificed to make room for it.

Beyond the complex, where the path narrowed and the shrubbery grew wild, lay the real Barbary Lane, a dwindling Bohemia of shingled lodges and garbage cans that weren't ashamed to stand up and be counted. As they opened the lych-gate at Number 28, the smell of pot roast wafted across the courtyard from the landlady's kitchen window.

When she buzzed them into her inner sanctum, the place reassured Michael with its constancy – that familiar, immutable hodgepodge of dusty books and dustier velvet. She greeted them effusively in a plum-colored kimono, a pair of ivory chopsticks thrust into the silvery tangle of her hair.

'Are you smoking?' she asked Michael.

He pretended to examine his extremities, 'I dunno, am I?'

'Now you mustn't make fun of my only sacrament.' She thrust a plate of joints into Thack's hands. 'Here, dear. You corrupt him. My biscuits are burning.' She spun on her heels and sailed back to the kitchen, all fluttering silk.

Thack smiled at the histrionic exit, then offered the plate to Michael.

Michael relented after only a moment's hesitation. This was a special occasion, after all.

When the landlady returned, he and Thack were both thoroughly buzzed, deep in the embrace of her worn-shiny damask sofa.

'Well,' she said, taking the armchair, 'I have some rather exciting news.'

'Really?' said Thack.

She beamed at them both, one at a time, heightening the suspense. 'I'm going away,' she said.

Michael felt an unexpected stab of anxiety. *Going away? Moving away?*

His distress must have been evident, for she made a

54

hasty amendment. 'Just for a month or so.'

'A vacation, you mean?' Thack looked just as amazed.

She answered with a wide-eyed nod, her hands clasping her knees. Apparently she was amazed too. Up to now she'd been the world's most committed homebody.

'Well,' said Michael, 'congratulations.'

'Mona wants me to meet her in Greece. And since I never get time with my darling daughter, I thought . . .'

'Greece?'

'Yes, dear.'

'Lesbos?'

The landlady's eyes widened. 'She's told you about it?'

'Well, not lately, but she's been talking about it for years.'

'Well, she's going this time. She's rented a villa, and she's invited her doddering old parent.'

'That's great,' said Thack.

Michael was already imagining the scenario. Ol' frizzy-haired Mona, sullen and horny in some smoky taverna. Mrs Madrigal holding court in her oatmeal linen caftan, doing that Zorba dance as the spirit moved her.

'I can hardly take it in.' The landlady sighed contentedly. 'The land of Sappho.'

Michael snorted. 'And about a zillion women who go there looking for Sappho. I don't suppose she mentioned that?'

'She did,' said Mrs Madrigal.

'It's practically a pilgrimage.'

'Yes.'

'She said there are so many dykes there at the height of the season that it looks like the Dinah Shore Open.'

Mrs Madrigal gave him a look. 'I think you've made your point, dear.'

'Of course, I'm sure they've got men too.'

'Yes,' came the dry reply. 'I'm sure they do.'

'When do you leave?' asked Thack.

'Oh . . . early next week.'

Michael wasn't expecting this. Nor was he expecting the mild anxiety that swept over him. Why on earth should this bother him? It was only a vacation. 'Not much time to pack,' he said lamely.

She seemed to be searching his face for clues.

'Of course, you won't need much,' he added.

'I'm not sure I know *how* to pack. I haven't been off Russian Hill for years.'

'All the more reason you should go,' said Thack.

Michael asked: 'Isn't it hot there?'

'Warm,' she replied.

'But you hate the heat.'

'Well, it's dry heat, at least.'

'They won't have dope,' he reminded her.

'Hey,' said Thack, looking at Michael. 'Stop being such a wet blanket.'

Michael shrugged. 'I just thought she should know.'

At dinner their talk drifted to Mary Ann and Brian, who apparently hadn't visited the landlady since Christmas.

'They've both been really busy,' Michael assured her, provoking a skeptical sneer from Thack, who was always prepared to believe the worst about Mary Ann.

Mrs Madrigal fussed with a wisp of hair at her temple. 'I'd be delighted to take Shawna for them. Brian hasn't asked me to sit for ages.'

'Well,' said Michael, feeling uncomfortable, 'she's in kindergarten now, of course. That takes care of a lot of it.'

'Yeah,' said Thack.

The landlady bit her lip and nodded. 'More potatoes, dear?'

Thack shook his head and patted his stomach. 'I'm stuffed.'

'There's lots more pot roast in the kitchen.'

'I'm fine. Really.'

'Michael?'

'Well . . .'

'Ah, he who hesitates . . .'

He smiled at her, abandoning the pretense of this week's diet.

'Come with me,' she said, beckoning him toward the kitchen. And then to Thack: 'Excuse us, will you, dear?'

In the kitchen she hovered a little too cheerily over the roast. 'Still like the crispy part?'

'Sure. Whatever.'

As she carved, her eyes remained fixed on her labors. 'Should I be doing this, dear?'

'What?'

'Leaving.'

'Of course,' he said. 'Why not?'

'Well . . . if everything's not all right with you . . .'

'Everything is fine,' he said. 'Don't you think I'd tell you?'

'Well, I'd certainly hope . . .'

He rolled his eyes. 'I'll come yelling. Trust me.'

She took her time arranging the slab on his plate. 'I'll be gone for a whole month.'

'Will you stop it!'

She set down the serving fork and wiped her hands on a dish towel. 'Forgive me.'

'Don't apologize.'

'I know it's irrational, but it's all I've thought about ever since . . .'

'Don't I look all right?'

She cupped her hand against his cheek. 'You look wonderful. As usual.'

The intensity of her gaze embarrassed him, so he looked away. 'Mona says it's a beautiful island. They've only had an airport for five years or something.'

'Mmm.' Her hand slid away, and she busied herself with dishes in the sink.

'Leave those,' he said. 'I'll get them later.'

'You could come with us,' she said, spinning around.

57

'Huh?'

'To Lesbos. I know Mona would love that.'

He smiled at her indulgently. 'I've got a business to run. And a house to pay for.'

Thack appeared in the doorway, holding his plate. 'Is it too late to change my mind?'

'Of course not,' said the landlady.

Michael stood aside while she heaped meat on Thack's plate. She seemed just as relieved as he that Thack had come along to put an end to their awkwardness.

They were washing dishes, the three of them, when someone rapped on the front door. Before the landlady could finish drying her hands, Polly Berendt had loped into the kitchen. 'Oh, hi,' she said, seeing Michael and Thack. Then she turned to Mrs Madrigal: 'I was on my way out, and I thought you could use this.' She unzipped a pocket on her black leather jacket and produced a check, obviously for the rent. 'Sorry it's late.'

The landlady tucked this offering into the sleeve of her kimono. 'No trouble at all, dear.'

Awkwardly, Polly rubbed a palm against a denimed thigh. 'Well, I didn't mean to interrupt or anything.'

'You aren't interrupting. We've finished our dinner. Come sit with us.'

'Thanks. I can't.' She looked at Michael. 'I'm meeting some friends at Francine's.'

'Oh,' chirped the landlady. 'Do I know her?'

'It's a bar,' Polly explained.

Michael couldn't resist. 'Guess where Mrs Madrigal's going.'

Polly looked faintly suspicious. 'Where?'

'Lesbos.'

'Uh . . . you mean . . . ?'

'The island,' Thack put in. 'Where Sappho's from.'

Polly nodded vaguely.

'Don't tell me you haven't heard of her,' said Michael.

'Well, of course I've *heard* of her. I'm just not up on my mythology.'

'Sappho wasn't mythological.'

'Hey,' Thack told him, 'lay off.'

'Yeah,' said Polly.

Mrs Madrigal was frowning now. 'If you children are going to quarrel . . .'

Michael shook his head reproachfully at Polly. 'How can you call yourself a dyke?'

His employee heaved a sigh and shifted her weight to her other hip. 'I don't call myself one. I *am* one. I didn't have to take a course in it, you know.'

'And that,' said Michael, keeping a straight face, 'is what's wrong with the young people of today.'

Polly groaned. Thack slid his arm along Michael's shoulder and gave him a vigorous shake. 'Such an old poop.'

'Indeed,' said Mrs Madrigal. 'And such a short memory.'

'What do you mean?'

'Well . . . if I'm not mistaken, dear, I had to explain Ronald Firbank to you.'

Michael frowned at her. 'You did?'

She nodded.

'You couldn't have.'

'I think so.'

'Well . . . Firbank is much more obscure than Sappho.'

'Now,' said the landlady, dispensing with the subject as she turned her attention to Polly, 'will you be all right while I'm gone?'

Polly shrugged. 'Sure.'

'I doubt you'll need heat, but if you do and it goes on the fritz, there's a knob on the furnace you can jiggle.'

Polly nodded. 'I remember.'

'I'm leaving the extra keys with the Gottfrieds on the third floor, so you can buzz them if you lose yours.'

'OK. Thanks.'

'Oh . . . if you could keep an eye out for Rupert. I think he's eating with the Treachers these days, but I keep some kitty food for him just in case. It's in the cupboard here. I'll give you a key before I leave.'

Hearing all this, Michael felt old and faintly alienated, like some decrepit alumnus who returns to his campus to find that undergraduate life has gone on without him. Who were these people, anyway – these Gottfrieds and Treachers who were privy now to the age-old mysteries of the lane?

He realized, too, that he was slightly jealous of Polly in her newfound role as junior lieutenant at 28 Barbary Lane. This was irrational, of course – it was he, after all, who had chosen to move away – but the feeling gnawed at him just the same.

When he and Thack left that evening, Mrs Madrigal took their arms like a dowager duchess and walked them down the foggy lane to the top of the steps. The very smell of this ferny place, pungent with earth and eucalyptus, released a torrent of memories, and Michael felt perilously capable of tears.

'Now listen,' said the landlady, as she released them for their descent. 'Let's do something fun before I leave.'

'You bet,' said Thack.

Mrs Madrigal tugged on Michael's sleeve. 'How about you, young man?'

'Sure.' Michael avoided her gaze.

'Make him call,' she told Thack. 'He'll forget.'

'I won't forget,' said Michael, and he hurried down the steps before she could see his face.

Well Enough Alone

So far, Brian realized, a whole day had passed without a peep out of Mary Ann about her lunch date with Burke Andrew. He had almost brought it up himself the night before, but something about her skittery, overpolite demeanor told him to leave well enough alone. If there was still something left between her and Burke, he didn't want to know about it.

This was paranoia, of course, but what could you do?

It was a clear blue evening, and he was heading home in his Jeep. The ivory towers of Russian Hill had gone golden in the sunset. All things considered, he had plenty to feel golden about himself, so this nagging insecurity would have to stop.

If anything, he decided, he should feel reassured by her behavior. The reunion had obviously been so uneventful that she had simply forgotten to mention it. What's more, if something *had* clicked between the two of them, she would have known better than to draw attention to the situation by keeping quiet; she would have mentioned it casually and let the subject drop.

He had put the matter behind him when he arrived at the twenty-third floor of The Summit.

'Yo,' he hollered, coming into the living room. The slanting sun cast a sherry-colored light on the carpet, where several dozen of Shawna's dolls were arrayed face-down in pristine rows. 'I'm home, people.'

His daughter emerged from the bedroom and stood scratching her butt. 'Hi, Daddy.' In her other hand she held the left foot of another doll.

'Hi, Puppy. What's this?'

'I'm giving them away.'

'You are?'

'Yes.' She knelt and placed the doll next to the others, solemnly arranging its limbs. 'To the homeless.'

'Was that your idea?' He was impressed.

'Mostly. Mostly mine and partly Mary Ann's.'

'Well, that's wonderful. Only not all of 'em, OK?'

'Don't worry.' She patted the doll's dress into place. 'I'm only giving away the ugly ones.'

He nodded. 'Good thinking.' Then he touched the tip of her nose. 'You're a regular Mother Teresa.'

In the kitchen his wife was shelling peas, looking raw-boned and Sally Fieldish in her Laura Ashley apron. When he kissed the nape of her neck, he caught a whiff of her ripe six o'clock smell and felt totally, stupidly, in love with her.

'Would you please tell me,' he said, 'what our daughter is doing?'

'I know.' She gave him a rueful look over her shoulder. 'It looks like Jonestown out there.'

He popped one of the raw peas into his mouth and munched on it as he leaned against the counter. 'You sure it's a good idea?'

She shrugged. 'Why not?'

'I dunno. What if she misses one? Remember how she was when we threw out her banky?'

'She wants to do this, Brian. It's a rite of passage. She's getting off on it.'

'I know, but if she . . .'

'If we'd listened to you, she'd still be sucking on that damn banky.'

'OK. You're right.'

'She's keeping her nice dolls, anyway.'

'Fine.'

'Whatcha want for potatoes?' she asked. 'Sweet or new?'

'Uh . . . sweet.'

'With baby marshmallows?'

He gave her a skeptical glance. 'Since when have you bought baby marshmallows?'

She shrugged. 'If you don't want 'em . . .'

'Oh, I want 'em. I just thought you said they were gross and middle American.'

She gave him a feisty glance and continued shelling.

'Want me to help with that?' he asked.

'No, thanks. I like having something to do with my hands. It soothes me.'

He moved behind her and nuzzled her neck again. 'Do you need soothing?'

'No,' she said. 'I just meant . . . it gives me something manual to do.'

'Mmm.' He nipped at her flesh. 'I know something manual you can do.'

She giggled. 'Go set the table.'

'Let's eat in front of the set.'

'OK. Nothing's on, though.'

'Sure there is. *Cheers*. Two shows in a row.'

'What else?'

'Well . . . Michael loaned us *The Singing Detective*.'

'No, thank you.'

'It's Dennis Potter.'

'Brian, I don't wanna watch some old guy having psoriasis while I'm having dinner.'

'You did a show on it last month.'

'All the more reason.'

'You're hard, woman,' he said, and pinched her butt.

She gave him a push toward the door. 'Go play with Shawna. Maybe after she's in bed . . .'

'Well, not if you don't . . .'

63

'Scoot. I've got shrimp to stuff.'

'You do?'

'Hey,' she said, mugging at his amazement. 'I'm a Total Woman.'

She hadn't stuffed shrimp for years.

In the living room he sat on the floor and listened as Shawna recited – a little too cheerfully, perhaps – the deficiencies of her soon-to-be-homeless dolls.

'This one doesn't talk anymore.'

'Oh, yeah?'

'And this one has dumb hair. And this one I hate.'

'You don't hate it, Puppy.'

'Yes I do. And this one has a really funny smell.'

Brian frowned, then sniffed the doll. The odor nipped his nostrils like tiny fangs.

'Pedro peed on her,' Shawna explained.

'Who?'

'The Sorensens' iguana.'

'Great.' He returned the doll to its resting place.

'Can we get a iguana?'

'No way.'

'I'd take care of him.'

'Yeah. Right.'

'I would.'

He thought for a moment, then picked up the reeking doll. 'I think we'd better retire this one, OK?'

'What do you mean?'

'Throw it out.'

'Why?'

'Because, Puppy, if it smells bad to us, it'll smell just as bad to some other little girl.'

'Uh-uh.' Shawna, miraculously, shook her head and scratched her butt at the same time. 'Not if she's homeless.'

'Yes she would. Trust me on this, Puppy.'

His daughter gave him a blank look. 'Whatever.'

'C'mon,' he said, taking her hand. 'Let's go help Mommy set the table.'

The first time he'd seen *The Singing Detective*, Mary Ann had been off networking at a cocktail party.

'It's amazing,' he told her now, back in the kitchen. 'This ugly ol' guy is in bed in the hospital, with like crooked teeth and this craggy-ass face, and he opens his mouth to sing and out comes "It Might As Well Be Spring." Only with like a crooner's voice – you know, whoever sang it originally – and with all the orchestration and everything.'

'I don't get it,' said Mary Ann.

'Me either,' said Shawna.

'You will when you see it,' he told his wife.

She wasn't convinced. 'Not if it takes six hours.'

'Well . . . we can watch it a little bit at a time.'

'Forget it,' said Shawna.

He turned to his daughter and tickled her under the arms. 'You're not watching it, anyway.'

The child squirmed, giggling. 'Yes I am.'

'Nope. You're watching *Cosby* in your room.'

'Says who?'

'Says me. And Freddy!' He stiffed his fingers into a claw and clamped it on the back of her head, getting a squeal out of her.

Mary Ann frowned at him. 'Brian . . .'

'What?'

'That isn't funny.'

'Oh . . . OK.' He let the claw wilt, then winked at Shawna. 'Mommy's making us sweet potatoes with teeny marshmallows.'

'Yummy,' said Shawna.

'Why do you think she did that?'

Shawna shrugged.

'He's a child-molester, you know,' his wife said.

He glanced at her. 'Who?'

'Freddy. In that movie.'

'Yeah. OK.' He turned back to Shawna. 'You think it was because we were good all week?'

'They've made a total hero of him. He's got his own posters, even. It's disgusting.'

'I guess it is,' he said.

'We're doing a show on it, actually.'

He nodded, having guessed as much already.

'I like him,' said Shawna.

Mary Ann frowned at her. 'Who?'

'Freddy.'

'No you don't,' she said. 'You do not like him.'

'Yes I do.'

'Shawna.' Mary Ann shot him a rueful look. 'See?' she said.

'I think he's funny,' said Shawna.

Brian gave his wife a glance that said: Lighten up. 'She thinks he's funny.'

'Right.' Mary Ann dumped a handful of peas into a saucepan. 'A child-molester.'

'You want wine with the meal?' he asked.

'Sure. Whatever.'

He went to the refrigerator and removed a bottle of sauvignon blanc, transferring it to the freezer so it would chill the way they liked it. Seeing Shawna wander off again, he sat down on the stool at the butcher-block island. 'I meant to ask you,' he said as nonchalantly as possible. 'How was your lunch with Burke yesterday?'

'Oh.' It took her a moment. 'Fine.'

He nodded. 'Get all caught up?'

'Mmm. More or less.'

'He still . . . married and all?'

She studied him a moment, then gave him a slow, honeyed smirk. 'You're a silly man.'

66

On its own, his eyebrow did something suggestive of Jack Nicholson in *The Shining*. 'Oh, yeah?'

Her eyes returned to the sweet potato she was slicing. 'I knew you were gonna get like this.'

'Hey,' he said, shrugging. 'What way have I gotten? It was a simple question.'

'OK, then . . . Yes, he is still married. Yes, he still has two kids.'

'How does he look?'

'What do you want me to say?' she said. 'Something really disparaging so you won't be insecure?'

'That would be good.'

She smiled. 'You're such a mess.'

'C'mon. Give it a shot. Has his ass gone froggy on him?'

She hooted, so he sidled up behind her and wrapped his arms around her waist. 'You used to like him a lot.'

'How do you know?'

'Hey,' he said, 'I was there, remember? I saw you guys together all the time.'

She rotated in his arms and raked the hair above his ears with her fingertips. 'Did Michael make a big deal about this lunch or something?'

'I didn't tell him,' he said. 'Did you?'

'No. Why would I do that?'

He shrugged.

'And what could possibly make you think that after eleven years I would even . . . ?'

'Nothing,' he said. 'You're right. I'm a silly man.'

Her eyes surveyed his with optometrical attention to detail. She gave him a dismissive rap on the butt and turned back to her sweet potatoes.

'If you wanna know the truth,' she said, chopping away, 'he's gotten kind of prosaic.'

'How so?'

'I dunno. Too serious and dedicated. Wrapped up in his career.'

'Which is?'

'Television,' she replied. 'Producing.'

'Small world.'

'He's nice, though. He was really concerned when I told him Michael was positive.' She paused. 'Actually, we spent most of the time talking about that.'

'They were close, huh?'

'Well, fairly. He asked if we could all get together sometime this week.'

'Oh, yeah? With Michael, you mean?'

She nodded. 'If you don't want to, of course . . .'

'No. That's fine.'

'I think you'd get along with him great.'

'I thought you said he was prosaic.'

She rolled her eyes. 'I meant . . . about his work. Is Wednesday a good night?'

'I dunno,' he said. 'I haven't checked the book lately.' By this he meant *their* book, of course, as opposed to his or hers. For years now, at her instigation, they had maintained three appointment books at home. It had saved them a world of trouble.

'We're free,' she said. 'Nguyet's available too.' Moments later she added: 'Probably.'

Hauling in the maid sounded a little too grand to him. 'We can do it without her, can't we?'

'We could,' she said. 'But it's five for dinner . . . six counting Puppy . . . and somebody's gotta dish it out. I just thought it would be more convenient.'

'I'll cook, then. I'll make my paella.'

'That's sweet, but . . .'

'Hey,' he said. 'It was a big hit last time.'

'I know that, but I want us all to be together. What's the point in doing this if you're holed up in the kitchen with the clams?'

'OK,' he said.

'You wanna ask Michael, or shall I?'

'Why don't you?' he said. 'He sees me all day. I think it would mean more. He hasn't heard from you for a while.'

She nodded and lifted the receiver of the wall phone.

His paranoia raged away in silence.

Dance with Me

Michael hung up the phone and went to the bathroom, where Thack sat naked in the empty tub, shampooing Harry. Sleek as a sewer rat in his coat of lather, Harry crooned softly in protest as Thack turned on the hand spray and rinsed the poodle's rump.

'Yes,' said Michael, talking to Harry. 'You're a good boy. What a good boy you are!'

'You should see the fleas,' said Thack.

'I bet.'

'We'll have to bomb the house, I'm afraid.'

Michael had expected this. As much as he pretended otherwise, Thack loved nothing better than 'bombing the house.' This adamant antimilitarist turned into Rambo incarnate when there were fleas to be annihilated.

'Who was that on the phone?'

'Mary Ann.'

Predictably, Thack winced.

Michael lowered the toilet seat cover and sat down. 'We're invited to dinner on Wednesday.'

Thack lifted Harry's head and sprayed around his neck. 'What brought this on?'

The implication was that Mary Ann had been keeping her distance lately. Fearing the truth of this, Michael didn't bother to argue. 'An old boyfriend's back in town. I think she thinks it might get heavy if it was just the three of them.'

'Which old boyfriend is this?'

'The one she met on the *Pacific Princess*. Who broke the story about the cannibal cult at Grace Cathedral.'

'Oh, yeah.'

'He's OK, actually. I mean, he was ten years ago.'

'He'd have to be,' said Thack. 'He got the hell away from her.'

Michael was tired of this kind of sniping. 'He didn't get away from her. He got a job offer in New York. He asked her to come with him, but she didn't want to leave San Francisco.'

Thack nodded. 'Too busy conquering it, no doubt.'

Michael stood up. 'I'll call her and cancel.'

'No.'

'If there's gonna be a scene . . .'

Thack flicked water at him. 'Sit down. Don't be such a prima donna.'

Michael sat down.

'Can't I just piss and moan a little?'

'If you pick a fight . . .'

'Who says I'm gonna pick a fight? Brian'll be there. I like him.'

Harry made a scramble for the side of the tub, his nails clicking frantically against the porcelain. Thack scooped him up and resumed rinsing.

'He doesn't like it too warm,' said Michael.

'I know.'

'And don't hit his balls with the spray. He hates that.'

Thack laughed. 'Yes, Alice.'

Michael gave him a dirty look.

'Well, you sounded like her,' said his lover. 'Just for a minute there.'

'Great.'

'Everybody's gotta sound like somebody.'

'Well, tell me what I'm doing, so I can fix it.'

Thack smiled. 'That wouldn't be the worst thing in the world.'

71

The hell it wouldn't. Homebody or not, he was damned if he was going to turn into his mother.

'Hand me Harry's towel,' said Thack.

This was a frayed blue beach towel bearing the logo of All-Australian Boy, a sentimental relic of Michael's tanning days at Barbary Beach. When his heart had still been hungry, he could spend an entire afternoon just getting his body ready for the night.

He snatched the towel off the shelf above the toilet and gave it to Thack. 'Let's go somewhere,' he said.

'When?'

'Tonight.'

'Like where?'

'I dunno. The Rawhide II?'

'Fine by me.' Thack wrapped the towel around Harry, then set him down on the floor and gave him a brisk rubdown under the terry cloth. 'What brought this on?'

'Nothing,' said Michael. 'I just thought it might be fun.'

'Oh.'

'We hardly ever go out.'

Thack peered up at him wryly. 'That's what I get for calling you Alice.'

They'd been talking about going for ages. Charlie Rubin had been there several times in the month before his death and had sent back glowing reports. Michael and Thack had planned on going with Polly and Lucy, but Polly had dumped Lucy – only hours before the date, in fact – for the first runner-up in the Ms International Leather competition. The new girlfriend preferred S & M to C & W, so Polly renounced the faith, and the boys were left dateless for the hoedown. To Michael's unending glee, Polly had spent the next three weeks being plied with jewelry for her clitoris.

When they arrived at the Rawhide II, a dance class

was in progress. The participants were in street clothes, pleasant looking but unextraordinary, as if the commuters on a BART train had acted on a sudden urge to waltz with one another. Fat and skinny, short and tall, couples of every configuration swirled around the room in a counterclockwise tide to the music of Randy Travis.

> *I'm gonna love you forever—*
> *Forever and ever, Amen:*
> *As long as old men live to talk about the weather—*
> *As long as old women live to talk about old men.*

Grinning uncontrollably, Michael found a stool at the bar and sat down. 'What do you want?' he asked, since Thack was undoubtedly headed for the john. He peed about as often as a dog in a palm grove.

'Beer,' said Thack. 'Miller's, I guess.'

'OK.'

'Do you see it?' He meant the men's room.

'It's the one marked Studs.' Michael rolled his eyes. 'As opposed to Fillies.'

'How sexist,' said Thack.

When he had gone, Michael ordered the drinks. As providence would have it, his beeper went off just as his Calistoga arrived. The bartender smiled at him. 'Another bionic man.'

Michael mugged ruefully. 'It usually goes off on a coatrack somewhere.' He dug out his pillbox and popped two, chasing them with the Calistoga. When he was done, the man on the stool next to him gave him a knowing look, then tapped the pocket of his Pendleton.

'I'm set to go off any second.'

Michael smiled. 'Last night at *Big Business*, there were enough to start a symphony.'

The man had dark, expressive eyes and the sweet ET.ish quality Michael had come to associate with guys who'd been sick for a long time.

73

'Do you take the middle-of-the-night dose?' Michael asked.

The man shook his head.

'Me either. Double doses at seven and eleven?'

'Yeah.'

'How's it going?'

The man shrugged. 'I've got six T-cells.'

Michael nodded and counted his own blessings in silence. The last time he checked, he had three hundred and ten.

'I'm feeling real possessive about them,' said the man. 'I may start giving them names.'

Michael chuckled. 'You've said that before.'

'Not tonight,' said the man.

Thack returned and leaned against Michael's stool, beer in hand. They watched the dance floor in silence as couple after couple revolved into view. This time the song was called 'Memories to Burn.'

'Look at her,' said Thack. 'Get a load of her.'

The object of his amazement was pantsuited, plump, and seventysomething. A tiny, pink-sequined sombrero was affixed to the side of her lilac hair, and she seemed to be enjoying herself no end. Her partner was a man about forty years her junior.

'She's a stitch,' said Michael.

'She's all yours,' said the man with six T-cells.

Michael turned and smiled at him. 'You know her?'

'I guess so. She's my mother.'

'Well . . .' Michael reddened. 'She's sure having a good time.'

'Isn't she?'

Thack laughed. 'She looks like a regular.'

The man grunted. 'A regular *what*, we won't say.'

'Does she live here?' Michael asked.

'She does now. She came out here five years ago from Havasu City. When I got sick.'

'Oh, yeah.'

'I guess she thought I didn't have too long, but . . . surprise, surprise.'

'She lives with you, then?' asked Thack.

'Oh, Lord, no. She lives with a friend of hers from Havasu City. The friend has a son here too.'

'Oh.'

'The two of 'em are real party animals.' He smiled dimly. 'She knows more queers than I do.'

Thack laughed. The old lady twirled into view for a moment, waggled her fingers at her son, and twirled off again.

'She's subdued tonight,' he said. 'She's got a whole outfit that goes with that hat.'

'You know . . .' Michael's brow furrowed. 'I think I've seen her before.'

The man looked at him. 'You play bingo at Holy Redeemer?'

'No.'

'How 'bout the Bare Chest Contest at the Eagle?'

Michael laughed. 'She goes to that?'

'Never misses one,' said the man.

'It must've been somewhere else,' said Michael.

The music ended, and the dance floor cleared. The old lady made a beeline for her son, dragging her partner by the hand.

'Ooowee,' she declared, patting her lilac wisps.

'How 'bout a Bud?' asked her son.

'Don't mind if I do. George, this is Larry. Larry, George.'

'Hi. Uh . . . this is . . .' The man turned to Michael and Thack, looking apologetic. 'We didn't actually get each other's names.'

'Michael.' He raised his hand in a sort of generalized greeting to all and sundry. 'This is Thack.'

Nods and murmurs.

75

The old lady cocked her head. 'Either of you boys feel like a go at it?'

'Oh, Lord,' said her son. 'She's worn out one and workin' on another.'

'You hush up,' said the old lady.

'You don't have to,' the man told Michael.

'I'd like to,' said Michael.

'You see, Larry,' said the old lady.

'I'm not sure I know *how*,' said Michael, seeing Thack's amusement out of the corner of his eye.

'Nothing to it.' The old lady took his hand and led him toward the floor.

'I thought you wanted a Bud,' yelled her son.

'Hang on to it,' she called back. 'Was it Michael, did you say?'

'Right.'

'Well, I'm Eula.'

'Hi,' he said.

Another song had already begun, so they waited for a space to open, then merged with the stream of waltzers. Custom seemed to demand holding your partner at arms' length, which worked out fine, really, since Eula's immense polyester-ruffled bosom had a few demands of its own.

'You're doin' good,' she said.

He chuckled. 'It's sorta the old, basic box step, isn't it?'

'That's it.' She nodded. 'Watch those girls ahead of us. They've got the knack of it.'

The 'girls' were a pair of fiftyish dykes in Forty-Niners jackets. They were good, all right, so Michael caught the rhythm of their movement and copied it.

'There you go,' said Eula. 'You got it.'

'Well, you're a good dancer,' Michael told her. And it was true, amazingly enough. She was remarkably light on her feet.

'First time here?' she asked.

76

'Uh-huh . . . well, no. I came here once in the early eighties, when it was called something else.'

'What was it called then?'

'I don't remember, actually.' This was a lie, pure and simple. It had been called the Cave, and the walls had been painted black. Its specialties had been nude wrestling and slave auctions. Why he was hiding this from a woman who frequented the Eagle's Bare Chest Contest, Michael did not know.

'That's my son you were talking to.'

'I know,' he said. 'He told me.'

'He don't like to go out much, but every now and then I make him.'

He didn't know what to say.

'Ronnie – that's his lover – he's even worse. All them boys wanna do is rent movies and stay home.'

'I know how they feel,' he said.

'Oh, now,' she said. 'You're more fun than that.'

The coquettish glint in her eye made him register finally on where he had seen her. 'You were at the Castro Theatre, weren't you? The Bow-Wow Beauty Pageant?'

'That was me,' she said.

'You had the Chihuahua, right? Dressed as Marie Antoinette?'

'Carmen Miranda.'

'Yeah. That was great.'

'Larry made the little hat,' she said proudly. 'He found all them little plastic bananas down at the Flower Mart, and he sewed 'em on a doll's bonnet.'

'Pretty clever.'

'He's good with a needle,' she said. 'He's been working on the AIDS Quilt.'

Michael nodded.

'He's already made ten panels for his friends.'

'That's nice,' he replied.

*

77

Five minutes later, at Eula's insistence, Michael led Thack on to the dance floor.

'Just once,' he said. 'Then we'll go home.'

His lover gave him a grumpy look but went along with it, faking a waltz step admirably.

'Look happy,' said Michael. 'She's watching.'

'She's not your mother.'

'I'll say.'

'And you wouldn't like it if she was.'

'I dunno,' said Michael. In his mind's eye, his mother was perpetually lunching at some mall in Orlando, telling anyone who insisted on knowing that her son lived 'in California' – never in San Francisco, because San Francisco was such a dead giveaway.

Thack said: 'You'd hate it if your mother was a fag hag.'

'Eula's not a fag hag.'

'That's her name? Eula?'

Michael smiled. 'She's just enjoying herself. Look, she's dancing with a dyke now.'

'OK,' said Thack. 'A dyke hag.'

'Be quiet. They're coming this way.'

Eula and her new partner waltzed alongside them. 'Lookin' good,' said Eula.

'Thanks,' said Michael. 'You too.'

Eula's partner was as short as Eula, only wiry and fortyish, with a delicate blue flower tattooed on her left bicep.

'Jesus,' said Michael, when they had danced out of sight. 'If Havasu City could see her now.'

Relieved to be done with nightlife for a while, they drove home to Noe Hill well before eleven. Harry greeted them deliriously at the door, toe-dancing like a carnival dog at the realization that they hadn't deserted him.

'Has he been walked?' Michael asked.

'Not by me.'

'I'll take him in a minute.'

78

While Thack shed his clothes, Michael sealed off the garbage with a twist tie and dragged it from its niche beneath the sink. Harry recognized this as a sign of impending departure and yelped indignantly for his walk.

'All right,' said Michael. 'I hear you.'

With the dog straining at the leash, he headed out into the darkness again and dropped the garbage into the curbside can. Thack had recently built a little weathered wood house for it, which looked homey and Martha's Vineyardish in the moonlight. Michael stopped and admired it long enough to receive another reprimand from Harry.

Dolores Park, Harry's daytime stomping grounds, was bristling with crack dealers and fag-bashers at night, so Michael opted for the safer circle route along Cumberland, Sanchez, and Twentieth streets. He freed the dog at the base of the Cumberland steps and watched as he rocketed through the oversized cacti to the softer, more welcoming green patch at the top. Before he could catch up with him, Harry was yapping in a way that could only mean he'd confronted an unidentifiable human.

'Harry!' he yelled, wary of being branded a noise polluter by the neighbors. 'Just shut up. Behave yourself.'

At the top of the steps, leaning against the rail, stood a chatty old geezer with a cane, who often 'took his constitutional' there.

'Little Harry,' said the man, as if that explained everything.

'He's a nuisance,' said Michael. 'I'm sorry.'

'That's just Harry. He's just announcing you.'

Harry circled the man, yapping obnoxiously.

'Harry!' Michael clapped his hands authoritatively. 'Get your fuzzy butt up the street!'

When the dog was gone, he gave the old man an apologetic smile and continued walking. It was odd to think that Harry had some sort of relationship, however abrasive, with at least half the people on this street. They all knew him by name, while Michael was regarded merely as Harry's owner. When he walked there by himself, the first thing they asked was: 'Where's Harry?'

He liked that, and he liked the talk that usually followed: good basic village chat about the drought or the wind, the graffiti problem, the roses in bloom, the ugly new house that looked like a Ramada Inn. What he had with the people on this block was an unspoken agreement to exchange pleasantries without exchanging names. It wasn't so different from the thing he'd enjoyed at the baths, the cordial anonymity that made strangers into equals.

Tagging after Harry, he passed the white picket fences of Cumberland, then turned right on Sanchez and climbed another set of stairs to Twentieth Street. Harry knew the route by heart, so since there was no traffic at night, Michael gave him freedom to explore at will. If the dog got too far ahead, he would wait patiently in the green darkness until Michael trudged into view.

When he reached Twentieth, a woman peeped from behind the curtains of her picture window. Recognizing him – or, more likely, Harry – she gave a chipper little wave. He waved back, realizing she was one of the Golden Girls, Thack's name for a group of Lithuanian ladies who played gin al fresco at a house down on Sanchez.

The moon hung fat and lemony over Twin Peaks when he reached the stairs leading down to Noe. He gazed at it contentedly, Harry by his side, until the beeper jolted him out of his reverie. Turning it off, he clipped the leash on Harry again and headed down the stairs toward home.

'You know what?' said Thack.

They were both – no, all three – in bed now, Thack snuggled against Michael's back, Harry burrowed under the new Macy's comforter, next to Michael's left calf.

80

'What?' asked Michael.

'I've got a great idea for a trellis.'

'OK.'

'We build it,' said Thack, 'in the shape of a triangle. And we grow pink flowers on it.'

'Cute.'

'I like it.'

'You would,' said Michael.

'Really,' said Thack. 'We wanted a trellis, and it would . . . you know, deliver a political message.'

'Do you think our neighbors really need the message?'

'Sure. Some of them. Anyway, it's celebratory.'

'Can't we just get a gay flag, like everybody else?'

'We could,' said Thack. 'Like everybody else.'

It really wasn't worth debating. 'OK, fine.'

'What? A flag or a pink triangle?'

'The pink triangle. Or both, for that matter. Go crazy.'

Thack chuckled wickedly. 'Be careful. My first idea was to write "Queer and Present Danger" above the door.'

He meant this, probably, so Michael kept his mouth shut.

'That would piss off ol' Loomis, wouldn't it?'

'Who's ol' Loomis?' asked Michael.

'You know. The guy who bitched about our Douche Larouche sign.'

'Oh, yeah.'

'Where the fuck does he think he's living, anyway? Homophobic old asshole!'

Michael chuckled and reached behind him to pat Thack's leg. 'You're such a Shiite.'

'Well,' said his lover, 'somebody's gotta do it.'

The Designer Bride

Smoldering, Mary Ann left the set and headed straight to her dressing room, barely acknowledging the associate producer who stumbled along beside her, pleading his case. 'Ilsa and I both talked to her last week,' he said, 'and she was a regular Chatty Cathy.'

'Swell,' she replied curtly. She had all but withered and died out there, and somebody was going to pay for it.

'If we'd had any *idea* . . .'

'That's your job, isn't it? To have some idea? The woman couldn't utter a complete sentence, Al. Forget sentence. I was lucky if I got "yes" or "no" out of her.'

'I know . . .'

'This is not television, Al. I don't know what it is, but it's not television.'

'Well, at least the audience could empathize.'

'What do you mean?'

'Just that . . . it was understandable.'

'Oh, really? How so?'

'Well, I mean . . . the traumatic aspect.'

'Al.' She sighed heavily, stopping at the door of her dressing room. 'It doesn't help much to know *why*, if she's not communicating with us.'

'I understand that.'

'Surely *somewhere* out there there's a woman who's been sodomized by her father and is capable of composing a few coherent sentences on the subject.'

82

'But she *did* when . . .'

'I know. When you and Ilsa talked to her. Terrific. Too bad nobody else got to hear it.' She opened the door, then turned and looked at him. 'I thought you said she was on Oprah.'

'She was.'

'Did she do that to Oprah?'

He shook his head.

'So what are you saying? It's my fault?'

'I'm not saying anything.'

'Good answer,' she said, and closed the door on him.

She was removing her makeup with broad angry swipes when the phone rang. She hesitated a moment, then picked it up, thinking it might be Burke. She hoped to God he hadn't seen the show. It was never too late for him to change his mind.

'Yes?'

'Mary Ann?' It was a woman's voice, fluty and frivolous.

'Who is this, please?'

'It's Prue, Mary Ann. Prue Giroux.'

She winced. 'Oh, yes.'

'They wouldn't put me through until I told them we were friends.' Prue giggled. 'You have marvelous watchdogs!'

Not marvelous enough, obviously. She'd done her damnedest for years to stay clear of this notorious climber. Prue's appetite for celebrities was such that she regarded Mary Ann as nothing less than a vital link in the foot chain. Mary Ann, after all, got first crack at the biggies.

'What's up, Prue?'

'Well, I know it's late notice, but I'm having a little impromptu session of the Forum this afternoon, and I'd love for you to come.'

The Forum was Prue's pretentious name for the

celebrity brunches she'd been throwing at her house for the past decade or so. They were almost always tedious affairs, populated by dubious local "personalities" and people who hoped to meet them.

'Oh, gosh,' she said, unintentionally mimicking Prue's gushy, little-girlish delivery. 'That's so sweet of you, but I'm up to my neck in work right now. We've got sweeps month coming up, you know.'

'You have to eat, don't you?'

How typical of this star-fucker not to take no for an answer. 'Prue,' she said evenly, 'I'd love to, but I'm afraid it's impossible.'

'That's such a shame. I just know you'd adore the Rands.'

What Rands? Certainly not *those* Rands.

'Russell just called up out of the blue last night and said that he and Chloe were in town.'

The very ones. How in the world . . . ?

Prue giggled. 'I told Russell he was naughty not to give me more warning, but . . . what can you do with creative people?'

'You're so right,' she replied. 'How long are they here for?' She had wanted to interview the designer for ages. The Forum might not be the ideal auspices under which to meet Russell Rand and his new bride, *but* . . .

'Just till Thursday,' said Prue. 'They're on their way to an AIDS benefit in LA.'

'Ah,' she replied, wondering why the hell none of her producers had heard about this. She might have been spared the indignity of dealing with Prue Giroux. 'Maybe, if I jiggle my schedule a little . . .'

'We aren't convening until two,' said Prue. 'You'll still have time to change.' There was a note of sly triumph in her voice; Mary Ann wanted to kill her. 'I've decided to wear the oldest Rand in my closet. Just to give him a giggle.'

'Well . . . sounds like lots of fun.'

'Doesn't it?' said Prue, thoroughly pleased with herself.

Mary Ann made a point of arriving late at Prue's Nob Hill town house. The usual crowd was assembled in the fussy Diana Phipps living room, converging on the famous couple like flies on carrion. Keeping her distance from this sorry spectacle, she headed for the canapés and waited for her hostess to track her down.

'Well,' came a voice from behind. 'Look who's here.'

It was Father Paddy Starr – red-faced, beaming, and resplendent in a raspberry shirt with a clerical collar.

'Hi, Father.'

'I saw you yesterday at D'orothea's, but I don't think you saw me.'

'No. I guess not.'

'Prue and I were in the front room. You were in the back with a gentleman.'

She fussed over the canapés, feigning disinterest. Father Paddy was too much of a fixture at the station to be entrusted with even the sketchiest information about Burke. The situation was ticklish enough as it was.

'Have you met them yet?' he asked.

She selected the palest cube of cheese she could find and popped it into her mouth. 'Who?'

He rolled his eyes impatiently. 'Dwight and Mamie Eisenhower.'

'If you mean them,' said Mary Ann, nodding toward the corner where the Rands were being eaten alive, 'I think they could use a little breather, don't you?'

Father Paddy selected an almond from a bowl of mixed nuts. 'They're used to it.'

'Maybe so, but it makes us look like hicks. So desperate and overeager.'

'Not me,' said the priest. 'I'm waiting my turn like a gentleman.'

'I didn't mean you.' She gave him a conciliatory look. 'It just makes me embarrassed for the city, that's all.'

This produced a sleepy, avuncular smile. 'Don't you worry about the city, darling.'

She recoiled privately at the 'darling' part, since it presumed the sort of cloying chumminess Father Paddy shared with Prue Giroux. Mary Ann simply didn't trust him enough to get campy with him.

The crowd parted a little, permitting a brief, dramatic glimpse of Chloe Rand. A pin spot intended for Prue's Hockney struck her face and rendered it classic: silky auburn hair, very short, and an elegant Castilian nose, which seemed to begin its descent in the middle of her forehead. Mary Ann was impressed.

'Isn't she stunning?' said Father Paddy.

'Very striking, yes.'

'Did you see the spread in *Vanity Fair*?'

'Yeah.'

'She's wearing a Rand Band,' said the priest. 'According to Prue.'

'A what?'

'That's what he calls his new line of wedding rings. Rand Bands.'

'Cute,' said Mary Ann. 'I thought they were supposed to be affordable.'

'They are.'

'And you think that's her real wedding ring?'

Father Paddy smirked. 'What a naughty girl you are.'

The crowd shifted again, and Russell Rand's famous profile came knifing into view. Scrubbed and tan, athletically lean, he looked uncannily like his wife, which lent a distinctly incestuous appeal to the intimacy they expressed so freely – and so frequently – in the presence of others.

'He bought her a Phantom jet for her birthday,' said Father Paddy.

'Really?'

The priest nodded, widening his eyes. 'Not a shabby little giftie, eh?'

'No,' she replied, almost mesmerized by the miraculous synchronism of those two shining faces. What must it be like to present such a picture of unity to the world? To share with someone else a life in which work and play are so artfully interwoven?

Why had she ever settled for less than that? Didn't she deserve the same thing? How had this happened to her?

'Let's go say hello,' said Father Paddy. 'It looks like there's an opening.'

'I think I'll wait.' The last thing she wanted was to face the Couple of the Year in the company of this gossipy old auntie. 'You go ahead.'

'Suit yourself,' he said, smiling. Then he clasped his hands across his stomach and glided off majestically, eyes on the horizon, like a wise man in search of a star.

She watched from several different places in the room as the priest bent their ear – and it did seem like one ear. Among the excited throng she spotted Lia Belli, several Aliotos, and the clownishly made up Frannie Halcyon Manigault, pushing seventy from the other side. She had half expected to see DeDe and D'orothea there – hadn't D'or once modeled for Russell Rand? – but the couple was nowhere in sight.

When the Rands were finally free of Father Paddy, she waited a moment before moving into their line of sight. As luck would have it, Chloe locked eyes with her almost immediately and gave her a sisterly smile.

'Hi,' said Mary Ann, extending her hand. 'I'm Mary Ann Singleton.'

Chloe took her hand cordially. 'Chloe Rand. And this is Russell.' Looking to her husband, she saw that he'd been set upon by someone else, so she gave Mary Ann a wide-eyed shrug and said: 'I think we lost him.' It came off as pleasant and schoolchummy.

'You must be exhausted,' said Mary Ann.

Chloe smiled without showing her teeth. 'It's been busy.'

'I'll bet.'

'Have we met before?'

Mary Ann shook her head and smiled.

'You look really familiar somehow. I guess I should know you, huh?'

'Not really. I know how many faces you see.'

'I know, but . . .'

'I host the morning talk show here.'

Chloe nodded. 'Right. Of course. We watched you on our last trip here.'

'Really?' She tried to sound pleased without getting gushy about it. Behave like a peer and they'll treat you like one. This was the first law of survival.

'It's a great show,' said Chloe.

She ducked her head graciously. 'Thanks.'

'Russell,' said Chloe, taking her husband's arm in such a way as to effect his escape. 'I hate to pull you away, but this is Mary Ann Singletary.'

'Singleton,' said Mary Ann.

'Oh, hell.' Chloe buried her elegant nose in her palm.

'It's OK,' she replied, shaking the designer's hand, reassuring Chloe with a look.

Russell Rand gave her a world-weary smile. 'It's been one of those days, if you know what I mean.' Like Chloe, he was making a gallant effort to draw her into their circle of intimacy.

Mary Ann wanted him to know that she sympathized, that she had a public every bit as demanding as his. 'I know exactly what you mean,' she said.

'Mary Ann has a talk show,' said Chloe. *'People Are Talking*, right?'

'No, actually. That's the other one.'

'We've seen you, though,' said Russell Rand. 'I remember your face.'

'Which one are you?' asked Chloe.

Mary Ann in the Morning.'

'Of course. How stupid.'

'You've got a partner,' said the designer, nodding. 'Ross something.'

Mary Ann wished he would just drop it. 'That's *People Are Talking*.'

'Right, right. Your partner's name is . . . ?'

'I work alone.'

'Sure. Of course.' He nodded authoritatively, as if he'd known that all along.

'I remember the show, though,' said Chloe. 'It was Cheryl Thingy . . . you know, Lana Turner's daughter.'

'Cheryl Crane,' said Mary Ann.

'Was that you?'

'That was me.' It wasn't, it was *People Are Talking*, but why not spare everybody the embarrassment? 'How long are you here for?' she asked, turning to the designer.

'Just a day or so, I'm afraid. We're doing an AIDS benefit in LA.'

'It's sort of spur-of-the-moment,' said Chloe, 'but Elizabeth asked us.'

Elizabeth. Just plain Elizabeth. As if Chloe and Mary Ann both knew the woman much too well to bother with her last name. Mary Ann felt worldly beyond belief. 'She's doing great work,' she said.

'She's the best,' said Russell Rand.

'I don't suppose,' said Mary Ann carefully, 'you're doing any press while you're here.'

'Not really.' Chloe looked sweetly apologetic.

'Well, I certainly understand.'

'I'm sure you do,' said Russell knowingly.

'If you wanna get away . . . I mean, just for some quiet

89

time . . . we have a place at The Summit, and I cook a mean rack of lamb.'

'Isn't that nice?' said Chloe. 'I'm afraid we haven't got a single free moment.'

'Well, I understand, of course.' She felt herself blushing hideously. Why had she even tried? They could have gone on talking about Elizabeth. All that was left for her now was a graceful retreat.

'Next time, for sure,' said Chloe, 'when our schedule's less hectic.'

'Great,' said Mary Ann.

'It was lovely meeting you,' said Russell.

'Same here,' said Mary Ann, backing away into the pressing throng.

As she had feared, Prue cornered her before she could make it out the door.

'Did you meet them?' asked the hostess, looking preposterous in her 'oldest Russell Rand'—a navy wool suit with a huge kelly-green bow across the bosom.

'Oh, yes.'

'Aren't they dear?' bubbled Prue.

'Very.'

'And so real.'

'Mmm.'

'They met at Betty Ford, you know. She was a counselor or therapist or something, and she just turned his life around. It's really the most romantic story.'

Mary Ann edged toward the door before Prue could regurgitate the entire *Vanity Fair* article. 'I'm afraid I've gotta dash,' she said. 'My little girl's waiting to be picked up at Presidio Hill.'

'Well, I'm glad you could make it.'

'Me too,' said Mary Ann.

'I didn't want you to miss out,' said Prue, making damn sure she got credit for the coup.

On her way out the door, Mary Ann caught a final

glimpse of the famous couple as they exchanged another look of excruciating intimacy. Their love was like an aura that surrounded them, protecting them from the crush of the crowd. *This is possible*, they seemed to be telling her. *You can have what we have if you refuse to settle for less.*

She knew in that instant what she would have to do.

A Picnic

At noon the next day Brian and Thack took a bag lunch to the top of Strawberry Hill, the island in the middle of Stow Lake. (Typically, a hassle with the nursery suppliers in Half Moon Bay had caused Michael to drop out at the last minute). As Brian looked out over the dusty greenery of the park, Thack ripped open the Velcro closure of his wallet and produced a joint.

'Hey,' said Brian. 'My man.'

Huddling under his Levi's jacket against the wind, Thack lit the joint, took a drag, and handed it over.

'Boy,' said Brian. 'It's been a while.'

'Has it?'

'Yeah. Mary Ann doesn't do this anymore.'

Thack shrugged. 'Why should that stop you?'

'Well, it gets in the furniture, she says. People can smell it.'

Thack nodded dourly, his wheat-straw hair whipping in the wind, his gaze fixed on a distant flotilla of pedal boats as they rounded the bend into view.

Brian knew what Thack was thinking. 'She's got a point,' he added, trying to explain himself. 'She's kind of a public figure.'

No reaction.

Brian found a flat rock and sat on it. Thack joined him, handing him the joint. He took another toke and said: 'She's not as bad as you think. You don't see the side of her I do.'

'Hey . . .' Thack held up his hands as if to say: Leave me out of it.

'I know how you feel about her, though.'

Thack said: 'I really don't have an opinion one way or the other.'

'Bullshit.'

'I don't. How could I? We don't see her that much.'

To Brian this sounded a lot like an accusation. 'Yeah. I guess so.'

'I didn't mean we expect you to . . .'

'She gets wrapped up in things. I don't see her that much myself.'

'I know.'

'She's missed you both. She told me so last night. That's why tonight is so important to her.'

Thack seemed puzzled.

'Dinner at our house.'

'Oh, yeah. Sorry.' A sheepish smile.

'That's OK. I don't remember that kinda shit either.'

'What's the story on this guy?'

'Oh . . .' He took another toke. 'Mary Ann used to date him.'

'Date?'

'OK, fuck . . . if you wanna get technical.'

Thack chuckled.

'He lives in New York now. He's in town doing research on an AIDS story.'

'Oh, yeah? As a reporter?'

'Producer,' said Brian. 'TV.'

Thack nodded.

'I've been your basic basket case, of course.'

'Why?'

He shrugged.

'When did she last see him?'

'Eleven years ago.'

Thack smiled. 'Nothing is the same after eleven years.'

93

'I guess not. Plus he's got a wife and two kids and a little dick . . .'

'Whoa,' said Thack. 'Who told you that?'

'Mary Ann.'

'When?'

'Last night.'

He laughed. 'You asked her . . . ?'

'She volunteered it, OK?'

'Just out of the blue, huh?'

Brian saw Thack's lip flicker slightly. 'You think she said that just to make me feel better?'

'Threw you a bone, so to speak?'

Brian laughed.

'I think you're being paranoid.'

'Yeah. I guess so. As usual, huh?'

Thack smiled, then twisted off the tops of the ciders and unwrapped the sandwiches. 'This is the one with mustard,' he said, handing Brian a sandwich. 'If you want more, there are some packets in that bag there.'

'This looks fine.'

'We can fight over who gets Michael's Yoplait.'

'We're not gonna fight over his sandwich?'

'Nope. All yours.' Thack munched away for a moment, then said: 'I wouldn't worry about it.'

'I'm not,' said Brian.

They left the park at one-thirty and took a bus up Twenty-fifth Avenue to the nursery. Thack would walk from there to a house off Geary he was assessing for the preservation people. When the bus stopped at Balboa, a pair of teenagers boarded with noisy ceremony. Some gut instinct told Brian to brace himself for trouble.

'Better not be,' he heard one of them say.

'Yeah,' said his much shorter sidekick. They were both overacting for their captive audience.

Brian glanced at Thack, who sat stock-still, cocking his head like a forest creature listening for alien footfall.

The tall teenager dumped his fare into the slot. 'Better not be . . . cuz I ain't gettin' AIDS.'

'Shit, no,' said the short one.

'You catch AIDS and die like a fuckin' dog.' He was moving toward the back now, brandishing the acronym like a switchblade. 'Whatcha think? Any *faggots* on this bus?'

There was a moment of excruciating silence before Thack did the predictable and piped up. 'Yeah,' he said, 'over here.' He was raising his hand with the kind of bored assurance a schoolkid gives off when he knows he's got the right answer.

Brian looked back at the teenagers, who stood slack-mouthed and silent, clearly at a loss for what to do next.

'There's one over here too.' This from a stout young black woman across the aisle.

'There you go,' said Thack, addressing the boys.

'Back here.' Two older guys in the back of the bus raised their hands.

'Yo,' called someone else.

Then came laughter, uncertain at first but growing to volcanic dimensions, rumbling from one end of the bus to the other. The short kid was the first to feel the heat, taking cover in the first available seat. The tall one muttered a half-assed 'Shit' and scanned the crowd desperately for allies. He seemed on the verge of rebuttal when his buddy grabbed his belt and yanked him down into a seat.

Grinning, Brian turned back to Thack. 'You're a crazy man.'

'Don't try it in New Jersey,' said Thack.

'New Jersey, hell. You could get killed doing that.'

'That's what Michael says.' Thack turned and looked out the window as the bus lurched down the avenue. 'Fuck it. I'm tired of this shit.'

Parlor Games

Archibald Anson Gidde, a prominent San Francisco realtor and social leader, died Tuesday at his home in Sea Cliff after a bout with liver cancer. He was 42.

Mr Gidde was a witty and flamboyant figure who distinguished himself by spearheading some of the City's most notable real estate transactions, among them the recent $10 million sale of the Stonecypher mansion to the Sultan of Adar.

A member of the Bohemian Club, he was active on the boards of the San Francisco Ballet, the San Francisco Opera, and the American Conservatory Theatre.

Mr Gidde is survived by his parents, Eleanor and Clinton Gidde of Ross and La Jolla, and a sister, Charlotte Reinhart, of Aspen, Colo.

'Well, I'll be damned.' Michael looked up from the *Examiner* just as his lover emerged from the bathroom.

'You knew him?' asked Thack, reading over Michael's shoulder.

'Not exactly. He bought some things at the nursery once or twice. Jon knew him. He was one of the big A-Gays.'

'Figures.'

'What do you mean?'

'Liver cancer,' explained his lover, scowling. 'How tired is that?'

For the past few years Thack had made a parlor game out of spotting the secret AIDS deaths in the obituary columns. Given the age of the deceased, the absence of a spouse, and certain telltale occupational data, he would draw his own conclusions and fly into a towering rage.

'Notice how they called him flamboyant? How's that for a code word?'

Michael was tired of this.

'Fuck him,' Thack continued. 'How dare he act ashamed? Who does he think he's fooling, anyway? He can sell his pissy houses in hell!'

'C'mon.'

'What do you mean, c'mon?'

'The guy is dead, Thack.'

'So what? He was a worm in life, and he's a worm in death. This is why people don't give a shit about AIDS! Because cowardly pricks like this make it seem like it's not really happening!'

Michael paused, then said: 'We've gotta move it, sweetie. We're gonna be late as it is.'

Thack shot daggers at him and left the room.

'Wear the green sweater,' Michael yelled after him. 'You look great in that.'

Mary Ann and Brian's condo-in-the-sky was not Michael's idea of a dream house. From twenty-three stories the city looked like a plaster-of-Paris model of itself, hardly the real thing at all. Lately Mary Ann had made an effort at jazzing up the chilly modern interiors with a lot of Southwestern stuff – painted furniture, steer skulls, and the like – but the effect was not so much Santa Fe as Santa Fe Savings and Loan. Maybe it just wasn't fixable.

The Vietnamese maid took their coats and led them into the living room, a place of too little texture and too much teal. Brian was ensconced behind the wet bar, looking unnaturally cheerful in a pink button-down. Mary Ann and Burke were at opposite ends of the big crescent-shaped couch.

'Michael,' said Burke, smiling as he rose.

'Hey, Burke.' Michael wondered if a hug was appropriate. It had been eleven years, after all, and the guy was straight.

He played it safe and stuck out his hand.

Burke shook it warmly, using both his hands in the process, suggesting that a hug might have been in order, after all. 'You look great,' said Burke.

'Thanks. You too.' Mary Ann's old flame seemed lean as ever in a blazer and gray flannel slacks. His fine, pale hair – very much the same color as Thack's – had receded significantly, but Michael thought it suited his air of quiet intelligence. True, the yup-yellow tie was a little off-putting, but you had to make allowances for New Yorkers.

Thack stepped forward, touching the small of Michael's back. 'Burke,' said Michael, 'this is my lover, Thack.'

Burke pumped Thack's arm energetically. 'Good to meet you.'

'Same here,' said Thack.

Mary Ann hugged Michael and pecked him chastely on the cheek. 'We were just talking about you,' she said. He was almost positive her scent was Elizabeth Taylor's Passion. When on earth had she started doing that?

He returned the peck. 'You want me to go out again, so you can finish?'

She giggled. 'No. Hi, Thack.' She hugged Thack, who made a passable show of hugging back. You would have thought they did it all the time. 'You guys both look *wonderful!*'

It was a little too gushy. Michael hated it when she over-compensated like this. What state of deterioration had she expected to find him in, anyway?

'What'll it be?' Brian asked from behind the bar. 'A couple of Calistogas?'

'Great,' said Michael.

'I'll take a bourbon, actually,' said Thack.

Michael shot his lover a glance. Thack rarely touched the hard stuff. Was he that uncomfortable about the evening ahead?

'Awriight,' crowed Brian. 'A serious drink.'

Burke grinned at this interchange, then addressed Brian: 'You used to be a real bartender, didn't you? Down at Benny's.'

'Perry's,' said Brian.

'That's right.'

'I was a waiter, though.'

'Oh.'

'He was a lawyer before that,' Mary Ann put in, 'but he took on so many liberal causes that he sort of burned out.'

Michael saw Brian's expression and knew what he was thinking: Why does she always have to say that? Wouldn't a waiter have been enough?

Brian locked eyes with his wife, plastered a sickly smile on his face, and returned his attention to Thack's bourbon.

'And now you guys are nurserymen.' Still a little over-jovial, Burke looked first at Michael, then at Brian.

'Right,' Michael answered.

'You need water . . . soda?' Brian was talking to Thack now.

'On the rocks is fine.'

'You got it,' said Brian.

'We've been partners for three years,' Michael told Burke.

'That's great.'

'Here you go, sport.' Brian handed Michael a Calistoga on the rocks. Michael and Thack went to the big curving couch and sat down in the space between Mary Ann and Burke.

Mary Ann reached over and gave Michael's knee a shake. 'I can't get over how good you look.'

Michael smiled and nodded and said: 'I feel good.'

'Hey,' said Burke. 'You know who I was thinking about today?'

'Who?' Mary Ann turned, letting go of Michael's knee.

'Our old landlady. Mrs Thingamabob.'

'Madrigal,' said Michael. 'Shit!'

Mary Ann frowned. 'What?'

Flooded with guilt, Michael looked at Thack. 'We were gonna call her. You were gonna remind me.'

'Oh, hell,' said his lover.

Brian settled into the big white leather chair across from the sofa. 'You can use the phone in the bedroom if . . .'

'No,' said Michael. 'It's too late.'

'She went to Lesbos,' Thack explained.

Burke laughed. 'Sounds like her.'

'*Damn* it,' muttered Michael.

Mary Ann looked lost. 'Why on earth did she go to Lesbos?'

'Because it's there,' said Burke, laughing.

'She's meeting Mona there,' said Michael. 'Her daughter.'

'Damn,' said Burke. 'I remember her. Frizzy red hair, right?'

'That's her,' said Michael.

'Didn't you use to go out with her?' Burke was addressing Brian now.

'Once or twice,' said Brian.

'She became a lesbian,' said Mary Ann.

There was an awkward silence before Brian told Burke: 'The two events were not related.'

This got an awkward chuckle.

Michael felt compelled to speak up on Mona's behalf. 'She was a lesbian long before she met Brian.'

'Thank you,' said Brian.

Mary Ann looked at her husband. 'I wasn't impugning your prowess, for God's sake.'

'Sorry.' Burke laughed, obviously thinking he had opened a touchy subject.

'No,' said Mary Ann, laughing to reassure him. 'Really.'

'Where is she now?' asked Burke.

'In England,' said Mary Ann. 'She married a lord and lives in this huge house in the Cotswolds.'

'Does the lord know she's a lesbian?'

'Oh, sure,' Michael told him. 'He's gay himself. They don't live together. He lives here. He drives a cab for Veterans.'

'Well,' said Burke. 'Thanks for clearing that up.'

As everyone laughed, Michael marveled at the apparent ease with which the four old housemates had reunited. Then, in a fleeting moment of self-torment, he pictured poor Mrs Madrigal sitting alone amid her carpetbags in some fly-specked Grecian airport without benefit of his bon voyage.

They were seated at the big green glass dining table when Michael realized who was missing.

'Hey, where's Shawna?'

'In her room,' said Mary Ann.

Brian glanced at his wife, then spoke to Michael: 'She's playing with her new Nintendo game.'

'Ah.' Michael nodded.

'She's not very good around new grownups,' said Mary Ann.

'She was fine,' said Burke. 'Really.'

Brian looked faintly apologetic. 'Sometimes it takes her a while,' he told Burke.

'No problem,' said Burke. 'Really.'

Michael and Thack communicated briefly with their eyes. Had Shawna been antisocial? Had she thrown a tantrum and been banished to her room?

When the maid appeared with a tray of mint-wrapped fish, Mary Ann jumped at the chance to change the subject. 'Nguyet,' she said, beaming up at the girl, 'those spring rolls were absolutely your best ever.'

Burke murmured in agreement, his mouth still full of the food under discussion.

The maid giggled. 'You like?'

'Very much,' said Thack, joining in the praise. 'Absolutely delicious.'

Nguyet ducked her eyes, then set down the tray and fled the room.

'She's shy,' said Mary Ann.

'But sweet,' said Burke.

'Isn't she?' Mary Ann waited until the girl was out of earshot. 'Her family had a horrible time getting out of Saigon.'

'She was a baby. She doesn't even remember that,' said Brian.

'Well, I know, but . . . you can't help but feel for her.'

Burke nodded, eyes fixed on the door to the kitchen.

'They live in some awful tenement in the Tenderloin, but they're the nicest, most industrious people.' Mary Ann handed the tray of fish to Burke. 'They're also incredibly clean. They're much cleaner than . . . almost anybody.'

Than who? thought Michael. Cleaner than who? Across the table he saw a homicidal glint come into Thack's eyes. Please, he telegraphed, just leave it alone.

There was one of those moments of total silence – a 'mind fart,' as Mona used to say – before Thack turned to Burke and announced: 'I just realized something.'

'What's that?'

'I saw you on CNN last month.'

'Oh, yeah?'

'It was some sort of panel discussion about television.'

'Oh, right.'

'You're producing something, aren't you? Some new show?'

'Well . . .' Burke looked vaguely uncomfortable. Or maybe it was modesty. 'There's a new project in the works, but it's not very far along yet.'

Mary Ann jumped in. 'Burke did that special on Martin Luther King last year.'

'I saw that,' said Michael. 'It was wonderful.'

'Thanks,' said Burke.

'I actually went to Selma,' said Brian. 'I mean, I participated.'

'Really?' Burke's response seemed a little patronizing, though he undoubtedly hadn't intended it that way. Michael found it touching that Brian had offered up this ancient credential for his guest's approval.

'What's this new show about?' asked Thack.

'Oh . . . just a general magazine format.' Looking distracted, Burke turned back to Brian. 'You were part of the civil disobedience and all that?'

'Oh, yeah.'

'That's when he was a lawyer,' said Mary Ann.

'No,' said Brian. 'That was earlier. I didn't pass the bar until 1969.'

'Right,' said Mary Ann. 'Of course.'

'I wish I'd been there,' said Burke.

'You were too young,' said Mary Ann.

Burke shrugged. 'Not by much, really. Anyway, it was a great time. Things happened. People cared enough to make them happen. I mean, look at the seventies. What a great big blank that was.'

Michael saw the cloud pass over his lover's face and realized with certainty what was about to happen. 'I don't know about that,' Thack said.

Burke offered him a sporting smile. 'OK. What happened?'

'Well,' said Thack, 'gay liberation for one thing.'

'How so?'

'What do you mean – how so?'

'In what form? Discos and bathhouses?'

103

'Yeah,' answered Thack, clearly beginning to bristle. 'Among other things.'

Burke, thankfully, was still smiling. 'For instance?'

'For instance . . . marches and political action, a new literature, marching bands, choruses . . . a whole new culture. You guys didn't cover it, of course, but that doesn't mean it didn't happen.'

'We guys?'

'The press,' said Thack. 'The people who decided that black pride was heroic but gay pride was just hedonism.'

'Hey, sport,' said Brian. 'I don't think he said that.'

'He means the press in general,' said Michael.

'Well, then don't blame me for . . .'

'I'm not,' said Thack, more pleasantly than before. 'I just think you should know that something happened in the seventies. It may not have been part of your experience, but something happened.'

Burke nodded. 'Fair enough.'

'The seventies were our sixties, so to speak.' Michael contributed this inanity and regretted it as soon as it tumbled out of his mouth. 'This decade talk is ridiculous. Everybody's experience is different.'

'Maybe so,' said Thack, still addressing Burke, 'but you should know something about the gay movement if you're doing a story on AIDS.'

Burke looked confused.

'Did I get that wrong?' Thack turned to Brian. 'Didn't you say he was . . . ?'

Brian shrugged and gestured toward his wife. 'That's what she said.'

'Oh.' Mary Ann looked flustered for a moment, then addressed Burke. 'I explained that that's why you're here. To do a story on AIDS.'

'Oh,' said Burke. 'Right. Of course. I drifted there for a moment.'

Mary Ann seized a bottle of wine and held it out. 'Who needs a little freshener?'

Almost everyone did.

After dinner, while the group was resettling in the living room, Michael headed off to take a leak. On his way back he passed Shawna's room and found the little girl wielding a crayon at her child-sized drafting table.

He spoke to her from the doorway. 'Hi, Shawna.'

She looked over her shoulder for a moment, then continued drawing. 'Hi, Michael.'

'Whatcha drawing?'

No answer.

'Just . . . art, huh?'

'Uh-huh.'

'Can I come in?'

'May I,' said Shawna.

He grinned. 'May I?'

'Yes.'

He stood behind her and studied her work, a jumble of brown rectangles scribbled over with green. In the corner, inscribed on a much smaller rectangle, was the number 28.

'I know what that is,' he said.

The child shook her head. 'Huh-uh. It's a secret.'

'Well, it looks to me like Anna's house.'

She gazed up at him, blinking once or twice, apparently surprised at his cleverness.

'That's one of my favorite houses,' he said.

She hesitated a moment, then said: 'I like it 'cause it's a on-the-ground house.'

He chuckled.

'What's funny?'

'Nothing. I agree with you.' He touched her shoulder lightly. She was wearing a white ruffled blouse and a midi-length blue velvet skirt, obviously meant for company. Yet here she sat, stately and alone at her easel, like some miniature version of Georgia O'Keeffe.

He went to the window and peered down on the silvery

plain of the bay. A freighter slid toward the ocean, lit up like a power station yet tiny as a toy from this height. Directly beneath him – how many hundred feet? – the house in Shawna's drawing slept unseen in the neighboring greenery.

He turned back to the child. 'Anna's gone to Greece on vacation. Did she tell you that?'

Shawna shook her head. 'I don't go see her anymore.'

'Why not?'

Silence.

'Why not, Shawna?'

'Mary Ann doesn't want me to.'

This threw him, but he didn't respond. The kid could make up some pretty off-the-wall stuff. Especially when it came to Mary Ann. It was bound to be more complicated than that.

Shawna asked: 'Are you gonna make that noise tonight?'

'What noise?'

'You know. Beep, beep.'

He smiled at her. 'Not for a few hours.'

'Can I see it? I mean, may I?'

'Well, you could, but it's in my overcoat, and that's on the bed in . . .'

'Is she giving you a hard time?'

Michael turned to see Brian standing in the doorway. 'No way,' he said.

'How's it going, Puppy?'

'OK.'

'She's done some beautiful work,' said Michael.

Brian looked at the picture and ruffled his daughter's hair. 'Hey . . . not bad. What do you call it?'

'Art,' said Shawna.

Brian laughed. 'Well, OK. Makes sense to me. Did you tell Michael what you're gonna be?'

Shawna gave him a blank look.

'For Halloween,' Brian added.

'Oh . . . Michaelangelo.'

Michael was impressed. 'The painter, eh?'

'No,' said Shawna. 'The Teenage Mutant Ninja Turtle.'

Michael looked to Brian for translation.

'You don't wanna know,' said Brian. 'It's an actual thing. She's not making it up.'

'Teenage Mutant . . . ?'

'Ninja Turtle,' said Shawna.

'We're going for Turtle mostly, with just a *hint* of Ninja. Wanna come along? It's Halloween morning. Mary Ann'll be at the station.'

'What is it?' he asked.

'Just a thing at the school. A parade or something.'

'Well . . .'

'We'd be back by eleven, tops.' Brian winked at him.

'OK, then. Great.'

'Yay,' crowed Shawna.

'See,' said Brian. 'I told you he'd do it.'

The child looked at her father. 'Can Michael be a Teenage Mutant Ninja Turtle?'

'Well, he *could* . . .'

'It's either that,' said Michael, 'or Ann Miller.'

Brian laughed. 'I think your Ann Miller days are over.'

'Why?' Michael grinned back at him. 'Ann Miller's aren't.'

Shawna looked at them both. 'Who's Ann Miller?'

'Oh, God,' said Michael, laughing. 'Don't ask.'

'Yeah,' said Brian, letting his eyes dart toward Shawna as a signal to Michael. 'Certain undersized personages know too much about lipstick as it is.'

Michael chuckled, remembering the incident – or at least Brian's version of Mary Ann's version of the incident. 'Is she still upset about that?'

'Who's Ann Miller?' Shawna persisted.

'She wasn't really upset,' said Brian.

The child, Michael was thinking, must have looked

uncannily like her natural mother once a stiff coat of makeup had been applied. No wonder Mary Ann had freaked. Tacky ol' Connie Bradshaw, the bane of Mary Ann's existence, back from the grave to do her embarrassing number all over again.

'Who's Ann Miller?'

'She's a lady who dances,' said Brian. 'A woman.'

'A lady,' said Michael.

Brian laughed and touched his daughter's shoulder. 'You wanna hit the sack, Puppy?'

'Yeah.'

'Kiss Michael good night, then.'

Shawna gave Michael a peck on the cheek.

'That's a cool dress,' said Michael.

'Thanks,' she replied solemnly.

'She got that special for tonight,' said Brian.

'Well, it's just right,' he told her. 'It brings out the blue in your eyes.'

Shawna basked in the attention for a moment, then looked at her father. 'Are you gonna tuck me in?'

'And anyway,' Mary Ann was saying when Michael returned, 'it's not exactly a state secret. Raquel Welch is absolutely notorious for being difficult . . .'

Burke chuckled. 'To put it mildly.'

Thack laughed, apparently enjoying himself. Seeing Michael, he asked: 'Have you heard this story?'

'Oh, God,' said Mary Ann. 'Too many times, I'm sure.'

'A few,' he said. 'It's a good one.'

'Well, it's over,' she said, laughing, 'so you're safe. Where's Brian?'

'Putting Shawna to bed.'

'Oh.'

The phone rang in the guest bedroom. Since Michael was nearest to it, he said: 'Shall I?'

'Leave it,' said Mary Ann. 'The machine's on.'

'Actually,' said Burke, 'I'm halfway expecting a call

from some friends. I left your number. I hope that's all right.'

'Of course.' Mary Ann hurried toward the ring.

Burke offered the rest of his explanation to Thack and Michael. 'They're just here for a little while, and they wanted to meet for drinks later. I thought, if no one minded . . .'

'Whatever,' said Michael.

'Yeah,' said Thack.

Mary Ann reappeared in the doorway. 'It's for you,' she told Burke quietly, almost reverently. 'It's Chloe Rand.'

Desperadoes

She couldn't help noticing how placidly Burke received this information. He smiled faintly and nodded, but his face betrayed nothing, not the slightest degree of amazement. She might just as well have told him his wife was on the phone.

When he was out of the room, she turned to find Michael gaping at her. 'Not *the* Chloe Rand?'

Thack gave Michael a cranky look. 'How many Chloe Rands can there be?'

'They're in town, you mean?' His expression was truly gratifying.

'Yeah.' She resolved to remain as nonchalant about this as Burke. 'Just for a day or so. They're doing an AIDS benefit in LA.'

This provoked a grunt from Thack, but nothing else. She wasn't about to ask him what he meant. He was forever grinding his axes in public, and she'd been singed by the sparks once too often.

Michael gave Thack a peevish glance and seemed on the verge of saying something, when Burke reappeared. 'Look,' he told her sheepishly, 'my friends have asked us to join them for drinks at Stars. If that's not OK . . .'

'No,' she said. 'It's fine.'

'It's Russell and Chloe Rand. I think you'd like them.'

'Fine. Whatever.'

'Guys?' Burke turned to Michael and Thack.

'Great,' answered Michael, apparently speaking for both of them. She couldn't tell *what* Thack was thinking. When he brooded, his face became an infuriating blank. She was halfway hoping he would make a fuss, or at least talk Michael into bowing out graciously. Four tagalongs was a bit much. The Rands were already getting more than they had bargained for.

Burke gave her another doggy look. 'I would've mentioned it earlier, but . . .'

'Look,' she said, getting a brainstorm. 'Why don't you invite them here?'

'Well . . .'

'They can just . . . kick back and relax.'

'That's nice of you,' said Burke, 'but I think they're kind of . . . entrenched.'

'Right,' she said evenly. But she was thinking: He hates the house. He thinks it's not chic enough for them.

'Shall I check with Brian?' Burke asked.

'No,' she said. 'He'll go.'

'Great,' said Burke, and he went back to the phone.

Where had she screwed up, anyway? The Indian blankets, the saguaro skeleton, the painted steer skulls . . . ?

The tiny, clear voice of her fashion sense told her that was impossible.

She had copied that stuff from a Russell Rand ad.

It was agreed that they'd arrive at the restaurant in two cars: Mary Ann, Brian, and Burke in Mary Ann's Mercedes; Michael and Thack in their VW. There was also the minor matter of a baby-sitter, and Nguyet, as usual, required nothing less than a bald-faced bribe before consenting to stay at the house past midnight. Brian, typically, knew next to nothing about the Rands, so while Burke was in the bathroom, Mary Ann dug into her stash of *Interviews* and gave her husband a hasty briefing.

On the way there, while Brian and Burke gabbed away in the front seat about Joe Montana's vertebrae, she filled her nostrils with the sweet scent of her gray leather interiors and took stock of herself. Had she known the evening would end with the Russell Rands, she might not have worn this uneventful little Calvin Klein cocktail dress.

Still, it showed she cared about such things. It seemed a bit much, anyway, to wear a Russell Rand outfit in the actual presence of Russell Rand. She conducted a hasty mental inventory of the women she'd seen with him in photographs. Had Liza worn his clothes when she went out with him? Had Elizabeth? Maybe only desperadoes like Prue Giroux did that.

For that matter, what about the Passion she had on? Was it gauche to wear Elizabeth Taylor's perfume around people who knew Elizabeth Taylor? People who knew what she actually smelled like? Maybe her real friends found the stuff laughable and pretentious. Certainly Cher's must. How could they not?

She would not dwell on it. The stuff wasn't cheap, after all, and Taylor had done so much for AIDS. Mary Ann had worn it mostly to please Michael, to show her support. She would say that, if the subject came up. It was the truth, anyway.

'And over there,' Brian was telling Burke with great authority, 'is the Hard Rock. It's OK, but it's kind of a kid's joint.'

'Brian,' she said, 'I think they've got one in New York.'

'I know that. I was just telling him about this one.'

'They're all the same,' she told him.

'The one in London is decent,' Burke put in. 'It was the first, I think.'

'Yes,' she said. 'It was.'

'Look at that fog,' said Brian. 'Look what it does to the neon. Isn't that great?'

Burke made an appreciative noise, obviously just being polite.

She shot Brian a quick look. 'Not everyone likes fog, you know?'

'Go on,' he replied with mock disbelief.

'Well, it's true.'

Brian looked at Burke. 'You like it, don't you?'

An easy grin and a shrug. 'Sure.'

'You gotta admit it beats the shit outa that stuff in New York. That stuff you have to scrape off your face.' Brian laughed, apparently to keep this from sounding hostile, but it didn't work. 'I mean . . . c'mon.'

Burke was gallant about it. 'Yeah . . . well, you're right about that.'

'He's such a San Francisco chauvinist,' she told Burke.

'And you're not?' Brian mugged at her.

'I like it,' she said calmly. 'I don't think it's the be-all and the end-all. And I don't think it's particularly nice to bad-mouth our guest's city.'

'C'mon,' said Brian, smiling to cover his tracks. 'He didn't take it that way.' He gave Burke a buddy-buddy wink. 'Anyway, I like New York. I wouldn't wanna *live* there . . . et cetera, et cetera.'

She clutched for a moment. Was that remark just coincidental, or was he on to her? Either way, she vowed to ignore it.

'How do you know the Rands?' she asked Burke pleasantly.

'Oh, you know,' he replied. 'Through friends.'

She started to tell him about meeting them at Prue's, but changed her mind in fear that they wouldn't remember her. If they *did* remember her and remarked on it, her silence at this point would simply come off as self-effacing. It was better to keep her mouth shut.

As Brian swung the Mercedes into Redwood Alley, she gazed out the window at a gaggle of opera-goers heading up the sidewalk toward the restaurant. Who among her associates, she wondered, might see her there tonight with the Rands?

It was almost too delicious to imagine.

The cavernous elegance of Stars never failed to seduce her. To enter this room full of feverish chatter and French poster art was to feel at one with a living tableau, something from the twenties, maybe, and certainly not from here. If you squinted your eyes just so, the illusion was more than enough to transport you.

As she had already envisioned, the Rands were imperially positioned on the platform at the end of the room. Chloe was in red leather tonight, her shoulders pale as milk under the stained-glass chandeliers. Russell looked wonderfully Duke of Windsorish in a herring-bone Norfolk jacket. Where had they been, anyway? The opera? Another party?

Chloe saw them first. She wiggled her fingers at Burke, then tilted her cheek to be kissed when he reached the table. 'You're so sweet to do this,' she said.

Burke kissed her, then clapped Russell amiably on the shoulder. Russell smiled at him for a moment, then turned his gaze toward Mary Ann. 'Did we sabotage your dinner?' he asked, as if they had known each other forever.

'Oh, no,' she replied, 'not at all.'

'Are you sure?'

'Yes. Really.'

'Aren't there some more?' asked Chloe.

'They're coming later,' she said, 'in another car.'

'This is Mary Ann Singleton,' said Burke.

'Yes, I know,' said Russell. 'I think we've met.'

'You have?' asked Burke.

'Russell, Chloe . . .' Secure in her identity again, Mary Ann felt a warming rush of self-assurance. 'This is my husband, Brian.'

114

Brian and Russell shook hands. Then Brian and Chloe. 'Please,' said Russell cordially, 'sit down, everybody.'

'When did you guys meet?' Burke asked her, taking the chair next to Chloe.

'At Prue Giroux's.'

'What's that?'

Chloe smirked. 'I don't think you wanna know.'

Russell gave his wife a brief, admonishing glance.

So, thought Mary Ann, she hates her too. Things were looking better all the time.

'She's kind of a local party girl,' Brian told Burke.

'Yeah,' Mary Ann said dryly. 'Kind of.' This was just enough, she felt, to let Chloe know she concurred without causing Russell further distress. Prue, after all, had been buying his dresses for years. She could see why Russell wouldn't want to appear disloyal. He had no way of knowing, really, which of these people might blab to Prue.

'I'm a real idiot,' Russell told Burke. 'When you told me about her, I just didn't make the connection.'

At first Mary Ann thought he meant Prue. Then it occurred to her that Burke must have briefed the Rands about the local talk-show hostess he wanted for his new venture. In a moment of abject panic, she realized that Russell was dangerously close to spilling the beans.

'OK,' said Chloe. 'Who needs a drink? Let's see if we can rustle up a waiter for these people.'

'Uh . . . right,' said Russell. 'Of course.'

He had the unmistakable look of someone who had just been given a swift kick under the table.

Half an hour later, in the john, Chloe said: 'Look, I'm sorry about ol' dummy out there. Burke told him not to bring up the talk-show stuff.'

'It's no problem,' said Mary Ann. 'Really.'

'Have you told him yet?'

'Not yet.'

Chloe fixed her lips in front of the mirror. 'It's a fabulous opportunity.'

'Yeah. I know.'

'Burke is so smart. He really is. I don't think you can go wrong with him.' She blotted her lips together once or twice, then turned and cocked her head apologetically. 'Sorry. I know it's none of my business.'

'No,' said Mary Ann. 'That's OK.'

'It's scary to move, isn't it? Gets you right in the gut. I felt that way exactly when Russell asked me to marry him. I mean, I knew what a life it could be, but all I could think of was how *foreign* everything would be. It's so stupid, isn't it?'

'You seem so collected,' Mary Ann remarked. 'I can't imagine that.'

'Sure,' said Chloe. '*Now*. Three years ago . . . forget it.'

'Actually,' said Mary Ann, warming to her, 'I'm pretty good about kicking over the traces. I did it when I moved here. I came here on vacation, and just . . . you know, had a few Irish coffees . . .'

Chloe giggled. 'And didn't go back?'

'Nope.'

'Damn. I'm impressed. Where was home?'

'Ohio,' said Mary Ann. 'Cleveland.'

'Well, no wonder!'

Mary Ann laughed uneasily. 'Really.'

Chloe stuck out her hand. 'Akron.'

'You're kidding!'

'Nope.'

'But you seem so . . . so . . .'

'Like I said, it takes a while. It didn't hurt to know Russell, of course. I was Geek City before I met him. Stringy hair, awful skin . . . and this honker on top of it.'

Mary Ann felt a mild protest was in order. 'C'mon. You have a beautiful nose. Like a Spanish aristocrat.'

'Try Lebanese.'

Thrown and a little embarrassed, Mary Ann changed the subject. 'And you really met him at Betty Ford?'

'Yep.'

'That's such a romantic story.' And what a movie it could be, she thought. She makes him clean and sober. He makes her beautiful and rich.

'It was just an administrative position. I wasn't a therapist or anything.'

'Still,' she said. 'You befriended him in his hour of need.'

'Yeah, I guess so. So what's the deal with your husband? He hates New York, huh?'

She nodded grimly. 'More or less.'

'Well, it's not like you wouldn't have contacts and everything. Burke and Brenda know practically everybody, and if you need help – you know, finding a co-op or something – Russell and I would be glad to help.'

Perhaps for the very first time the package she was being offered became vividly clear to her, and it was almost too much to take. Real fame, bright new friends, a home that would be her salon. She could see the place already: big pine cupboards, an antique harp, paper-thin Persian carpets against bleached floors. Something in SoHo, maybe, or just down the hall from Yoko at the Dakota . . .

'That's so sweet of you,' she told Chloe.

'Not at all.' Gazing into the mirror, Chloe swiped at the corner of her eye with her little finger. 'We could use some new faces.'

'That's great to know. That dress is genius, by the way.'

'Oh, thanks.' Chloe turned and smiled at her. 'I can't wear it at home. Ivana Trump has one just like it.'

'Bad luck,' said Mary Ann. She was dying to ask what Ivana Trump was really like, but thought it might sound too hungry, too much like a desperado.

*

When they returned to the table, Mary Ann found Brian regaling the men – Michael now among them – with his current pet opinion. 'I mean, give me a break, man. I'm no Republican, but the woman is being ragged about not dyeing her hair. In the old days, dyeing it was the scandal! What the fuck is going on here?'

Russell Rand, she noticed, made a valiant effort at laughing. Brian had a way of demanding too much from his audience when his turn came for center stage. It put people on the defensive, embarrassed them. He had no way of knowing this, of course, and she had never thought of a nice way to tell him.

That was her problem now, wasn't it? *A nice way to tell him.*

'Where's Thack?' she asked Michael as she slid into her chair.

It was Brian who answered. 'He pooped out on us.'

'His stomach's bothering him,' Michael added.

'I'm sorry.' she said. 'Hope it wasn't the spring rolls.'

'No.'

'He dropped you off?'

'Yeah.'

They've had a fight, she thought. It was just as well. Thack would only have made trouble.

'You haven't met Chloe,' she said. And she touched Chloe's shoulder lightly, just to prove to Michael she could do it. 'Chloe Rand, Michael Tolliver.'

They greeted each other across the table. Michael was clearly captivated.

'Anyway,' said Brian, blundering on, 'Barbara Bush is a whole shitload better than that bitch we've got in the White House now. All she ever does is have her hair done and con free dresses out of designers.'

Dead silence all around.

Brian looked from face to face for reinforcement.

How typical of him, she thought. If he'd thought for half a second before shooting off his mouth . . .

118

'Oh,' said Brian, looking at Russell Rand. 'I guess this means you . . . ?'

The designer managed a thin smile. 'It wasn't a con, really.'

'Well . . . it's good advertising, at least. I mean, the people who like her are probably the ones who . . . anyway, it doesn't imply a personal endorsement on your part.'

'I'm very fond of Mrs Reagan, actually.'

Brian nodded. 'Well, I don't know the lady.'

Mary Ann gave him a look that said: No, you don't, so shut up.

Russell Rand remained gracious. 'She's gotten kind of a bum rap, you know. She's not at all the person she's perceived to be.'

'Yeah, well, I guess, since I can only go by things generally available to the common man . . .'

'I don't blame you for thinking that way. I really don't.'

Brian nodded and said nothing. Michael sat perfectly still, staring at his Calistoga and looking mortified.

Somebody had to lighten things up, so Mary Ann said: 'Can't take him anywhere.'

'Not at all,' said Russell Rand. 'We're all entitled to our opinion.'

'Thank you,' said Brian, speaking to the designer but casting a quick, sullen glance in her direction.

A Bad Dream

The dream was still vivid as life when Michael stumbled out to greet the dawn. A thick coat of dew covered the deck, and he was reminded of how Charlie Rubin once referred to this phenomenon as 'night sweats'. Below, in the neighboring gardens, the wetness on the broad, green leaves suggested deceitfully that the drought had passed. Only the garden of his dead neighbor told the truth, its ravaged tree fern blunt as a crucifix in the amber light of morning.

He lifted his eyes until they jumped the fence and fled into the valley below, where a thousand Levolored windows were ablaze with sunrise. Sometimes, though not at the moment, he could see other men on other decks, watching the valley like him from their own little plywood widow's walks.

What he loved most about this view was the trees: the wizened cypresses, the backyard banana trees, the poplars that marched along the nearest ridge like Deco exclamation marks. There were some, of course, the cypresses in particular, that could only be appreciated through binoculars, but he knew where they were just the same.

Suddenly, a flock of parrots – forty strong, at least – landed in the fruitless fig tree of the house next door. While they screeched and fussed with their feathers, he stood stock-still and debated waking Thack for the event. He had never seen them this close to the house.

'Wow,' came a voice behind him.

Thack stood in the kitchen doorway. Clad only in Jockey shorts, his smooth body looked heroic in the morning light, but his thinning, sleep-bent hair muddled the effect, lending it a comical, babyfied air.

'Should I come out?'

'Yeah,' said Michael, 'but make it graceful.' He couldn't help but feel vindicated. He'd been raving about these creatures for almost a year now, without so much as a flyover to prove to his lover that he hadn't been hallucinating.

Thack joined him at the rail. 'Noisy little fuckers.'

'Yeah, but look how beautiful.'

'Not bad.'

'They used to be pets,' Michael told him.

'That's what you said.'

'See those little ones? Those are the parakeet groupies.'

In the midst of this appreciation Harry scampered on to the deck, causing the birds to ascend in a whirling flurry of green.

'Well, good morning,' said Michael as he scratched the poodle's rump.

Thack knelt and joined him, studying Michael's face before he spoke. 'Don't be mad at me,' he said.

'I'm not mad.'

'Yeah, you are.'

'Go back to bed,' said Michael. 'It's too early for you.'

'Nah,' said Thack. 'I'm up now. I'll make us breakfast.'

It was oat bran, Sweeney style, black with raisins. They ate it at the kitchen table, while Harry watched them.

'Well, how was it?' asked Thack.

'Fine. They were nice. She's really an extraordinary-looking woman.'

'I'm sure.'

This could have been snide, but Michael decided that it wasn't.

Thack poked at his cereal for a while, then asked: 'Did he drop any hairpins?'

'What do you mean?'

'C'mon. You know what that means.'

'I know, but . . . in this case . . .'

Thack sighed impatiently. 'Did he just assume that everyone knew he was gay, or did he spend the whole evening playing breeder?'

'It wasn't really one way or the other.'

'Did you tell him you were gay?'

'No.'

'Why not?'

'Because, Thack, it didn't come up. Besides, I'm your basic generic homo. Who needs to be told?'

'He does. He needs to be surrounded by fags and told what a fucking hypocrite he is.'

'I thought we were done with this,' said Michael. 'Is there more milk?'

'In the refrigerator.'

Michael brought the carton to the table and splashed milk on his cereal.

'The thing is,' said Thack, 'he was famous for being gay.'

'Not to me he wasn't.'

'Oh, c'mon. I heard about it down in Charleston. Everybody in New York knew about him. He fucked every porn star in town.'

'So?'

'So now he's out selling wedding rings and singing the praises of heterosexual love.'

'It's his profession, sweetie.'

'OK, but it doesn't say shit about his character.'

Michael was beginning to get irked again. 'You don't know him,' he said. 'Maybe he really loves her.'

'Right. And maybe she's got a dick.'

'Thack . . . people get married for all sorts of reasons.'

'Sure. Money and image, to name two.'

Michael rolled his eyes. 'He's got much more money than she does.'

'And he plans to keep it too. Can't have America knowing he's a pervert.'

'They're doing an AIDS benefit in LA,' Michael reminded him.

'Uh-huh. Welded at the hip, no doubt. A nice liberal married couple helping out the poor sick gay boys. Only you can be damn sure they won't be mentioning the G-word.'

'Why are we arguing?' Michael asked. 'You know I agree with you. Basically.'

'Why'd you go, then?'

'Look, it was a question of not busting up the party. Mary Ann obviously wanted to go.'

'No, that's a cop-out. You wanted to go too. This shit matters to you.'

'OK,' said Michael. 'Maybe it does.'

Thack sulked a moment. 'Well, at least you admit it.'

'Admit what? That I was curious? Big deal. Thack, I can't go through life being some sort of Hare Krishna for homos. I just can't. I'd rather find out what I have in common with people and go from there.'

'Fine. But what you have in common with Russell Rand you could never talk about in public. Not if you wanted to be his friend.'

'Who said I wanted to be his friend?'

After a long, brooding silence, Thack said: 'She should never have bullied us into going. She invited us to her house for dinner, and then she just let Burke take over. It was fucking rude.'

'I agree with you,' Michael said calmly. 'It could have been handled better.'

This seemed to placate him. Eventually, Thack began to smile.

'What is it?' asked Michael.

'She told Brian that Burke has a little dick.'

'Brian told you that? When?'

'Yesterday at lunch.'

'It's not true,' said Michael.

Thack gave him a sly look. 'How would you know?'

'We double-dated to the mud baths in Calistoga. Him and Mary Ann and me and Jon. They have a girls' side and a boys' side, so we ended up in . . . you know, adjoining vats.' He shrugged. 'It was kind of glopped with mud, but it looked fine to me.'

'Figures,' said Thack.

'What do you mean?'

'Brian thinks she said that to make him feel better.'

'About what?' asked Michael.

Thack shrugged. 'Them still having a thing going.'

'Burke and Mary Ann? Please.'

'Well, you saw them last night.'

'Saw what?'

'Those looks she kept giving Burke.' Thack looked peevish. 'She kept catching his eye all night long. Didn't you see it?'

'No.'

'Well, something's going on.'

'So why were we invited to witness it? That makes a helluva lot of sense.'

'Maybe she wants your blessing,' said Thack. 'She usually does.'

'Oh, right. Why are you so down on her all the time? Does she always have to have an ulterior motive?'

'No, but . . .'

'Just save it, OK? I'm sick of arguing with you!'

This flare-up came so suddenly that Thack frowned. 'What brought this on?' he asked.

'Nothing. I'm sorry. It's not you. I had a bad dream.'

'About what?'

'Oh, it's stupid. You and I went to Greece, looking for Mrs Madrigal.'

124

Thack smiled. 'What's so bad about that?'

'Well . . . she was hiding from us. She was afraid we were gonna take her back. She had this little lean-to sort of thing on a cliff . . . with lots of her stuff from home. When we finally found her, she invited us in for sherry, and I told her how much we missed her, and she said: "Life is change, dear." It was really horrible.'

Thack reached across the table and stroked Michael's hand. 'You're just feeling guilty about not calling her.'

'I know.'

'Do you have a number for her?'

'No.'

'Well, maybe . . .'

'I just have the creepiest feeling about this trip. There's no real reason for it . . . I just do.' Michael knew how neurotic this sounded, but there was no point in denying his dread. Its roots apparently reached far deeper than that ridiculous dream.

Thack observed him for a moment. 'You know,' he said gently, 'you didn't betray her when you moved out.'

'I know that.'

'Do you?'

'Well . . . if you wanna get technical, I didn't give her that much notice. I lived there for ten years . . .'

'OK, here we go.'

'That's not it, though. It really isn't.'

Thack gave him a dubious look.

'She wanted this to happen,' he said. 'She wanted me to fall in love. For Christ's sake, how can you betray your landlady?'

'Exactly.' Thack smiled victoriously and took another bite of his oat bran.

The call came when Michael was rescuing an English muffin from the jaws of their recently acquired antique Deco toaster. Mary Ann's voice was subdued enough to suggest that Brian was still in bed. 'Is this too early?' she asked without announcing herself.

'Not at all,' he told her.

Thack cast a curious glance at him.

'We loved having you last night,' she said.

'Thanks. It was fun. We really enjoyed ourselves.'

His lover rolled his eyes.

'Aren't the Rands nice?'

'Very.' He was keeping it cryptic now to avoid further commentary from Thack.

'Look, I wondered what you were doing tomorrow. I thought we could go down the Marina Green or something, take one of our walks.'

One of our walks. As if they did this all the time. As if they'd never stopped taking them.

'I could pick you up,' she added.

He hesitated only because Thack had reserved Saturday for building his pink triangle trellis. 'God,' he said, 'I've got so many chores . . .'

'I could have you back by early afternoon. Please, Mouse, I really need to talk to you.'

He marveled at the potency of an old nickname. 'OK. Fine. What time?'

'Ten o'clock?'

'Great. Shall I bring anything?'

'Just your sweet self,' she said. 'Bye.'

'Bye.'

When he hung up, Thack said: 'Mary Ann?'

He nodded. 'We're getting together tomorrow morning. The two of us.'

Thack said 'Fine' and left it at that, but Michael knew what he was thinking.

He was thinking the same thing himself.

126

Lesbian Sauce

Taking her usual shortcut through the churchyard, Mona Ramsey headed into the high street of Molivos, where a pack of German tourists had already set forth on a predinner prowl through the gift shops. The street, which was barely wide enough for a car, was roofed at this point by a mat of ancient wisteria, so that to enter it was to find herself in a tunnel – cool, dim, and cobbled – descending to the village center.

The tailor shop lay near the upper end of the tunnel, across from a pharmacy where a dough-faced old lady made proud display of condoms with names like Dolly, Squirrel, and Kamikaze. Dick-worship, Mona had found, was as rampant in Lesbos as it was everywhere else in Greece. You couldn't buy a pack of breath mints at the local newsstand without running into a shelf or two of those plaster-pricked Pans.

The patriarchy was out in full force when she entered the tailor shop. The proprietor, who also functioned as vice-mayor of the village, was gabbing away to half a dozen of his male constituents. Seeing her, he rose behind his antique sewing machine and gave a little birdlike bob. His cronies receded noticeably, realizing she was a customer.

Hoping it would speak for itself, she held up the skirt that Anna had torn on her hike to Eftalou. Two days earlier, upon greeting the baker on her morning raisin bread run, Mona had made a stab at '*kalimera*,' but it

127

had come out sounding a lot like '*kalamari*.' This had provoked gales of laughter from the other customers, who must have thought she had come to the wrong store. Who else but a stupid tourist would ask for squid at a bakery?

'Ahhh,' said the tailor, recognizing the skirt. 'Kiria Madrigal.'

Thank God for that. Another fan of Anna's. 'Just . . . you know . . .' She held up the tear, laid her palm across it like a patch, and looked up at him hopefully.

'Yes, yes,' said the tailor, nodding. The other men nodded with him, reassuring her. He understands, they seemed to be saying. Now let us get back to our gossip.

She headed out into the high street, glad to be rid of this daughterly duty. An army truck came rattling up the viny tunnel, probably bound for the bakery, so she retreated into a gift shop to let it pass. The island was bristling with soldiers – the dreaded Turks being only six miles away – but the troops were too fuzzy-cheeked and funky to invoke her anti-militarist indignation.

She had been in the shop only a moment or two when she noticed a pair of English girls – one heavy, one slim – both with the same sculpted black-and-blond haircut. They were bent over a calendar called *Aphrodite 89*, obviously ogling the nudes. When the heavy one realized she was being watched, she tittered idiotically and pressed her fingers to her lips.

Mona reassured them with a worldly smile. 'Not bad, eh?'

The skinny one made a fanning motion, pretending to cool herself off.

The three of them laughed together, reveling in this shared lechery. Mona couldn't help but notice how good it felt to be a dyke among dykes again. There weren't nearly enough of them in Gloucestershire.

*

128

The Mermaid was on the water, down where the esplanade became a sort of cobbled off-ramp to the little harbor. When she arrived, there were already three or four people staking claim to tables along the wall. On the wall itself, almost at eye level with the diners, stood a phalanx of alley cats, oblivious to the sunset, waiting for leftovers.

She tested a couple of tables and chose the less wobbly, then did the same with chairs. The sky was a ludicrous peach color, so she turned her chair to face it while it did its number. She wondered if the gushy couple next to her would burst into applause when it was over.

Costa, the proprietor, swept past her table with a bottle of retsina. 'Your lovely mother,' he said. 'Where is she?'

'She's coming,' Mona told him, trying not to sound crabby about answering this question for the fourth time today. 'She's meeting me here.'

Costa set the retsina down at the next table, then swung past her again on his way to the kitchen. 'We have very good swordfish tonight.'

'Great. You're on to me.' She watched as he continued his progress into the restaurant, nodding to his customers like a priest dispensing absolution. Then he seized a sheet of fresh plastic and returned to her table, whipping it into place with a flourish. As custom seemed to demand, she helped him tuck the edges under the elastic band.

'Well,' he said, giving the tablecloth a final whack, 'you got some sun today.'

'Did I?' She poked doubtfully at her forearm. 'Think I should try for one big freckle?'

'It looks good,' he insisted.

'Right.'

'Would you like wine now?'

'No, thanks. I'll wait till she gets here.'

'Very good,' said Costa, and he was gone.

Out on the water, a blue-and-green fishing boat was putt-putting back to the harbor. In this orange explosion of evening it looked oddly triumphant, like something about to be hoisted into a mother ship. She wondered if its captain felt heroic, knowing that all eyes were upon him. Or did he just feel tired, ready for his dinner and a good night's sleep?

She looked up the esplanade, to see a pair of strollers stopped at the wall: the mousy little straight couple from Manchester who had bored her so thoroughly two nights before at Melinda's. Next to them, but farther along, stood the sixtyish German dykes she had already dubbed Liz and Iris, after a similar pair she knew at home.

Two by fucking two. The whole damn town was paired off.

Where in the name of Sappho did the single girls go?

The sign in Costa's window said: TRY MY LESBIAN SAUCE ON FISH/LOBSTER. She had laughed at that on their first night in town, pointing it out to Anna, and they had both been charmed by its naïveté. Naïveté, hell. Costa had served plenty of lowercase lesbians – plenty of city people in general – who must have registered amusement over the years. Certainly he had wised up by now, leaving it there only to get a rise out of tourists on the esplanade.

Like, for instance, those babes with the two-tone haircuts. They had stopped in front of the restaurant, lured by that absurd sign, to smirk the way they had smirked in the gift shop. The little one tried to take a picture of it, but her black-hosieried friend glanced at the nearby diners and shook her head disapprovingly.

Go ahead, girl, thought Mona. Don't be such a wimp.

'Ah . . . Mona?'

Startled by this voice, she turned to confront the

130

handsome old codger who had shown Anna the sights this week, while Mona held down her post in a high-street taverna,watching the lovesick librarians go by. 'Stratos,' she said.

Short and dapper, he was wearing a blue sharkskin suit and smelling faintly of some piny aftershave. In the sunset his oversized white mustache had turned to pink cotton candy. 'May I join you?' he asked.

'Of course.' She waved toward a seat.

'I thought perhaps . . .' He lowered his compact frame into the flimsy little chair. 'I hoped we could dine together tonight. You and your mother and I. But perhaps she has made plans already.'

'No. Not really. I mean . . . she's joining me here any moment.'

'Oh, yes?'

'You're welcome to join us.'

'But perhaps your mother may . . .'

'I'm sure it's no problem, Stratos.'

He looked pleased. 'Then I insist that you both be my guests.'

'Whatever.'

'Good, good.' He clamped his leathery little hands on his knees. 'We must have wine, then. Retsina, yes? Or do you still think it tastes like mouthwash?'

She smiled at him. 'I can handle it.'

He flagged down the twelve-year-old who was busing tables and placed his order in Greek, patting the boy's shoulder when he was through. 'So,' he said, turning back to Mona, 'have you been enjoying Molivos?'

'It's beautiful,' she said, avoiding a direct answer. 'Bored shitless' might lose something in the translation.

He murmured in agreement, then gazed out to sea with an air of doggy wistfulness. 'The season is over,' he said. 'The people are leaving. The shops are closing. You can feel a difference in the streets already.'

'Fine by me. The sooner that disco closes, the better.'

131

He seemed to know what she meant, giving her a look that was almost sorrowful. 'It is a great shame,' he said.

'It gets louder and louder after midnight. And it's no good closing your shutters, because it just gets hot and stuffy, and you can still hear the damn thing, anyway.'

He nodded gravely. 'Many people feel the way you do.'

'Why doesn't somebody do something, then? Pass a noise ordinance or something.'

'There is such an ordinance,' said Stratos. He seemed on the verge of explaining this, when the bus-boy arrived with the retsina and three glasses. The old man dismissed him, then filled two of the glasses. 'There is such an ordinance, but the police have refused to enforce it.'

'Fire the damn police.'

Stratos smiled warmly, showing a gold tooth. 'The police are the national police. They are right-wing.'

This made no sense to her. 'The right wing hates rock-and-roll.'

'Yes, but the police hate the mayor. The mayor is communist, and they have no wish to help him in any way. The mayor has appealed to the police, but they are indifferent. This is not their regime, so . . .' He shrugged to finish it off.

'But this is their village. Everybody's gonna suffer in the end. People came here for peace and quiet, not for Bruce Fucking Springsteen. They'll stop coming.'

'Yes.' Stratos remained placid in the face of her outburst. 'And the mayor will be blamed, you see. The communist regime will be blamed.'

Mona groaned. 'Disco Wars in the Aegean.'

'Ah,' said Stratos, raising eyebrows that looked like albino caterpillars. 'Here is your mother.'

Mona looked over her shoulder to see Anna striding down the esplanade, tanned and majestic in her linen

132

caftan. It was gathered at the waist with a lavender scarf – a recent purchase, apparently – and her hair was up and spiked with her favorite chopsticks. There was even purple eye shadow to match the new scarf.

'Stratos,' said Anna, extending her hand. 'What a pleasant surprise.'

For a split second, Mona thought he was going to kiss it, but he simply bowed and said: 'It's a very small village.'

'Yes,' said Anna, smiling demurely. 'I suppose so.' She descended gracefully into a chair and folded one hand across the other on the table. Such a femme, thought Mona. 'Will you join us for dinner, Stratos? I'm sure we'd both be delighted if you would.'

'He asked us,' Mona told her. 'I said we would already.'

'Oh.' Anna seemed to redden slightly. 'How nice.'

Stratos gestured toward the retsina. 'I took the liberty. I hope you don't . . .'

'Wonderful,' said Anna, holding out the empty glass.

Stratos poured rather elegantly. 'Mona has been telling me about your unpleasantness with the disco.'

'Oh, yes,' said Anna. 'Can you hear it where you live?'

He shook his head. 'Not much. My house is protected by the hillside.'

'Lucky you,' said Anna. 'We're just above it. The sound bounces off the water and heads straight for our place. There's a sort of amphitheater effect, I suppose.'

'It will end soon,' he said.

Mona was irked by his typical Greek complacency. 'I'm gonna cut the wires one night.'

Anna gave her an indulgent little smile, then turned to Stratos and said: 'My daughter is an anarchist, in case you haven't noticed.'

'She thinks I'm kidding,' said Mona.

Stratos chuckled and raised his glass in Mona's direction.

'Perhaps I will join you. We will be guerrilla patriots.'

Mona clicked her glass against his. 'Death to disco,' she said.

During dinner, four or five cats climbed down from the wall and did a weird little gavotte around Anna's legs. 'This one reminds me of Boris,' she said, tossing a scrap of fish to an ancient tabby. 'Do you remember him?'

Mona nodded. 'Is he still alive?'

'No.' Anna looked wistful. 'No, he's gone. I have Rupert now.'

Stratos filled their glasses again. 'Did you tell Mona about Pelopi?'

'No,' came Anna's soft reply. 'Not yet.'

Was she blushing, Mona wondered, or was that just the sunset? 'What's Pelopi?'

'It's a village in the mountains. Stratos has kindly offered to . . . show it to me.'

'Oh.'

Stratos said: 'It is the birthplace of the father of Michael Dukakis.'

'Oh . . . right.'

How could she have forgotten about Pelopi? The taverns of Molivos were abuzz with media pilgrims on their way to the sacred birthsite. Several local farm trucks even sported Dukakis bumper stickers. The mayor of Molivos, it was said, had already made plans to ship a traditional Lesbian dance troupe to the White House in the event of a Democratic victory.

She wasn't holding her breath.

'Stratos says it's lovely,' Anna put in, giving Mona a meaningful look. 'His cousin has a house there.'

'That's nice. Another day trip, then?'

'Well . . . no. We thought we'd stay over.'

Nodding slowly, Mona saw the light.

Of course. They were fucking. Or at least wanted to be very soon. How could she have been so thick?

Anna regarded her peacefully with a slight, beatific smile, which said: Don't make me spell it out.

'It is much smaller than here,' said Stratos. 'Very beautiful.'

Mona nodded. 'Is your cousin away or something?'

'Mona, dear . . .'

She flashed her parent a crooked smile, acknowledging the conquest. That it was Anna, and not her dyke daughter, who was about to be laid on the Sapphic isle was an irony lost on neither one of them.

Oh, well. This was what you got for believing in brand names.

'So,' Stratos jumped in, 'you will have the villa to yourself for a few days.'

'Fine.' She smiled at them both. 'No problem. Have a good time.' After thinking for a moment, she added: 'But don't leave on my account.'

'We're not, dear.'

'Because I can always take a room . . .'

'I'm leaving on my own account,' said Anna, cutting her off with a vengeance. 'I'm eager to see Pelopi.'

'Mmm. Well, I can see why.'

Her parent gave her a hooded look.

'That's pretty awe-inspiring. The birthplace of Dukakis's father.' Mona shook her head in mock amazement, enjoying herself to the fullest.

Anna avoided this gentle harassment by staring at the big greasy clock on the wall of the Mermaid. Eventually she asked: 'What time is it in San Francisco?'

Mona did some quick arithmetic. 'Uh . . . nine o'clock in the morning.'

'Oh, good.' Anna rose suddenly and gave Stratos an apologetic look. 'Would you be a dear and keep my daughter company for about ten minutes?'

'With pleasure.' Stratos's smile turned cloudy after a moment. 'Nothing is wrong, I hope?'

'No, no. Not a thing. I just want to call the children.' Anna turned back to Mona. 'I'll just dash up the phone lady and be back in three shakes. We'll all go someplace for dessert.'

She gave them both a final glance and hurried off into the gathering dark.

The waiter appeared, distressed about Anna's departure. Mona assured him she would return, then ordered a Sprite-and-ouzo.

'What about you?' she asked Stratos.

He shook his head.

The waiter left.

'You have brothers and sisters?' Stratos asked.

Mona smiled at him and shook her head. 'She calls her tenants her children.'

The old man absorbed this without changing his expression.

'She runs an apartment house,' Mona explained. 'I guess she told you that already?'

He nodded. 'Yes.'

There was a long, uncomfortable silence before Stratos said: 'I have an idea for you.'

'What's that?'

'Perhaps . . . if the disco noise is too much for you at the villa . . . you should go to Skala Eressou.'

Mona blinked at him, wondering if Anna's sudden trip to the phone lady had been a setup. Were they trying to get rid of her, after all?

'There is a beach there,' he added.

'Like this one?' This sounded harsher than she'd intended, but the local strip was a horror – narrow, rocky, and strewn with garbage.

'No,' he replied. 'With beautiful sand. It is a simple place, but I think you might like it.'

She decided that he was just being nice. Still, she wanted to stay put at the villa. It was paid for, after all, and this 'simple place' might be even less exciting than here. 'Thanks,' she told him, 'but I'm OK.'

'It is the birthplace of Sappho, and there are many tents on the beach.'

'Tents?' she asked.

'Yes.'

'What sort of tents?'

'Many women . . . feminists . . . from everywhere. Many more than here.'

She studied the face, but it betrayed nothing.

'Perhaps you would like it,' he said.

She gave him a slow-blooming smile. 'Perhaps I would.'

The Wave Organ

Beneath the blue porcelain dome of Noe Valley a lone kite chased its rainbow tail. Mary Ann watched it for a moment, admiring its reckless indecision, then swung the Mercedes into Michael's driveway. October's false springtime gave her an unexpected surge of optimism. The task ahead of her might not be as terrible as she'd once imagined.

Thack called from the garden. 'He'll be right out.' He was on a ladder, nailing planks to the side of the house.

'Thanks.'

'You've got a nice day for it, looks like.'

'Yeah,' she said. 'It does.' It occurred to her that he could be very pleasant when he wanted to. 'What's that you're building?'

'Just a trellis.'

'It looks interesting.'

'Well . . . it will. I hope.'

Michael hollered at her from the doorway. 'Do I need a jacket?'

'No way.'

Seconds later, he bounded out of the house in cords and an ancient pale-green Madras shirt, that yappy little poodle toe-dancing around his heels. 'No, Harry. You're staying here, poopie. Stay. Here. Understand?'

'Has he been walked?' Thack asked, gazing down from the ladder.

'This morning. To the p-a-r-k.' Michael grinned at

Mary Ann as he climbed into the car. 'We have to spell around him, or he gets unnecessarily excited.'

'I know exactly what you mean.'

He laughed. 'Only, Shawna can spell, remember?'

'Yeah. We're thinking of having that fixed.'

She joined in his laughter as they pulled out of the driveway. He always made her feel so reckless.

Down at the marina, they parked in the lot next to the yacht club. The bay was anemic with sails, the volleyballers so jammed on to the west end of the green that they seemed to be playing a single, riotous game. Michael suggested they walk out the seawall to the Wave Organ, which suited her fine, since there were less people out there and she needed all the privacy she could get.

She had done a short feature on the Wave Organ once, but she had never actually seen it. It was basically a series of plastic pipes that ran underwater and surfaced at a stone terrace at the end of the seawall. By pressing an ear against one of several openings on the terrace, you could hear the 'music' of the organ, the very harmonies of the sea itself, if you believed the press releases.

Michael knelt by one of the openings.

'How is it?' she asked.

'Well . . . interesting.'

'Does it sound like music?'

'I wouldn't go that far.'

She found a neighboring outlet, sort of a stone periscope, and listened for herself. All she heard was a hollow hiss, overlaid with a lapping noise. Not exactly a symphony of Neptune.

'Maybe it's better when the tide changes.' As usual, Michael refused to abandon his fantasies.

'What is it now? High or low?'

'Who knows?' He looked around, assessing the structure. 'The design is nice, though. It's kind of neoclassical

139

postmodern. I like those carved stones.'

'They're from cemeteries,' she told him.

'They are?'

'That's what I heard.'

He sat down in an alcove and caressed the contours of the stones. Joining him, she gazed out at the billowing sails, the gulls swooping low over the water. After a silence, she said: 'I'm sorry we've lost touch lately.'

'That's OK.'

'My schedule gets the best of me sometimes.'

'I know.'

'Brian fills me in on you, so . . . I feel connected somehow.'

'Yeah.' He nodded. 'He does that for me too.'

'I don't want us to drift apart, Mouse. I count on you for too much.'

He studied her for a moment. 'Was that what you wanted to tell me?'

She shook her head.

'What is it, then?'

'Burke has offered me a job.'

'A job?'

'In New York. As host of a syndicated talk show.'

He took a while to absorb this, but he seemed more amazed than horrified. 'You're kidding.'

'No.'

'Like . . . national?'

'Yes.'

'Hot damn!'

'Isn't it incredible?'

'Are you taking it?' he asked.

'Looks like it. Burke doesn't know that yet, but I've pretty much decided.'

'What does Brian think?'

'I haven't told him yet. I wanted to sort things out first.'

A couple approached, checking out the Wave Organ. 'How is it?' asked the woman.

'Iffy,' Michael told her.

The man pressed his head against one of the stone periscopes. He was wearing enough polyester to have been a member of Mary Ann's studio audience. 'What are you supposed to hear?' he asked.

'We're not sure,' said Mary Ann.

The man listened for a while, then grunted and walked away. This was apparently enough for his wife, who didn't bother to listen. As they left, she stopped abruptly in front of Mary Ann. 'I have to tell you,' she said. 'I loved your show on phone sex.'

Mary Ann did her best to be gracious. 'That's very sweet of you.'

The woman fled, her message delivered, joining her husband as he left the seawall.

Michael turned and grinned at her. 'Are you sure you want to be bigger than this?'

She pressed her finger to her temple and pretended to ponder the issue.

'OK,' he said. 'Stupid question.'

This was what she loved about him. He could wriggle in closer to her real self than anyone she had ever known. He could stay there longer too, snuggled up against her burning ambition like a cat against a coal stove.

'Will you be . . . like the main host?'

She nodded. 'They're gonna keep the name. *Mary Ann in the Morning.*'

'Perfect. How star-making.'

'Isn't it?'

'So what's the problem?' he asked. 'Are you afraid that Brian won't want to go?'

'No,' she answered. 'I'm afraid that he will.'

His face remained composed, but he obviously understood.

'I don't love him any more, Mouse. I haven't loved him for a long time.'

141

Looking away, he said 'Shit' so softly that it sounded like a prayer.

'I know how this must seem to you. We haven't exactly talked about . . .'

'What about Shawna?'

She paused to measure out her words. 'I wouldn't take her away from him. She belongs here as much as he does.'

He nodded.

'Even if I did still . . . feel something, it wouldn't be fair to make him leave. The nursery means more to him than anything he's ever done. He wouldn't be happy in New York. It's a whole different world. You saw him the other night with the Rands.'

'What was wrong with him?'

'Nothing was *wrong*. He just wasn't . . . comfortable. It's not his game; it never has been. He says so himself, all the time.' She searched Michael's long-lashed brown eyes for a response. 'You know that's true. It would kill him to be reduced to being my escort again.'

'Yeah,' he replied, somewhat absently.

'There was a time when we had something, but it just isn't there any more.'

He kept his eyes on the water. 'Are you still in love with Burke?'

She had expected this, of course. 'No. Not a bit.'

'Is he in love with you?'

She gave him a small, ironic smile. 'I'm not sure he even *likes* me. This is business, Mouse. I swear. Nothing else.'

Michael watched a gull as it trooped solemnly along the edge of the seawall. 'How long has it been like this?'

'I don't know.'

'You must.'

'No,' she said. 'It sort of crept up on me. It was a lot of little things that just added up. It's not like I've been thinking about it for a long time.'

'But the talk-show thing forced the issue?'

'Well, it made things clearer. I saw how long I've been settling for less than the whole package. I need a partner, Mouse. Someone who dreams about the same things.' Suddenly, she felt hot tears welling behind her eyes. 'Sometimes I look at Connie Chung and Maury Povich and get so *jealous*.'

'Do you want a divorce?'

'I don't know. Not for a while. It might just complicate things. This would be more like Dolly Parton.'

He obviously didn't understand.

'You know. She has a husband back in Tennessee, doesn't she? Who digs ditches or something?'

'Paves driveways.'

'Whatever,' she said.

'So . . . a separation?'

'I want whatever's easiest on everybody, that's all.'

'Maybe you should wait, then. See how this job turns out.'

'No. How fair would that be? It's over, Mouse. He has to know that. There's just no other way out.' She began to sob, mangling her words. 'I'm not a monster. I just can't . . . make him give up his life here for . . . something that isn't working any more.'

'I understand.'

She dug a Kleenex from her purse and blew her nose. 'Do you? Really?'

'Yes.'

'I was so afraid that you wouldn't. That you'd hate me for this. I can't stand the thought of losing you.'

'When have you ever lost me?'

'I don't want to now,' she said. 'Especially not now.'

He slipped his arm gently around her waist. 'When are you gonna tell him?'

'I don't know. Soon.'

'He won't be ready, you know.'

She blotted her eyes with the wadded Kleenex, feeling

143

a twinge of anxiety. 'You won't tell him, will you?'

'Of course not, but . . . he loves you a lot, Babycakes.'

'No,' she said. 'It's a habit. It's something that just happened to us because we didn't have anywhere else to go. He knows that himself. Deep down.'

'C'mon.'

'I mean it. It's the truth.'

'You and I just happened,' he said.

'No we didn't. We've always chosen each other, Mouse. From the very beginning.' She looked at him but didn't touch him, knowing it would be too much. 'We're gonna be friends when we're both in rockers at the old folks' home.'

A tear slicked his cheek. He swiped at it with the back of his palm, then smiled at her. 'Did you pick this spot on purpose?'

'What do you mean?'

'Where we met. The Marina Safeway.'

'Oh, yeah.' It was down at the end of the green. She hadn't been there in years, she realized. How like him to think that she had brought him here for commemorative purposes.

'Remember Robert?' he asked. 'The guy I was with that day?'

'Do I! He was the one I was trying to pick up!'

'Well, thanks a lot.'

She smiled. 'What about him?'

'I saw him the other day,' he explained. 'I couldn't believe how boring he was.'

'Of course.'

'All I could think was: What if he hadn't dumped me? I'd be living in some tract home in Foster City. And I never would've met Thack.'

She didn't know exactly what to say to that, so she gazed out at the water. Angel Island squatted in the distance like a dusty shrub in the midst of a wide blue prairie. She and Michael used to picnic there, years ago.

They would spread a blanket on one of the old gun emplacements and talk about men for hours on end.

'I want you to come visit me,' she told him.

'OK.'

'Promise?'

'Of course.'

'If you do,' she said, 'I'll introduce you to everybody in the world.'

'It's a deal. And you'll call me every week?'

'With dish like you won't believe!'

When he laughed, she knew that the worst was over. Ten minutes later they strolled to the Marina Safeway in quest of lunch. Out on the seawall, another bewildered couple knelt in homage to the Wave Organ, listening for the music that wasn't there.

Interrogations

On Monday morning, in the greenhouse at Plant Parenthood, Brian turned to Michael and said: 'Mary Ann says you guys had a good time catching up.'

Michael was thrown, but he tried not to show it. She had been right, of course, to tell him about their outing at the marina. Why harbor any more secrets than absolutely necessary? 'Oh, yeah,' he replied as breezily as possible. 'It was nice. We bought pasta salad at the Marina Safeway.'

His partner's sandpaper cheeks dented in a smile. 'Is that place as cruisy as it used to be?'

'Got me. I was too busy lusting over the pasta.'

'I hear that.'

Polly burst into the greenhouse, looking less collected than usual. 'It's for you, Michael. The cops.'

'What?'

'On the phone. Sounds important.'

Shit. His parking tickets. How many were there, anyway?

'He says he knows you.'

Brian chuckled. 'An old boyfriend, probably.'

'What's his name?' Michael asked.

'Rivera, it sounded like.'

Michael looked at Brian. 'He *is* an old boyfriend.'

'What did I tell you?' Brian looked pleased with himself. 'I know you better than you do.'

*

He took the call in the office. 'Bill. How's it going?'

'You remember, huh?'

'Of course. Good to hear your voice.' How long had it been, anyway? Six years? Seven?

'Same here.'

'What's up?' He half wondered if he was about to be asked for a date. For all Bill knew, Michael was still single, still looking for somebody to play with.

'I'm down at Northern Station. We've got a friend of yours. At least, he gave us your name. He's not making much sense, I'm afraid.'

'What's his name?'

'Joe something. He won't tell us anything else.'

He thought for a moment. Joe Webster. The guy Ramon Landes was looking after. The one with dementia.

'He's got no ID on him, but I didn't wanna turn him over to a hospital unless . . .'

'Real tall and skinny? About thirty, with brown hair?'

'That's him,' said Bill. 'You know him, then?'

'Not very well. I took an AIDS workshop with him. We have some friends in common. I'm surprised he even remembered my name.'

'Do you know where he belongs?'

'Well, I know his Shanti buddy . . .'

'Could you call him, tell him to come pick him up?'

'Sure. Did he . . . uh . . . do anything wrong?'

'Well,' said Bill, 'he kind of . . . accosted someone. It was nothing serious. We haven't charged him with anything.'

'I see.'

'We just need to get him home safely.'

'OK. Thanks a lot, Bill. I'll take care of it.'

As luck would have it, Ramon wasn't at home, so he left a terse message on his machine and took off for Northern Station on his own. When he announced himself, the sergeant at the desk hollered 'Rivera' over his shoulder and

147

buried his beefy face in the pages of *Iacocca*.

Bill was there in a matter of seconds. 'Hey . . . long time, buddy.'

Resisting the urge to hug him, Michael shook the cop's hand with exaggerated heartiness. 'Hey, kiddo. You're lookin' great.' Bill had thickened a little around the waist, but he wore it well in his uniform. His civilian clothes of yesteryear – Qiana shirts and overstitched designer jeans – had never done justice to his sex appeal.

'You still over there . . . what's it called?'

'Barbary Lane.'

'Yeah, that's it. Damn.' He shook his head, seemingly lost in memory. 'I haven't been there for a long time.'

'Actually, I moved away a few years ago. I'm over in Noe Valley now.'

'Take a load off,' said Bill, pointing toward a row of plastic chairs. 'I'll get him.'

'Wait.' Michael grabbed his arm.

'Yeah?'

'What exactly did he do?'

'Oh . . . well, he kind of . . . harassed some Jehovah's Witnesses.'

Michael repressed the first comment that came to mind. At the moment his job was to look responsible. 'He assaulted them, you mean?'

'Not really.' Bill made a notation on his clipboard. 'Just waved something around for a while.'

'What?' Michael scanned the room guiltily, as if there were Jehovah's Witnesses present, or grownups who might overhear them. 'You mean his . . . ?'

The cop shook his head with a dry smile. 'Somebody else's.' Reaching below the desk, he retrieved a plastic shopping bag and handed it to Michael. 'Check it out.'

Inside the bag was a box bearing a glossy likeness of Jeff Stryker, the porn star.

'What the hell?'

148

'Read it,' said the cop.

The label said: *The Realistic Jeff Stryker Cock and Balls. Incredibly awesome in size! Molded directly from Jeff's erect cock! Looks and feels amazingly realistic!*

He opened the end of the box, to reveal a velvet bag with a drawstring.

'I wouldn't take it out,' said Bill.

'Right.'

'The balls are squeezable.'

'You're kidding.'

'Nope.'

'What's the world coming to?' said Michael.

Bill chuckled, but it was a dry, professional chuckle. 'Got an address for him?'

'I'm sorry. I don't.'

'Think you could phone it in later? For my report.'

'Sure,' said Michael. 'No problem.'

'So.' The cop looked up from the clipboard. 'How have you been?'

'Pretty good. I'm alive.'

'Yeah. Really. Are you still . . . on your own?'

'No. I've got a lover now.'

'Hey. All right. Where'd you meet him?'

'Alcatraz, actually.'

This got a smile. 'A tourist or a ranger?'

'Tourist.'

'And then he moved here?'

Michael nodded. 'About three years ago.'

'Well, good for you.' If Bill was racked with heart-break, his police training had taught him to conceal it pretty well.

'How 'bout you?' asked Michael.

'Same as always. Bachelor Number Three.'

'Well . . . it suits you.'

'You got that right. What would I do with a lover at Pigs in Paradise?'

Michael drew a blank.

149

'You know, the big party. Gay and lesbian law enforcement. I took you to one, didn't I?'

'Nope.'

'You sure?'

Michael rolled his eyes. 'I would've remembered, Bill. Trust me.'

'Come to the next one, then. Bring your lover.'

'Thanks. Maybe we'll do that.'

'I'll go get him,' said Bill.

He gave Michael's shoulder a brotherly shake and ducked into the back room.

Joe Webster emerged looking gaunt and exhausted, his rangy frame slumped into a sullen pterodactyl stance. When his eyes met Michael's they registered no recognition whatsoever.

'Here's your friend,' the officer told him.

'He's not my friend.'

'This is Michael Tolliver. You said to call Michael Tolliver, didn't you?'

No answer.

Bill smiled indulgently and looked at Michael. 'Is this the guy?'

Michael nodded. 'He's right, though. We're not really friends.'

Bill shrugged. 'Well . . .'

'The bastards wouldn't give me a room,' said Joe, scowling. 'And they're outa fuckin' towels.'

'Did you reach his Shanti buddy?'

'Not yet.' Michael turned to Joe and tried to appear as benign as possible. 'Why don't we go see Ramon? OK?'

'Where is he? Where's Ramon?'

'He's at home. Or he will be soon.' He hoped to hell this was so. 'I'm gonna take you there, OK?'

'No fuckin' towels. What the fuck do they think I'm doing? I paid, didn't I? Didn't I pay?'

'What's he talking about?' asked Michael.

150

'Got me. What're you gonna do if you can't find his buddy?'

'I dunno.'

'You have a work number for him?'

'He works out of his house. He must be out shopping or something.'

'No fuckin' towels, no fuckin' rooms . . .'

'Maybe you should call again,' said Bill.

This time Ramon was home. Michael told him what had happened and offered to drive Joe to Ramon's house in Bernal Heights. Ramon thanked him profusely and was waiting on his front steps when they arrived half an hour later.

'Sorry about this.'

'No problem,' said Michael.

Joe unfolded his lanky frame from the VW and headed up the steps without a word. 'Hey,' Ramon called after him. 'Say thank you to Michael.'

Joe stopped and looked down at them. 'Why?'

'Because I asked you to.'

Michael felt uncomfortable. 'That's OK. Really.'

Ramon lowered his voice. 'He's been losing it a lot lately. Last week he set fire to a trash can at a Louise Hay seminar.'

'I see.'

'He must really like you, or he wouldn't have given them your name.'

'It doesn't matter,' said Michael.

'He gets these periods when he's just a different person.'

Michael nodded. 'He kept talking about towels at the police station.'

'He does that at the hospital too. The post office, for that matter. He thinks he's at the baths.' Ramon shrugged. 'It must be the little window or something.'

Joe was watching them from the top of the steps. 'You

know,' he yelled down, 'you don't get points for this. Nobody's keeping score in heaven. If you get it, you get it.'

Michael ignored him as he handed Ramon the bag with the rubber cock. 'I'd keep an eye on this.'

Ramon winked at him. 'I owe you one.'

'That's OK.'

'Did you hear me?'

'I better go,' said Michael.

Ramon nodded. 'Yeah.'

'It's time to get mad, Michael. Niceness doesn't count for shit!'

'Believe it or not,' said Ramon, 'he has moments when he's really clear.'

Michael had the creepy feeling that this was one of them.

A Blind Item

'So anyway,' Polly was telling Brian in the greenhouse, 'Madonna and Sandra Bernhard are there on Letterman, their arms totally *draped* around each other. And they're like giggling and making jokes about the Hole, which is the Cubby Hole, this famous dyke bar in New York, and the whole damn thing is going straight over Letterman's head . . . the stupid pig.'

Brian didn't buy this at all. 'You're not gonna tell me Madonna . . .'

'Why not? Get real.' She was scraping out plastic pots, stacking them in the corner. 'Just because you can't stand the thought of it . . .'

He chuckled.

'What?'

'I like the thought of it.'

'Yeah. Well, OK. That figures, doesn't it?'

He looked at her sideways. 'Which am I supposed to do? Like it or not like it?'

'Hand me that pot, please.'

He complied, grinning.

'The real question is: What the fuck does Madonna see in Sandra Bernhard? If I were Madonna, I'd be going for the serious stuff. Jamie Lee Curtis, at the very least.' She stood up and dusted off her hands. 'Shouldn't Michael be back by now?'

'Seems like it, doesn't it?'

'How long does it take to bail somebody out?'

'He didn't need bail,' Brian said.

'Oh, yeah.'

'I guess he could've had trouble finding the Shanti volunteer.'

'Was that Mary Ann in the paper this morning?'

The change of subject threw him. 'What do you mean? Where?'

'In Herb Caen's column.'

'She was there? What did it say?'

'It might not have been her,' said Polly. 'It was a . . . you know. What do they call it when they don't use the name?'

'A blind item,' said Brian, feeling queasy already. What the hell were they saying about her now? 'Is there a paper in the office?'

'Yeah,' she said, and followed him out of the green-house.

Five minutes later, when Polly had left the office, he collected himself and called Mary Ann at the station.

'Was that you?' he asked without announcing himself.

No answer.

'Was it?'

'Brian.' Her voice assumed its most businesslike armor. 'This is as much a surprise to me . . .'

'I didn't figure there could be *that* many perky morning girls being wooed by New York producers.'

'It wasn't even supposed to be there.'

'Oh. Well, then.'

'I want to talk to you about this,' she said, 'but I don't want to do it on the phone.'

'Shall I plant an item somewhere?'

She sighed. 'Don't be like that.'

'Like what?'

'All wounded and alienated. I was going to tell you about it.'

'When?'

'Tonight.'

'Wrong. We're talking now. Right this minute.'

'No,' she said quietly. 'Not on the phone.'

'Then meet me somewhere.'

'I can't.'

'Why? Do you have to be wooed some more?'

She made him pay for this with a long silence. Finally, she asked: 'Where do you want to meet?'

'You name it.'

'OK, then. Home.'

He gathered from this that she was afraid of risking a public scene.

When he arrived, she was standing by the window, dressed in her traditional garb of apology – jeans and the pink-and-blue flannel shirt he liked so much. It was an obvious gesture, but it soothed him just the same. He was already beginning to feel as if he'd overreacted.

'I sent Nguyet home,' she said.

'Good.' He sat on the sofa.

'I'm really sorry about this, Brian. I don't know how it got into Herb Caen.'

He didn't look at her. 'Is it for real?'

'Yes.'

'Do you wanna do it?'

'Very much.'

'How long have you known about it?'

'A while.'

'Since that lunch, right?'

She nodded.

'And what did you think? That I would be so jealous of some old burned-out boyfriend . . . ?'

'No. Never. You know there's nothing there.'

'Well, OK. Then what?'

'What do you mean, what?'

'Why wouldn't you tell me? This is what you've been working toward. Didn't you think I'd be happy for you?'

'Brian . . .'

'Am I that much of a self-centered bastard?'

'Of course not.'

'Did you think I'd be so attached to the nursery that I'd try to stand in your way?'

'Well...'

'You did, didn't you? That's exactly what you thought.'

'I know how much you love it,' she replied somewhat feebly.

'I love you, sweetheart. Your victories are my victories. That's always been enough for me. What do I have to do to convince you of that?'

She left the window and sat down on the chair across from him, tucking her legs neatly under her butt. 'I don't think bad things of you, Brian. I really don't. I know how much you have to put up with.'

She said this with such tenderness that he felt the last vestiges of his anger melt away. He gave her a chipper smile to let her know. 'So what's he offering?'

'Just a show.'

'Just? Syndicated, right?'

'Yeah.'

'Out of New York?'

'Uh-huh.'

'You don't seem very excited,' he said.

'I am. There's just... a lot to think about.'

'What have you told him?'

She shrugged. 'That I'd have to talk to you.'

This was suddenly making sense to him. 'Is that why you brought him here for dinner? So I could see how unthreatening he was before you told me about it?'

She made a sheepish face.

'I don't have a problem with it. Really.' He saw that doubts still lingered. 'Your ship has come in, sweetheart. We should be celebrating.' He gazed at her for a while, then patted the sofa cushion next to him. She left her chair and joined him, leaning her head against his shoulder.

'Call Burke,' he said. 'Tell him we'll do it.'

'No.'

'Why not?'

'He's in L.A. I don't know how to reach him. He's gonna call me.'

'Oh.' He thought for a moment. 'Did you tell Michael about this?'

'No. Of course not.'

'Should I tell him?'

'No,' she replied, almost fiercely. 'Just leave it alone for a while.'

'He's gonna ask. He must've seen the item.'

'Oh, yeah.' She frowned, deep in thought, obviously concerned about hurting her old friend.

'He'll understand,' he told her, squeezing her shoulder. 'It's not like he didn't run the place on his own before I came along.'

When he got back to the nursery, Michael sauntered toward him in the slanting afternoon light.

'How did it go?' asked Brian, remembering the call from the cop.

'OK. They didn't book him or anything.'

'What did he do?'

'Nothing. Waved a dildo at some Jehovah's Witnesses.'

Brian laughed. 'You sure he's sick?'

Michael's smile was forced. He seemed unusually subdued.

'I'm sorry,' said Brian. 'It's not funny, I know.'

'No. It is. You're right.'

'Are you OK, man?'

'Yeah. Fine.'

'We were worried when we didn't hear from you.'

'Oh, well . . .'

'I guess it took a while with the cops.'

'Not really,' said Michael. 'I drove out to the beach. I needed some air.'

'Don't blame you a bit.'

157

'I should've called, I guess.'

'No. Not at all.' Poor guy, thought Brian. It must've really gotten to him.

'Polly said you had to leave. I hope it didn't make things tight.'

'Nah.' He wondered if Michael was hinting around about the blind item. At any rate, there was no point in avoiding the subject. 'Did you see Herb Caen's column this morning?'

Michael nodded. 'Polly showed me.'

'It's Mary Ann.'

'Oh, yeah?'

'She's gonna do it, I think.'

Michael seemed to avoid his gaze. 'Well, it's . . . definitely an opportunity.'

'Yeah, it is.' He hesitated a moment. 'We may have to work something out, Michael.'

'What do you mean?'

'About the partnership.'

Michael blinked at him, uncomprehending.

'If I leave,' he explained.

'Oh.'

He hoped a smile would soften the blow a little. 'If it helps any, this is pretty much of a surprise to me too.'

'Well . . . that's OK.'

'I'll work it out so you aren't strapped for help. I promise you that. If you want me to remain an absentee owner, fine . . . or whatever you want.'

Michael nodded, looking faintly distracted.

'I know this is sudden. I'm really sorry.'

'Hey.'

'It's not like I love New York, you know.'

'No.'

'But I'd be a real shit to oppose her on this. It's really a great . . .'

'Maybe we should talk about this later, huh?'

It was obvious that Michael was hurt. 'Well . . . OK.'

158

'It seems a little premature at the moment.'

'OK . . . Sure. I just didn't wanna hide anything. I wanted you to be in on it.'

'I appreciate that,' said Michael as he headed off toward the office.

Mary Ann was already in bed when Brian got out of the shower that night. As he came into the bedroom she was hanging up the phone.

'Who was that?' he asked, sitting on the edge of the bed.

'Michael.'

'What did he want?'

'He says to bring the lap-top with you when you come in tomorrow.'

'Oh . . . OK.' He turned and looked at his wife. 'Did he say anything about New York?'

She shrugged. 'He congratulated me. Not much else.'

'I think he's kind of freaked out about it.'

'Why?'

'You know. Busting up the partnership.'

'Oh.'

'To tell you the truth,' he said, 'I was too.'

'Was what?'

'Freaked out.'

'Oh.'

'I'm over it.' He reached across and stroked her thigh beneath the bedcovers. 'We've got a real adventure ahead of us. It was all I could do to keep from telling Shawna.'

She seemed to stiffen. 'You didn't, did you?'

'No. But I don't see what harm . . .'

'It's completely premature, Brian.'

'Why?'

'Well . . . it's not a deal yet. She'll blab it all over school.'

'Oh, yeah.'

'I'm having a hard enough time as it is. Kenan called me into his office today over that fucking item.'

'Oh, Christ.' He pictured the indignation of the station manager, his piggish panic at losing this lone jewel in his crown. 'Is he on to you?'

'Oh, yeah.'

'You denied it, though?'

'Of course.'

'Attagirl.' He turned off the light and climbed into bed, snuggling up to her.

'He's such an asshole,' she said.

'Absolutely.'

'I can't wait to watch him twisting in the wind.'

For a moment, for the hell of it, he imagined them lying like this in another city, another season. There was fresh snow on the windowsill, and a streetlight outside, and Shawna was asleep in a wallpapered bedroom down the hall. 'You know what?' he said.

'What?' she answered drowsily.

'If we got a place on the ground this time . . . with a garden, I mean . . .'

'Go to sleep,' she said sweetly.

She beat him to it several seconds later, purring rhythmically against his back. She was dreaming of the future, no doubt, a land of riches and proper recognition and assholes twisting in the wind.

The Third Whale

Their villa, like most of the houses around it, was a two-story stone building with a red-tile roof and big pine shutters that could be battened against the noonday sun. There was a kitchen (which they never used), a terrace dripping with dusty wisteria, and a pair of huge, high-ceilinged bedrooms overlooking the Aegean. When Mona awoke in hers, it usually took her a while to determine whether it was morning or late afternoon, since she hardly ever missed a siesta.

At the moment, it was morning. She knew because she could hear roosters and the tinny radio in the taverna on the hillside below. (There were entirely different sounds in the afternoon – church bells and asthmatic donkeys and the piratical shouts of children as they clattered down the streets to freedom.)

A frisky zephyr had found its way through the crack in her shutters and was teasing the long, filmy curtains. Out on the landing between the bedrooms she heard her parent's graceful footfall and the unmistakable piglet squeal of the refrigerator door.

The double doors creaked open, and Anna stood there in her caftan, backlit by the morning, holding a bottle of mineral water.

'Are you awake, dear?'

Errant beams bounced off the shimmering blue plastic like rays from a holy scepter. Our Lady of the Liter,

161

Mona thought, rubbing her eyes. 'Yeah, I guess so. What time is it?'

'Eight o'clock. I thought you might like an early start, so you don't have to travel in the heat of the day.'

Oh, yes. Her long-awaited pilgrimage to Sappho's birthplace. That was today, wasn't it?

'I bought some lovely raisin buns at the bakery. Shall I bring you one with some tea?'

Mona swung her legs off the bed. 'No, thanks. I'll come down.'

'Stratos says he can find a driver for you, if you like.'

'That's OK. I'll just get one on the esplanade.'

'Oh . . .' Anna reached into the pocket of her caftan. 'I thought perhaps you could do with these.' She dropped a handful of joints on Mona's dresser and smiled beatifically. 'I'd hate for you to miss anything.'

Mona smiled back at her. 'Thanks.'

'Its name is Sigourney.'

The grass, which Mona had already sampled, was from the garden at Barbary Lane. Anna – who named all her dope after her favorite people – had mailed it to herself before leaving home. Despite the buffer of several boxes and four or five layers of shrink wrap, the package had reeked to high heaven when they picked it up in the tiny post office next to the Molivos police station.

No one had said a word, however. Anna could get away with anything.

An hour later Anna and Stratos left for the Dukakis natal site in a beat-up Impala convertible that, to hear Stratos tell it, was all but legendary in Lesbos. Trim and tanned, gold tooth glinting in the sun, the old guy looked almost rakish behind the wheel. Arranging herself next to him, Anna set about doing picturesque things with scarves. 'If you can,' she told Mona as the car bumped away down the cobblestones, 'find something Sapphic for Michael.'

'OK.' She trotted alongside the car. 'If you don't like

Pelopi,' she said, 'feel free to come back and use the house.'

Anna gave her an enigmatic smile.

'I'll be gone for a few days . . . is what I mean.'

'Yes, dear. Thank you.'

As the car pulled away from her, Stratos yelled: 'Sappho the Russian.' It sounded like that, anyway.

'What?'

'It's a hotel. Remember.'

She yelled after the Impala. 'Sappho the what?'

His answer was drowned out by a chorus of barking dogs.

She finished up the breakfast dishes, then packed a change of clothes, locked up the villa, and hired a cab on the esplanade. The cabs here were all Mercedeses, beige and battered, with lurid and elaborate shrines to the virgin obstructing every dashboard. This was Mary's island, really, not Sappho's, and they never let you forget it.

The trip across the island took several hours along winding mountain roads. For most of the journey her driver plied her with cassettes of bouzouki music, so there was blessedly little call for conversation. Beyond the olive groves the landscape became barren and blasted, made vivid here and there by roadside memorials to people who'd gazed too devoutly at the virgin and missed a hairpin turn. She was thoroughly nauseated by the time they descended into the green farming outskirts of Skala Eressou.

It was a beach town, basically: two-story concrete buildings with tile roofs, a row of thatched tavernas forming a sort of boardwalk along the littered gray sand. At the edge of town, where she got out, a jumble of homemade signs offered various services for tourists. Among them, almost as crudely lettered, was one that purported to be official:

163

How fucking dare they? How many odes to discretion had Sappho ever written? She wondered if busloads of visiting dykes had become too demonstrative in the lap of the motherland and somehow horrified the Mary-worshipers. It made her want to rip off her shirt and grab the nearest woman.

She walked along the seafront tavernas to get the lay of the land. Most of the other tourists were Greek or German. The British voices were North of England, people on package tours, pale as larvae, buying sunshine on a budget. She spotted several pairs of lowercase lesbians along the way, but hardly enough to qualify the town for mecca status.

Thirsty and still a little queasy, she stopped at the nearest taverna and ordered a Sprite-and-ouzo, the drink she'd learned to tolerate in Molivos. She sipped it slowly, watching the beach. A bare-breasted fräulein with huge mahogany thighs was sprawled towelless on the coarse sand, reading a German tabloid. Her hair was bleached so white that she looked like a negative of herself. Mona made a mental note to pick up some sun block.

The beach curved down to a big gray mountain crumbling into the sea. There were wind surfers in the sparkling water and, just beyond the next taverna, a queue of bathers waiting for an outdoor shower. Despite obvious civic efforts at making the place look like a resort, there was an irrepressible seediness to Skala Eressou, which she found completely endearing.

But what of Sappho? Was there a marker some-where commemorating her birth? Something noble and weatherworn, bearing a fragment of her work? Maybe she could buy a volume of the verses and read it while she strolled on the beach.

She tried three different gift shops and found not so much as a pamphlet on the poet's life. The guidebooks she checked devoted a paragraph or two to the subject, but the details, at best, were sketchy and embarrassed: The poet had been born in 612 BC in Skala Eressou. She had run a 'school for young girls'. Her passionate odes to the beauty of women had often been 'misinterpreted'.

Fuming, Mona stalked a statuary shop, where she passed row after row of plaster penises before pouncing on the only female figurine in sight. 'Sappho?' she asked the clerk, pronouncing it 'Sappo,' the way the Lesbians did.

The clerk frowned at her, uncomprehending.

'Is this Sappho? The poet?'

'Yes,' he replied, though it sounded suspiciously like a question.

'Forget it,' said an American voice behind her. 'It's Aphrodite.'

Mona turned to see a woman her own age, handsome and lanky, with a big Carly Simon mouth. 'They don't do Sappho. Not as a statue, anyway. Somebody told me there's an ouzo bottle shaped like her, but I haven't been able to find it.'

Mona returned the figurine to the shelf. 'Thanks,' she told the American.

'You'd do better in Mitilíni. They've got a statue of her down by the harbor.' The wide mouth flickered. 'It's ugly as shit, but what can you do?'

Mona chuckled. 'I can't even find a book of her poetry.'

'Well, there's not much left, you know.'

'Oh, yeah?'

'The church burned it.'

Mona grunted. 'Figures.'

'You might try the gift shop on the square. They've got some fairly decent Sappho key rings.'

'Thanks,' said Mona. 'I'll do that.'

The woman went back to her browsing.

In the shop on the square Mona found the key rings – a crude profile on an enameled chrome medallion. They weren't much, but they did say SAPPHO, so she bought a green one for Michael, thinking that it looked vaguely horticultural. Then she set off in search of a hotel that sounded like Sappho the Russian.

She found it on the boardwalk after a five-minute search. Sappho the Eressian. The room she rented there was spare and clean – blond wood, a single bed with white sheets, a lone lamp. She showered off the grit of the road, then anointed herself with sun block and changed into a crinkly cotton caftan she'd bought in Athens. She was much more comfortable when she returned to the beach and felt her wet hair kinking in the warm breeze.

She headed toward the big gray bluff, since the beach seemed less crowded at that end. The bathers grew sparser – and nuder – the longer she walked. When everyone in sight was naked, she skinned off her caftan and rolled it into a tight little ball, stuffing it in her tote bag. She spread a towel on the sand and lay on it, stomach down, feeling a warmth that seemed to rise from the earth's core.

The nearest sunbathers were a dozen yards away on either side. She raked her fingers through the coarse sand and felt it roll away magically, like tiny gray ball bearings. There was a breeze off the water, and the sun lay on her big white bottom like a friendly hand.

This was all right.

The last time she'd done this had been in San Francisco in the mid-seventies. She and Michael had gone to the nude beach at Devil's Slide. She had shed her clothes with great reluctance, feeling white and blobby even then. Michael, of course, had wussed out at the last minute, supposedly to preserve his tan line.

She missed him a lot.

She had wanted him to explore Lesbos with her, but the little fool had fallen in love on her and never found the time.

He wasn't sick, Anna had insisted. He might have the virus, but he wasn't sick.

But he could be. No, he would be. That was what they said now, wasn't it?

Unless they discovered a drug or something. Unless some scientist wanted the Nobel Prize bad enough to make it happen. Unless one of the Bush kids, or Marilyn Quayle, maybe, came down with the goddamned thing . . .

She laid her cheek against the warm sand and closed her eyes.

Later, in the heat of the day, she strode out into the sea. When she was thigh-deep, she turned and surveyed the broad beach, the prosaic little town and distant dung-colored hills. She didn't know a soul for miles. Anna and Stratos were on the other side of the island, napping by now, no doubt, or making love behind closed shutters, stoned to the tits.

She smiled at the thought of them and splashed water on her pebbling flesh. This has been a good idea, she decided, taking a holiday from her holiday. She felt wonderfully remote and unreachable, even a little mythical, standing here in the cradle of the ancients, naked as the day she was born.

On an impulse, she tilted her chin toward the sky and had a few words with the Goddess.

'You can't have him yet,' she yelled.

She was pink by nightfall, but not painfully so. In her monastic room at Sappho the Eressian, she smoked one of

167

Anna's joints and watched as the lights of the tavernas came on, string by string. When she was pleasantly buzzed, she glided down to the pristine little lobby and asked the desk clerk, just for the sound of it, where she could find a good Lesbian pizza.

By the strangest coincidence, they sold just such an item at the hotel taverna. It was a truly awful thing, dotted with bitter-tasting little sausages. She polished it off with gusto, then she began to speculate about the quality of Lesbian ice cream.

'Hello,' crooned a familiar voice. 'Find those key rings?'

It was the woman with the Carly Simon mouth, a good deal browner than before. She was still in her walking shorts, but her crisp white shirt was a more recent addition.

'Yeah, I did,' said Mona. 'Thanks.'

'What did you think?'

'Well . . . I bought one.'

The woman smiled. 'It's all there is, believe me.'

'It's so stupid,' said Mona. 'You'd think they'd notice there was . . . some interest.'

The woman chuckled. There was a comfortable silence between them before Mona gestured to a chair. 'Sit down,' she said. 'If you want.'

The woman hesitated a moment, then shrugged. 'Sure.'

'If you're about to eat, I don't recommend the pizza.'

Wincing, the woman sat down. 'You didn't eat the pizza?'

'I can't help it,' said Mona. 'I'm sick of Greek food.' She held out her hand. 'Mona Ramsey.'

'Susan Futterman.' Her grip was firm and friendly, devoid of sexual suggestion. Mona's current contentment was such that she didn't care one way or the other. It was just nice to have a little civilized company.

*

Susan Futterman lived in Oakland and had taught classics at Berkeley for fifteen years.

'I'm surprised it isn't Futterwoman,' Mona told her.

'It was, actually.'

'C'mon!'

'Just for a little while.'

'Oh, shit,' said Mona, laughing.

Susan laughed along. 'I know, I know . . .'

'I had a lover once from Oakland.'

'Really?'

Mona nodded. 'She runs a restaurant in San Francisco now. D'orothea's.'

'Oh, yeah.'

'You know her?'

'Well, I know the restaurant.' Susan paused. 'Do you live in San Francisco?'

'No. England.'

She looked surprised. 'For good?'

'I hope so.'

'What do you do?'

Mona thought it best to be vague. She hadn't been Lady Roughton for almost a month and was beginning to enjoy the anonymity. 'I manage properties.' she said.

Susan blinked. 'Real estate?'

'More or less.' She gazed out at the strollers along the boardwalk. 'There really are a lot of women here.'

'Oh, yeah.'

'It's funny how just a *name* can do that much.'

'Isn't it? Have you been down to the tents yet?'

'I don't think so,' said Mona.

'You'd know,' said Susan.

Susan was a seasoned Grecophile and tossed back several glasses of retsina without flinching. Mona stuck with her Sprite-and-ouzo and was feeling no pain by the time they set off in quest of the famous tents.

169

They were down at the end of town, some yards back from the beach in a dusky thicket. Most of them weren't tents at all but 'benders,' like the ones the antinuke women had built on Greenham Common – tarps flung over shrubbery to form a network of crude warrens.

She was astounded. 'Where do they come from?'

'All over. Germany mostly, at the moment. I saw some Dutch girls too.'

'Is it always like this?'

'Usually more,' said Susan. 'This is the tail end of the season.'

Like pilgrims in a cathedral, they kept their voices low as they passed through the encampment. Here and there, women's faces beamed up at them in the lantern light.

Sappho's tribe, thought Mona, and I am a part of it.

Susan, it seemed, knew a woman in one of the benders: a young German named Frieda, square-jawed and friendly, with a blond ponytail as thick as her forearm. She poured vodka for her visitors and cleared a place for them to sit on her sleeping bag. There were faltering efforts at an English conversation before Susan and the girl abandoned the effort and broke into frenetic German.

Unable to join them, Mona downed her vodka, then let her eyes wander around the bender. There was a battered leather suitcase, a bottle of mineral water, a pair of blue cotton panties hanging out to dry on a branch. On the ground next to her knees lay a pamphlet for something called Fatale Video, printed in English; the headline FEMALE EJACULATION leapt out at her.

She glanced at it sideways and read this:

FATALE VIDEO – By and for women only.
Thrill to Greta's computer-enhanced anal self-love!

170

Sigh with scarf play, oral and safe sex with Coca Jo
and Houlihan!
Gasp at G-spot ejaculation and tribadism with Fanny
and Kenni!

She smiled uncontrollably, then looked up to see if
she'd been noticed. Susan and the girl were still
nattering away in German. The return address on the
pamphlet was Castro Street, San Francisco. While
she'd been becoming a simple English country dyke, her
sisters in the City had been building their own cottage
industries.

The conversation across from her grew quieter, more
intense. Then Susan said something that made the girl
laugh. They're talking about me, thought Mona.

'Well,' said Susan, addressing Mona again. 'Ready to
mosey?'

'Sure.'

Susan spoke to the girl again, then led the way out of
the bender.

Mona's leg had gone to sleep, so she felt a little shaky
as she left.

Smiling at her, the girl said: 'Bye-bye.'

'Bye-bye,' said Mona.

They didn't talk until they were out of the thicket and
walking back to town on the moon-bleached sand.

'How long have you known her?' asked Mona.

Susan chuckled. 'Since . . . oh, four o'clock.'

They had seemed like old friends.

'I met her coming back from the beach today. She
paints houses in Darmstadt.'

'Why was she laughing just before we left?'

Susan seemed to hesitate briefly. 'She thought you
were my lover. I told her you weren't.'

'Oh.'

'She wasn't laughing at you.'

Mona accepted this, but she had the uncomfortable feeling she was cramping Susan's style. 'Well, look,' she said, 'if you wanna go back . . .'

'No, no.' The broad smile seemed brighter by moonlight. 'She didn't want *me*.'

Mona stopped in her tracks.

'Or *just* me, anyway. She was looking for a couple.'

'You're shitting?'

'No.'

'Both of us?'

'Exactly.'

'Christ,' said Mona.

'Welcome to Lesbos,' said Susan.

Just before midnight they drank thick Greek coffee at a restaurant near the square. The breeze off the sea was chillier now, and Mona was sorry she hadn't brought a jacket.

'It's almost winter,' said Susan. 'You can practically smell the rain coming.'

'Yeah.'

'I always come this time of year. I like it when I'm right on the cusp. When the tourists are leaving, and they start to batten everything down. There's something so poignant about it. And so purifying.' She stirred her coffee idly. 'All those leaves being washed clean.' She looked at Mona. 'What's it like where you are?'

'Right now?'

'Well . . . anytime.'

Mona thought for a moment. 'It's in the country. Gloucestershire.'

'Oh, that's magnificent.'

She nodded. 'It gets cold and damp any day now, but I really don't mind it.'

'Sure. You can sit by the fireplace with a cup of tea.'

More often than not, Mona stood *in* her fireplace

with a cup of tea, but it seemed pretentious to say so. She flashed for a moment on winter at Easley House: the lethal drafts, the frost on the diamond-shaped panes, the smoke curling out of the limestone cottages in the village. Then she saw the silly grin on Wilfred's face as he dragged some lopsided evergreen into the great hall.

Susan asked: 'Do you live alone?'

She shook her head. 'I have a son.'

'How old?'

'Twenty. I adopted him when he was seventeen.'

'That's nice. Good company.

Mona nodded. 'The best.'

'I have a daughter myself. She starts at Berkeley next year.'

Mona smiled and sipped her coffee. If they weren't careful, they'd start dragging out snapshots.

Later she got another joint from her room and shared it with Susan as they strolled through the maze of deserted streets behind the promenade.

'This is nice,' said Susan, holding a toke.

'It's Northern Californian.'

'No.' Susan laughed, expelling smoke. 'I mean this. Getting to know you.'

'Well, thanks.' Mona gave her a wry smile. 'Futter-woman.'

After another leisurely silence, Susan said: 'You think she's found her couple yet?'

Mona had been wondering the same thing herself. 'Maybe not.'

'Poor baby.'

'I know. Must be tough, being so specialized.'

Susan seemed lost in thought. 'Did you know that whales do it in threes?'

Mona mugged. 'Pardon me?'

'It's true. Certain types of whales perform the sex

act in threes. The gray ones, I think. The third whale
sort of lies against the female and holds her steady
while the other two are fucking.'

Mona mulled this over. 'Is the third whale male or
female?'

'I don't know.'

'Well, what good are you? We need *facts* here,
Futterwoman.'

Susan chortled, obviously feeling just as giddy as
Mona. 'It was only a footnote.'

'Are you sure you heard her right?'

'Absolutely,' said Susan.

'What would she want with a couple of old dames?'

'Fuck you.'

Mona laughed.

'She's not that young, anyway. It's just the ponytail.'

'Yeah . . . but . . .'

'But what?' said Susan.

'If we go back . . .'

'Yeah?'

'Well . . . I don't wanna be the third whale.'

Susan laughed. 'Who does?' She stopped at an inter-
section, got her bearings, and reversed her course.

'The tents are back this way,' Mona told her.

'I know. I have to get something in my room.'

'What if she doesn't want us? I mean . . . what if she
requires actual lovers?'

'We'll fake it,' said Susan, picking up steam.

Her room was in a boardinghouse off the square. Mona
waited for her downstairs while Madonna serenaded
the patrons of a nearby taverna. Susan returned about
three minutes later with an oblong box in one hand.

'Saran Wrap?'

Susan winked. 'Don't leave home without it.'

'What do you mean?'

'C'mon. Where have you been?'

174

Mona started to answer, but 'Gloucestershire' didn't seem to cover it.

'Better safe than sorry,' said Susan.

'Oh.' The light dawned. 'Right.'

They hurried arm in arm down the pitch-black beach, giggling like a couple of teenagers.

Disguises

In the sun-splashed courtyard at Presidio Hill School, Brian knelt amid the other parents and children and applied the finishing touches to his five-year-old. 'Stop squirming, Puppy. I'm almost through.'

'Hurry up,' she told him. 'He's gonna be here.'

'Yes, Your Majesty.'

He dabbed his forefinger in the gunky green makeup and obliterated the last patch of white on her cheek. 'This is looking pretty good, actually.'

'Lemme see.'

'Hang on.'

She had brought along a little hand mirror, something from a doll's wardrobe, and was consulting it to the point of obsession. She had already used it to check the angle of her 'shell' – two shallow cardboard boxes he had covered with green garbage bags – and to adjust the roll of her turtleneck sweater.

'Where is he?' she asked. 'He's gonna miss it.'

'He has to open the nursery first.' He checked his watch and saw that Michael was half an hour late. He'd probably hung around the place too long and gotten entangled in a sale.

Shawna pawed through her bag of costume supplies. 'Where's my ninja mask?'

'In my pocket. You don't wanna put it on yet. The parade won't start until . . .'

'I wanna have it on when Michael gets here.'

'Oh . . . OK. Good thinking.' He produced the mask – really an orange blindfold with eyeholes – and knotted it behind her head. 'Can you see?'

'Yeah.'

He drew back a little and appraised her. 'I think we've got it.'

She grabbed the little hand mirror.

'See?' he said. Out of the corner of his eye he spotted Michael climbing the stairs from Washington Street.

'Puppy . . . he's coming.'

Shawna tossed the mirror aside and assumed what was apparently the stance of a Teenage Mutant Ninja Turtle.

'Where's Shawna?' Michael asked, playing along.

Shawna giggled and gave his leg a halfhearted little karate chop.

'Oh, no,' said Michael. 'The dreaded Michaelangelo.' He knelt and Shawna attached herself to his shoulder, laughing wickedly. 'You look fabulous,' he told her.

'Thanks.'

'You're welcome.' Michael turned back to Brian. 'Sorry I'm late.'

'No sweat. It hasn't started yet.'

'Yeah,' said Shawna. 'No sweat.' She let go of Michael's shoulder and darted across the courtyard to the spot where her classmates were assembling for the parade.

'How was it?' asked Brian.

'OK.' Michael stood up. 'Polly's there with Nate and the new guy.'

'I thought it might have gotten busy on you.' He hoped this sounded conscientious enough. He had already begun to feel guilty about leaving Michael in the lurch.

'No,' said his partner. 'It was slow. I got the shits, that's all.'

'Oh.'

Michael smiled ruefully. 'Nothing dramatic. Just . . . garden variety.'

'Well, look . . . nobody's gonna hold you to this.'

'I know.'

'If it gets too much . . .'

'I'll tell you. Don't worry. I'm over it, anyway. Shawna looks great.'

'Doesn't she?'

'Did you make the costume?'

'Yeah.'

'Not bad, Papa.'

Brian said: 'She's been waiting for you. You're the one she did it for.'

'That's nice.'

'She's gonna miss you, guy.'

Though Michael didn't respond to this, something registered in his eyes. Brian couldn't decide what it was. Embarrassment, maybe? Sadness? Resentment?

'Where does the parade go?' asked Michael.

'To Saint Anne's,' Brian told him, glad to change the subject. 'The old folk's home.'

The procession included a fairly predictable array of witches, ghosts, pirates, Hulks, and Nixons. To her delight, Shawna was the only Teenage Mutant Ninja Turtle. Brian and Michael tagged alongside with the other grownups, like paparazzi at a royal wedding – there but not there.

The general idea was to cheer up the old folks, but most of the functioning inmates of Saint Anne's were off at mass somewhere when the kids arrived. The deserted halls were modern, devoid of soul and pungent with piss. Nuns in white habits – the Little Sisters of the Poor, Michael said – smiled the tight smiles of sentinels as the parade of tiny pagans passed them by.

Michael touched Brian's arm. 'Look.'

A ghost in a white sheet had left the procession long enough to stop and stare in stupefaction at one of the white-habited sisters. From this angle, the child and the nun looked like a pair of Mutt-and-Jeff Klansmen.

'Saint Casper the Friendly,' said Michael.

Brian smiled.

'This is sort of surreal, isn't it?'

'Sort of?'

At the core of the building lay a mini-mall meant to suggest a city street. There were flimsy aluminum lampposts and plastic plants and an assortment of pseudoshops providing amenities for the residents. At the ice cream parlor one of the ghostly sisters was constructing a cone for a nearly hairless old woman in a wheelchair.

Michael leaned closer to Brian's ear. 'Sister Mary Rocky Road.'

The old woman heard the chatter of the children and stared, slack-mouthed and uncomprehending. One of the teachers yelled, 'Happy Halloween.' The old woman squinted at the alien invaders, then turned away, clamping a palsied claw on her ice cream cone.

'Christ,' Brian murmured, almost involuntarily.

'What?'

'Is this what it comes to?'

'If you're lucky,' said Michael.

Brian left it alone.

'Oh, no.' Michael made a face suddenly.

'What?'

'I gotta find a nun.'

'Huh?'

'Or a toilet. Whichever comes first.'

Brian looked around. 'There's a nurses' station up ahead.'

'See you later.'

'I'll meet you out front. In case we get separated.'

'Right.'

Michael all but bolted to the nurses' station.

They reunited on the lawn at Saint Anne's, twenty minutes later.

'Are you OK?' Brian asked.

Michael nodded, looking decidedly pale. 'I made many new friends. Where's Shawna?'

'They just headed back. We can catch up with them, though.' He threw his arm over Michael's shoulder. 'Sorry you're feeling bad.'

'Thanks.'

'You wanna get some breakfast after this . . . or would that just make it worse?'

'No. I'm hungry, actually. Ravenous.'

'Good,' said Brian. 'I've found a great new place on Clement.'

It was time they talked.

Back at the school, climbing out of her shell, Shawna pronounced the parade an unqualified success.

'We're doing a pageant at Christmas,' she told Michael. 'Wanna come?'

'Sure.' Michael looked uncomfortable. It had obviously occurred to him that Shawna wouldn't be here then.

Brian swiped at her face with a Kleenex. 'You're gonna be green till Christmas. I think you'd better try some soap and water on this.'

'No,' she said. 'Cold cream.'

'Great. But we don't have any cold cream.'

'Nicholas does.'

'See if you can borrow his, then.' He gave her behind a pat as she darted off to one of the classrooms. When she was gone, he said: 'We haven't told her about the move yet.'

Michael nodded but wouldn't look at him.

'You think that's unwise?'

'Brian . . .'

'Well, you look like it does.'

'It's none of my business.' Michael's tone was reasonable enough, but something was bugging him.

'Mary Ann hasn't firmed it up with Burke yet, and she thinks Shawna might spill the beans.'

'Yeah, well . . .'

'Plus I don't wanna hit her with this until we can be . . . you know, more specific about her new home. So she feels like she's moving to something instead of just away.'

Michael shrugged.

'If you think it's a rotten idea, tell me.'

'I don't think anything.'

'You're lying.' Brian said this jovially, then smiled, hoping it would get a rise out of him. 'You're right, though. It's her life too. She has a right to know what's going on.'

He had always believed that kids could sense it when you held out on them. At least on some subliminal level. Secrecy was unhealthy in the long run. He would talk to Mary Ann again and insist that they tell her.

Shawna returned breathlessly, clutching a jar of cold cream. 'We have to give it back,' she said.

'Sure thing,' he said, and winked at Michael.

Michael ordered dry toast and ate it slowly.

'There's a bug going around,' Brian assured him. 'A lot of people have it.'

His partner nodded.

For a moment, perversely, Brian's imagination went berserk. He saw Michael at ninety pounds, the way Jon had been, an old man at thirty-two. 'Sometimes,' he added hastily, 'when you change your diet or eat too many fruits and vegetables . . .'

181

Michael gave him a small, indulgent smile as if to tell him to drop it.

'OK,' said Brian.

'What time is it?'

He looked at his watch. 'Eleven.'

'We should be going. I told Polly we'd be back by now.'

'I have to say something first.'

Michael looked uncomfortable. 'What?'

'I just . . . I want you to know that this isn't easy for me.'

'What isn't?'

'Leaving.'

'Oh.'

'You're my best friend, you know, and . . . being your partner has meant more to me . . .'

'Brian, c'mon . . .'

'No, wait a minute, dammit. I have to say this.'

Michael looked down at his toast.

'If you're embarrassed, I'm sorry but . . .'

'I'm not embarrassed.'

'I've thought about this a lot, Michael. We've been through so much together. I'm really aware of . . . what it must be like for you right now.'

'Look, don't exaggerate the . . .'

'I'm not, OK? I'm looking at the way things are. I couldn't handle it if you thought I was . . . you know, deserting you.'

'You're not. I don't feel that way. Stop overanalyzing things.'

Brian smiled dimly. 'That's what Mary Ann always says.'

'Well, in this case, she's right.'

'But something's bothering you,' said Brian. 'I can tell.'

'Look, my stomach . . .'

'Not your stomach. C'mon. I know you, man. I love you. Tell me what's on your mind.'

Refusing to meet his gaze, Michael picked up a piece of toast. 'It's got nothing to do with you and me.'

'I know that's not true.'

'It is. Can't you just leave me out of this?'

'Nope,' Brian told him, smiling. 'Sorry. You're in my life. There's nothing I can do about it. C'mon now. Tell me.'

Michael sighed and set down his toast.

Completely Amicable

The show that morning had been about modern witch-craft, but the broomstick graphics and spooky music that accompanied it had not exactly jibed with the panelists: three paisley-clad crystal enthusiasts from Oakland. They had been desperate last-minute replacements; all the really serious occultists had defected to the networks for Halloween.

As she passed this funky trio afterward in the green room, Mary Ann fully expected a complaint to be lodged. Witches were a minority group nowadays, and one of these aging hippies was bound to accuse her of negative stereotyping, or possibly even 'witchist' behavior.

But they were all smiles.

'That was a ball,' said the oldest one.

The other two agreed, grinning like idiots.

'Good,' she told them. 'Let's do it again soon.'

Well, it figures, she thought, heading for the dressing room. They had gotten high off their first dose of television, and all other potions had paled by comparison. Witches were just as susceptible as anyone else.

The phone was ringing when she reached her inner sanctum.

'Yeah?'

'It's Burke, Mary Ann.'

'Oh, hi.' She collapsed on her sofa, toed her shoes off. 'You're back. How was LA?'

'Good. Useful. I've lined up some more talent.'

184

'Terrific.'

'Is this a good time?'

'Sure.'   'Have you had time to think it over?'

'Uh-huh.'

'And?'   'I think we can do business.'

She wasn't sure what she'd expected. Maybe a small preppy cheer of some sort. Or at least a burst of boyish laughter. What she got was a brief silence and the sound of breath being expelled. 'Well,' he said. 'All right.'

She said: 'I think we've got a hit on our hands.'

'You bet.'

'What's our timetable?'

He didn't hesitate. 'I need you in New York by the end of the month.'

She'd expected this but gave a whistle, anyway.

'I know. I'll make it as easy as possible for you. I'll get you the best movers in the business.'

'Actually,' she said, 'I won't need to move that much.'

'You're gonna sell your stuff?'

'No. Brian wants to stay here with Shawna.'

'But, I mean, eventually . . .'

'No,' she said. 'They'll stay here for good.'

Silence.

'He thinks it's best,' she said, 'and so do I.'

'Well . . .'

'It's not fair to uproot Shawna, and he's got his own business.' She paused, wondering how Burke was taking this. 'I'll really just need a furnished place for the time being.'

He seemed to hesitate. 'Is this resolved?'

'Yes.'

'Completely?'

'Yes,' she said quietly. 'This has been coming for a long time.'

'I'm sure you understand.' He cleared his throat. 'There's a contract involved here.'

'I know.'

'Are you getting a divorce?'

'Does it matter?'

After a moment he said: 'No. Not really.'

'It's all completely amicable. You don't have to worry about it.'

'All right . . . OK.'

'Shall we meet?' she asked.

'No. I'm flying back to New York tonight. There's nothing we can't work out on the phone.'

Another call came in. 'Hang on,' she said. 'Would you?'

'That's OK. I'll sign off. We'll talk at the beginning of the week. I'm delighted about this, Mary Ann. I've got a great feeling about it.'

'Me too,' she said. 'Talk to you later.'

She punched the flashing button. 'Yeah?'

'It's Security, Mary Ann.'

'Yeah?'

'Your husband's here.'

What the hell was this about? 'To pick me up?' she asked.

'I dunno.'

'Well, ask him, please!' 'I can't. He's on the way up.'

'Terrific.' She slammed down the phone, suddenly filled with panic.

The rap on her door came moments later.

'Yes?' she called evenly.

'It's me.'

She opened the door, to find him looking wretched and drawn, like a lost man stumbling into a ranger station.

'What is it? What's the matter?'

'You tell me,' he said.

'Huh?'

'Michael says you don't want me to go with you.'

That little snitch, she thought.

'Is it true?'

186

She eased the door shut and gestured toward a chair.

He sat down at once, obedient in his shock, and gazed up at her with red-rimmed eyes, waiting for an answer.

'He shouldn't have said that,' she told him.

He nodded slowly, obviously taking that for a yes. 'I thought maybe that . . . ?' He cut himself off as his eyes filled with tears and overflowed.

She sat on the arm of his chair and touched his arm gently. 'Please don't think . . .'

There was a rap on her door.

'Yes?' she called irritably.

Raymond's head poked through the doorway, prickly with mousse. 'Sorry. Need some autographs for the studio audience.'

'Come back later, please.'

'But they're leaving in . . .'

'Raymond . . .'

'Right. Sorry.' He shut the door.

'I'd hoped we could talk tonight,' she told Brian.

'How long have you felt like this?'

She didn't answer.

'A month? A year? What?'

She stroked his arm and used the gentlest tone she could muster. 'I think you've felt it too.'

'No.' He shook free of her and stood up, his cheeks slick with tears, his voice choked with anger. 'I don't think I have. I don't think I've felt that at all.'

She paused for a moment, still on the edge of the chair. 'I'm sorry you had to hear it like this.'

'Yeah, well . . .' He was flailing around for something to hunt her with. 'What else is new? I'm always the last fucking one to know anything. Of course, I realize that when you're destined for stardom . . .'

'Brian . . .'

'What did I do? Embarrass you in front of those lounge lizards at Stars?'

'You've never embarrassed me.'

187

'Bullshit!'

She kept herself centered by smoothing the material on the arm of the chair. 'If it makes you feel better to cast me as the villain . . .'

'Oh, yeah! It does. It makes me feel fucking great! I'm on a major high right now!'

'If you would just . . .'

'Goddamn that asshole!'

She had been waiting for this and resolved to remain calm. 'You know perfectly well Burke and I . . .'

'He's taking you away, isn't he? He's paid for your expensive ass, and you're outa here!'

'Lower your voice, please.'

'Does he know about this?'

'About what?'

'That you're dumping your husband and child.'

She flinched. 'I'm not dumping anybody.'

'You got that right! That's one luxury you're not gonna enjoy.' He lunged toward the door.

'Stop, Brian. Don't be silly. Where are you going?'

'What the fuck do you care?'

'C'mon. Sit down. We can have lunch somewhere.'

'Fuck your lunch!' He flung open the door, then turned to face her for his parting shot. 'You're one coldhearted bitch, you know that?'

He slammed the door so hard that it knocked one of her awards off the wall.

She took off her makeup, then called the nursery.

'Plant Parenthood.'

'It's me, Michael.'

'Oh . . . hi.' He sounded guilty already.

'Brian was just here,' she told him.

'Yeah. I kinda figured.'

'I just want you to know I feel totally betrayed by you.'

'Well, I'm sorry. What was I supposed to do?'

'You were supposed to keep your mouth shut. You promised me you would.'

'And how long ago was that?' he snapped.

'What difference does that make?'

'You told me you'd tell him, that's what. It's been days. The poor bastard was making plans about New York. He was apologizing to *me*, for God's sake. I couldn't just pretend I didn't . . .'

'Why couldn't you? I asked you to.'

'Oh, well,' he said snidely, 'in that case . . .'

'You've hurt him very deeply. I think you should know that.'

'*Me?*'

'How do you think it felt for him to hear that from you? To know that you and I had discussed something so personal before he even knew about it.'

'Well, OK, but . . .'

'If you had seen how destroyed he was . . .'

'You have got one helluva goddamn nerve!'

'Well, think about it.'

'I am thinking about it! You're the one who's leaving him, sister, not me!'

He hung up on her.

She sat at her vanity and cried.

Sooner or later, men were all the same.

A Long Evening

'If it rains a lot this winter,' said Thack, 'it'll be nice and weathered by spring.'

He was talking about his pink triangle trellis, now a *fait accompli*. All that was left was to plant the pink clematis, or maybe roses (they hadn't decided which), and wait for nature to do her stuff. 'It looks great,' Michael told him, standing back to admire the carpentry. 'I really like the way you've joined the corners.'

'It's not bad, is it?'

Michael didn't have the heart to tell him that the whole thing might not read, that flowers – roses especially – might refuse to conform to the perimeter of the triangle.

They admired it together in silence. Eventually, Thack said: 'I'm worried about Brian.'

'Me too.'

'He didn't come back to work at all?'

'No.'

'You'd think he would've called, at least.'

'Well, she said he was really upset.' Michael felt awful about this. Maybe Mary Ann was right. Maybe he had only made it worse – actually contributed to Brian's humiliation – by spilling the beans. 'You think he's pissed at me?'

'No. Is that what she said?'

'No, but . . . if he sees me as her ally . . .'

'What did he say when you told him?'

'Nothing, really. He was just kind of numb.'

Thack nodded.

'Do you think I fucked up?'

'I don't know, baby.'

'Well, thanks for the vote of confidence.'

'It doesn't matter. He had to find out.' He slipped his arm around Michael's waist. 'How's your stomach?'

'Still there,' Michael told him.

'Why don't you run a hot tub and relax?'

Michael did so for half an hour. He was changing into his nightshirt when the phone rang.

'Hello.'

'It's me, Mikey.'

'Oh . . . hey, Mama.' He collapsed on the bed and slipped into his mother mode.

'I hadn't heard for a while, so . . .' She stopped there, as she always did. He had never known her to finish this sentence.

'I've been really busy. I'm sorry.'

'I left a message on your machine.'

'I know,' he said.

'Didn't Thack tell you . . . ?'

'Yeah. I just forgot. I've had a lot on my mind. How are you?'

'Oh . . . can't complain.'

'Well, that's good.'

'How are you feeling?'

'OK. I seem to be responding to the AZT. My T-cells are holding steady.'

She was quiet for a moment. 'Now which are they?'

He'd expected this, but he was still annoyed. 'Mama, did you get the pamphlet I sent you?'

'I got it. It's mighty confusing, though.'

'Right.'

A long silence. 'You haven't got it, though, have you?'

'No, Mama,' he explained one more time. 'I have the

191

virus. I'm OK now, but I could get it eventually. I probably will.' God, how he hated this 'it' talk. How could he ever explain to her that he had had 'it' – or it had had him – from the very moment he learned of Jon's diagnosis, over seven years earlier? Most people thought you got this thing and died. In truth, you got this thing and waited.

'Well . . . I think you should be positive about it.'

How like her not to know that she'd made a pun. 'I am, Mama.'

'Your daddy's worrying killed him, sure as I'm sitting here. More than that cancer ever did.'

'I know,' he said. 'I know you think that.'

'I just can't help thinking if you found yourself a nice church, with a pastor you liked . . .'

It never took her long to get back to this. 'Mama.'

'OK. Never mind. I've had my say.'

'Good.'

Thack passed through the room naked, bound for the tub with a bottle of Crabtree & Evelyn bath gel. 'Is that Alice?' he asked.

Michael nodded.

'Tell her I said hey.'

'Thack says hey,' Michael told his mother.

'Well, tell him hey back.'

'Hey back,' he told Thack.

Thack leaned over the bed and sucked Michael's big toe. Michael yanked his foot away and tried to slap Thack's butt, but his lover dodged the blow and gamboled off to the bathtub, laughing under his breath.

'So what have you been up to?' he asked his mother.

'Well . . . me and Etta Norris went to the new multiplex and saw that movie with Bette Midler you told me about.'

'Oh, yeah? What did you think?'

'I liked her.'

'I told you.'

192

'I guess I didn't like her near as much as Etta. She like to laughed herself silly.'

Michael hollered into the bathroom, where Thack was splashing about like some creature at Marine World. 'She likes Bette Midler.'

Thack laughed.

'What was that?'

'Nothing, Mama. I just told Thack you like Bette Midler.'

Thack yelled back. 'I knew this would happen when they fucked up the ozone layer.'

'What did he say?'

'Nothing important, Mama.'

'Listen, Mikey, they finally put in Papa's tombstone last week. It looks real nice.'

'Well . . . good.'

'I took some pictures of it, so you can see.'

For a moment all he could picture was the floral arrangement that had stopped him short at his father's funeral the year before. Some doting, Bible-toting aunt from Pensacola had sent it, and his mother had displayed it proudly – and conspicuously – at the funeral chapel.

A bed of white carnations formed the backdrop for a child's toy telephone, also white. JESUS CALLED was written across the top in fat, glittered letters. Down below, it said: AND HERB ANSWERED. To Michael's dismay, no-one else there that day – not even his younger cousins – had found the slightest humor in this. He had ended up calling Thack from a neighboring Taco Bell, just to laugh with someone about it.

He tried, and failed, to picture his mother's idea of a 'nice' tombstone. 'I'm glad it turned out,' he told her.

'It's so pretty there.'

Apparently she meant the cemetery.

'Your papa was a smart man to buy that plot. You know they're so expensive now you can't hardly afford 'em at all.'

193

'That's what I hear.'

'And he made sure there was room enough for the whole family.'

For her, this was subtlety. Not to worry, she was saying, we've saved a place for you. He let it pass without comment, knowing she meant well, the way she had years before when she'd lobbied annually for him to spend Christmas 'with the family' in Orlando. It had never even occurred to her that his family might be elsewhere.

She rambled on for another half hour, filling him in on people he hadn't seen for at least fifteen years. Most of her gossip was second generation, since his high school buddies were now the parents of children old enough to drink and take dope and 'get into trouble with the law'.

It wasn't the same Orlando any more. He'd seen as much when he went home for the funeral. In the years since his departure, the trees at Disney World had thickened into plantation oaks. The Mickeys and Goofys who plied their trade there could now be found off duty at Parliament House – the PH to those in the know – an antiseptic gay mall offering a choice of leather, western, or preppie saloons.

The cemetery, as he recalled, had been two minutes off the interstate, with a broad avenue of palms and a heart-stopping view of the Piggly Wiggly.

No, thank you, ma'am.

Thack emerged from the bathroom in his terry-cloth robe. 'How was she?' he asked.

'Fine.'

'What's she been up to?'

'Well . . . among other things, trying to bury me in Florida.'

'Huh?'

'My father's tombstone arrived, and she's working on a family reunion.'

Thack rolled his eyes and sat on the edge of the bed. 'Leave it to me,' he said.

'She'll fight you over it.'

'No she won't. She likes me.'

'That has nothing to do with it. Trust me.'

Thack picked at the comforter for a moment. 'Did you tell her what you wanted?'

'No.'

'Are you going to?'

'I guess I'll have to write her,' said Michael. 'It's kind of hard to get chatty about.'

Thack smiled. 'Turn over.'

Michael turned over. Thack straddled his back and kneaded the muscles at the base of his neck.

'These people are serious Christians,' Michael told him. 'They'll put me in the living room and bring casseroles.'

His lover laughed. 'Shut up.'

'I mean it. You don't know.'

'Yeah, yeah.'

'And next to me there'll be this huge philodendron on a spinning wheel . . .'

'Just relax.'

'Lower,' said Michael. 'That feels wonderful.'

'There?'

'Yes.'

Thack seized the tightest rope of muscle between his thumb and forefinger. 'What is this, anyway? Mary Ann?'

'Do you have to name it?' said Michael. 'Can't you just rub it?'

The new doorbell made them both jump. This particular model had caught Michael's eye at Pay 'n Pak with its simple design and lyrical name – the Warbler. What this meant was that it fired away like a machine gun as long as there was a finger on the bell. Only the briefest poke would produce the lone dingdong usually associated with a doorbell.

And the damn dog went nuts over it.

'Harry,' said Thack, springing off Michael's back. 'Shut the fuck up.'

'Who are we expecting?'

'Nobody.'

Harry was in the living room now, yapping like crazy. Michael scooped him up and stashed him in the guest bedroom. Peeping through the spy hole in the front door, he saw Brian's distorted face, golden as a carp's under the orange porch light. He was the only person they knew who never remembered not to lean on the doorbell.

Michael opened the door. 'Hi.'

'Hi. Sorry I didn't call first.'

'No problem.'

'Is it a bad time?'

'Not at all.'

Thack let Harry out of the guest bedroom. The dog did a barkless little jig around Brian – the one he saved for members of the immediate family.

'How's it going, Harry?' Brian let the dog sniff his hand for a moment, then gave it up, seemingly drained of energy. 'You guys were in bed, weren't you?'

Thack shook his head. 'On it. Back rub.'

'Oh.'

'Sit down. Can we warm up some polenta lasagna for you?'

'No, thanks.' He sank into the armchair as if he might never get up again.

'There's some wine,' said Michael. 'Sauvignon blanc.' He had just noticed how wrecked Brian's eyes were.

'Any Scotch?'

'Not really.'

'How 'bout rum?' Thack suggested.

Michael looked at his lover. 'Where do we have rum?'

'Under the sink, next to the cleaning stuff.'

196

'Since when?'

'We bought it for the eggnog last year.'

'Oh, yeah.'

'Rum would be great,' said Brian.

Michael brought back the bottle with a glass. Somehow, the mission seemed fraught with urgency, like serum being dog-sledded across the Yukon. 'There's not much to mix it with. Diet Cherry Coke, maybe?'

'Straight up's fine.'

Michael poured several inches. Brian downed it in one gulp and handed the glass back. 'I know that's a cliché, but it had to be done.'

Michael smiled. 'Want another?'

'Nope. That was it. Thanks.'

'No problem.'

Brian looked down at his hands, dangling between his legs. 'I talked to her,' he said.

'Did you?' It was best, Michael decided, not to tell him she had called. That could only lead to trouble. He put down the glass and sat next to Thack on the sofa.

'Why didn't I see it coming?' said Brian. 'How out of it could I have been?'

There was a long silence, during which Harry hopped on to the armchair and settled his chin against Brian's leg.

'I was actually picturing it, you know.'

'What do you mean?' asked Michael.

'New York,' explained Brian. 'We had a brownstone on the Upper West Side. And a cat. And Shawna and I knew the museums by heart.' Brian stroked the dog's back. 'I was just cruising along like everything was copacetic.'

'Why shouldn't you?' Thack said quietly.

'But . . . if I'd communicated more . . .'

'Look,' said Thack, 'it's not your fault.'

Michael, who was thinking what a straight word 'copacetic' was, cast a nervous glance at his lover.

197

Neutrality was in order here, and Thack, as usual, seemed on the verge of blowing it. 'I don't think it's a question of fault, really.'

Thack gave him a dirty look.

'I can't go back to the condo,' said Brian. 'Not while she's still there.'

Silence all around.

'Somebody's gotta talk to Shawna, I know, but . . .' Brian's face balled up like a fist, rubbery with grief. He began to sob soundlessly.

Michael and Thack remained still.

'I'm sorry, guys.'

'That OK,' said Michael.

'It's just there, you know?' Brian took a couple of swipes at his eyes. 'I thought I had it under control.'

The doorbell fired off another sally, making them all jump. Harry sprang off Brian's lap and barked vigorously at the latest intruder.

'Who the fuck is that?' Thack looked at Michael.

'Got me.' Michael picked up the poodle, causing him to downgrade his yap to a low growl. Brian gave Michael an apprehensive look, as if he thought Mary Ann herself was waiting behind the door.

Thack peered through the spy hole. 'Christ.'

'What?' said Michael.

'What day is this? Think.'

It took Michael a moment. 'Oh, shit.'

'Do we have anything?' asked Thack.

Michael racked his brain. There hadn't been candy in the house for months. None, at any rate, that had survived their last tumble off the sugar wagon. There weren't even any apples. This was the second year in a row they had forgotten to stock up on treats for the kids. In this neighborhood it wasn't just the grownups who did Halloween.

The doorbell rang again.

'Maybe they'll go away,' offered Thack.

'We can't do that,' said Michael. He dashed to the kitchen and found a package of dried apricots in the back of the cupboard. 'How many are there?' he hollered.

'Just one,' yelled Thack. 'At the moment.'

Michael returned with the apricots and opened the door to a three-foot Roger Rabbit. 'Well, hello there.'

The kid held out a Gump's bag without a word. In a single, guilty movement, Michael deposited the apricots, hoping they would sound like Tootsie Rolls. The kid said 'Thanks' and ran back to a cluster of older children waiting on the sidewalk. Michael closed the door and leaned against it, feeling like a total fraud.

'If you'd done that to me,' said Brian, 'I would have TP'ed your house.'

There were bound to be more trick-or-treaters, so Michael made an emergency run to the Noe Hill Market, where he found a giant assortment of miniature candy bars. If they didn't give them all away, he could always throw them out in the morning.

Back at the house, while Brian played listlessly with Harry in the living room, Thack confronted Michael in the kitchen. 'Shouldn't we offer him the guest room?'

'I don't know, sweetie.'

'We can't just . . . send him off.'

'Yeah, but it would seem like taking sides.'

'Who cares?'

'I care. Mary Ann's my friend too.'

'Some friend. She just blamed the whole damned thing on you.'

Michael threw him a medium-sized dagger. 'We'll just make it worse if he stays here.'

'For God's sake,' said Thack, 'he's your partner.'

'Don't preach to me, all right? I know who he is.'

'OK, fine. Call the Motel 6.'

*

'It's no problem,' said Michael. 'Really.'

He and Thack were back in the living room. Brian was still on the floor with Harry. 'Are you sure?' he said, looking up. 'I can get a motel.'

'Nah. That's ridiculous.'

Brian shrugged. 'I've done it before.'

'Well, it's . . . You have?'

'Sure. Couple of times.'

'When?'

'I dunno. Last year.' He raised his brows sheepishly.

'You should stay here,' said Thack.

Michael nodded. 'Yeah.'

'OK, then. Thanks.'

Thack looked at Michael. 'Are there sheets on the guest bed.'

'No, but . . .'

'The couch is fine, guys.'

'Don't be noble,' said Michael. 'We've got a guest room for just this purpose. Well, not *exactly* this purpose . . .' The doorbell rang.

'Shit.' Michael peered out through the spy hole. This time there were five of them. More plastic capes and plastic faces.

'It's gonna be a long evening,' said Thack.

Brian helped Michael make the bed in the guest room.

'What about Shawna?' Michael asked. 'Who's gonna take her to school in the morning?'

'Nguyet can do it.'

'Are you sure? I'd be more than happy . . .'

'No. That's OK. Thanks.' He looked at Michael earnestly. 'Can we not talk about this for a while?'

'Sure.' Michael finished tucking in the top sheet and plumped a feather pillow into place. 'There are some little hotel toothbrushes in the top of the medicine cabinet.'

'Thanks.' Brian smiled feebly. 'Trick toothbrushes.'

'What?'

'Isn't that what you used to call 'em?'

Michael chuckled. 'What a memory.'

'I'm sorry about this, Michael.'

'Don't be.'

'I can't go back there. I can't just . . . wait for her to leave.'

'I understand.'

'I knew I could count on you,' said Brian.

The Kastro

Mona felt a twinge of homecoming when her cab rounded the seafront bend and Molivos sprang into view. The bright shutters and stone terraces, the smoke-stack of the old olive oil factory, the Genoese castle crowning the hill – all had lost their exoticism and become suddenly, ancestrally familiar. She had been here before and now she was back, an Amazon returning from the Sapphic Wars.

It pleased her somehow to be able to identify the noise coming from the esplanade. It was the laundry truck, which announced itself by what appeared to be a top-mounted gramophone, and which, once or twice a week, transported the dirty clothes of tourists into Mitilíni, sixty kilometers across the mountains. The people of Molivos were a proud lot, who did their own washing but no-one else's.

The first time she'd heard the blare of that loud-speaker, she'd held her breath and waited for word that a coup had been declared. Even now, almost three weeks later, she suspected it of fascist leanings. Who knew what it was saying, anyway? Maybe it wasn't just a laundry truck. Maybe it was issuing some sort of public edict.

Attention all dykes, attention all dykes. The season is officially over. Please vacate the streets immediately and return to your home countries. This is your last warning. I repeat: This is your last warning . . .

She smiled and peered out the window. A lot of the shops and restaurants had been boarded up in her absence, now citadels against the coming rains. In the tiny high street, the sea-green grotto of Melinda's Restaurant harbored the last of the tourists. The men at the Old Guys' Café – her name for the place where Stratos usually ate – seemed tickled to death that Molivos was about to be returned to them.

Who can blame them? she thought. I wouldn't want to share it either.

She disembarked at the wisteria-covered end of the high street and paid her driver. She had chosen this approach to the house, rather than the easier one from the esplanade, for the sheer navigational thrill of threading her way down the maze of cobbled walkways. She enjoyed knowing where she was going in such a completely foreign place.

When she reached the Turkish fountain that identified the base of their terrace, she stopped and, looking up, saw the flutter of silk against the sun. Anna cooed a greeting. 'You're home.'

'I am,' said Mona, and smiled at her, one seasoned traveler to another.

'It was truly elemental.'

They were on the terrace now, under big hats. The waning sun had turned the sea to blue Mylar, and there was a breeze. The wisteria on the terrace had lost its thick coat of dust in what Anna said had been a torrential rainstorm.

'No shit?' remarked Mona. 'It barely drizzled in Skala.'

'Indeed?'

'How long did it last?'

'All night. We were giddy on the ozone. We flung open the shutters and let it just tear through the house.' Anna smiled winsomely. 'I was quite the madwoman.'

'Did it knock out the electricity?'

'No. Why?'

'There are candles all over the place.'

'Oh. Those were for' – Anna dropped her eyes – 'atmosphere.'

'Atmosphere?'

'Yes.'

Mona didn't pursue this, but the image that leapt to mind was of Anna buck naked in a thunderstorm, head wreathed in laurel, arms aloft, like some transcendental Evita. 'Did you enjoy the house?'

Anna nodded.

'You didn't throw him out, just because I was . . .'

'No, dear. We both wanted a little distance for a while.'

'A breather,' said Mona.

Her parent glowered.

'He seems nice.'

'He is. Very.'

'How was the birthplace of Dukakis's father?'

'Lovely.'

Mona tilted her hat and gave Anna a friendly smirk. 'You never even went, did you?'

'We most certainly did.'

'For how long?' She wasn't letting her off the hook this easily.

Anna hesitated, then said: 'Most of a day, at least.'

'You could've just asked me to leave, you know. I wouldn't have minded.'

'Dear, I assure you . . .'

Mona laughed.

'How was Sappho's birthplace?'

'Fine.'

'Did you meet any nice people?'

'Several,' said Mona, and let it go at that.

*

When Mona woke to the three o'clock church bells, the air was much cooler, and there were fat, bruised clouds lolling outside her window. This had been her last siesta; tomorrow she'd be back in Athens, sitting on her luggage, waiting for her flight to Gatwick. Wilfred had insisted on meeting her plane, so she felt compelled to be strict about her schedule.

'What haven't you done?' Anna asked her over tea.

Mona rolled her eyes. 'Don't ask.'

'I mean here,' said Anna, smiling. 'Have you seen the *kastro*?'

'They have gay boys here?'

'The castle, you philistine.'

'I know.'

'It's extraordinary, if you haven't seen it. Fourteenth century.'

'Fine. Let's do it.'

'It's a bit of a walk.'

'Something told me,' said Mona.

Higher and higher they trekked through the cobbled labyrinth, until the houses fell away and the castle gate loomed above them. Two black-sweatered old ladies with apple-doll faces were on their way down, so Anna chirped a cheery '*Kalispera*' before taking Mona's arm and pointing to the squiggly writing above the gate. 'The Turks ruled this place for over four hundred years. They didn't leave until 1923.'

Mona imagined Stratos on the same spot, telling Anna the same thing. And the goofy look in Anna's eyes when he said it.

'The *kastro* itself is Genoese, built by a titled Italian family.'

Mona grunted and followed her through the gate and up a scrubby incline to another entrance, more mammoth than the first. Thirty feet above their heads, a gnarled fig tree grew from the very stone itself. The ground was sticky from a recent bombardment of fruit.

The door to the keep was ironclad on the outside, but its wooden inside had proved vulnerable to tourist graffiti. It was Greek, for the most part, and the quaint fraternity lettering of the ancients somehow reduced its offensiveness. The only English word she recognized was AIDS, emblazoned in red against the medieval wood.

She averted her gaze and kept walking, her temples pounding as she strode into the open air of the inner fortifications.

Her parent seemed unaffected. 'They use this part for a stage,' she explained. 'Stratos says they did a production of *The Trojan Women* several summers ago.'

'Oh, yeah?'

Anna forged ahead, ignoring the lackluster response, climbing until the castle began to resemble an opera set – all turrets and fragments and stony niches framing the sea. There were Wagnerian clouds to match, and the wind had picked up considerably, invading Anna's hair to create a sort of Medusa effect.

She looked at Mona, then swept her arm toward the distant Turkish coastline. 'Troy,' she sighed. 'Imagine.'

'That's it, huh?'

'That's it.'

Mona leaned against the battlement and studied her parent's face, struck suddenly by its radiance. 'You've enjoyed yourself, haven't you?'

'Oh, yes.'

'I'm glad.'

'I've never known anyone like him.'

Mona hesitated, surprised at the sudden appearance of 'him'.

'He's asked me to stay, in fact.'

'For how long?'

Blinking at her, Anna made a vague gesture in the direction of Troy. 'This long.'

Mona laughed, suddenly tickled. 'Really?'

Anna nodded.

'A Lesbian wedding?'

'Heavens, no!'

'OK, then. A Lesbian shack-up.'

They laughed together, sharing their distrust of institutions.

'Is he rich?'

'Mona!'

'I just meant . . .'

'He's comfortable. We'd have plenty between us. His brother-in-law is a Dukakis.'

Mona smiled.

'I forgot to tell you,' said Anna. 'He lost.'

'Who?'

'Dukakis. Stratos told me this morning.'

'Oh.' She wasn't in the least surprised. America was already fucked.

'Stratos is really rather bleak about it.'

'What did you tell him?'

'About the election?'

'About you.' She smiled. 'Don't be coy.'

Anna raked her Medusa locks with her fingers. 'I haven't told him anything yet.'

'Is he . . . important to you?'

Anna nodded.

'Enough so that . . . ?'

'Oh, yes. More than enough.'

'What would you do?' asked Mona. 'Sell the house?'

'I suppose.'

'Could you do that?'

'I don't know. The Treachers have made me an offer.'

'Who are the Treachers?'

'They're on the third floor.'

'Oh.'

'They're a nice young couple. They're looking for a place to buy. I'm sure they'd take good care of it.'

207

'You'd probably get a fortune for it.'

'I'm not interested in a fortune.'

'I know, but . . . it wouldn't hurt. You could travel all over Europe, visit me at Easley. Hell, I'd come see you here. I'd make the sacrifice.'

Anna chuckled, then held Mona's arm and gazed down at the toy-boat harbor, the train-set village flung against the mythic hillside.

'I can see you here,' said Mona.

'I am here,' said Anna.

Mona smiled at her. 'You know what I mean.'

'Yes.'

'Are you afraid he's not for real?'

'No. Not at all.'

'Don't you want a companion?'

'In my old age?' A smile darted across Anna's lips.

'C'mon.'

'I have plenty of companions. Wonderful company. Just like you.'

'You want to do this,' said Mona. 'I can tell you do.'

Anna fidgeted with the sleeve of her caftan. 'The children would never understand.'

'If you mean Michael, he's got his own life. You should do the same.'

'And there's Mary Ann and Brian . . .'

'They're all gone, for God's sake.'

'Nevertheless . . . I have responsibilities.'

In her mind's eye Mona saw the writing on the castle wall. She knew exactly what Anna was thinking. 'Look,' she said, 'Michael would never forgive you if you passed this up on his account.'

'Dear . . .'

'If that's the reason, I'll tell him, so help me.'

'You'll do nothing of the kind.'

'You've spent your whole life telling other people to live and be free. Why don't you stop blowing smoke and take a little of your own advice?'

'That's quite enough.'

'You know I'm right.'

'It's starting to rain . . .'

'Go home and tell them. See what they say, at least.'

Her parent didn't answer as she scurried along the battlement, in flight from the downpour.

Cock-and-Bull-Stories

When Brian pulled up in front of the summit, Shawna was downstairs as arranged, scribbling furiously in her coloring book.

'How's it goin'?' asked the doorman, leaning into the Jeep. He was obviously curious as hell about the change in their daily routine. This was the fourth morning in a row Brian had arrived from somewhere else to pick up his daughter.

'Not bad, not bad.' He made a point of sounding jaunty.

'Hey, are those rumors true?'

'What rumors?'

'Mary Ann taking her act to the Big Apple.'

'Oh.' He shrugged. 'Looks like it.' He opened the door and let Shawna in. 'Where's your lunch box, Puppy?'

'We don't have to,' Shawna told him. 'Solange's mom is fixing burritos.'

'I guess we'll be losing you guys.' The doorman wasn't giving up.

'Well, it hasn't really been ...'

'We don't have to go with her,' Shawna offered brightly.

'Puppy.' Brian gave his daughter a scolding look before turning back to the doorman. 'Nothing's really definite.'

He pulled away from the curb, causing his inter-rogator to slap the side of the Jeep and say: 'Hang in there.' There was a sympathetic, man-to-man air about

210

this, which made Brian wonder if the guy had already guessed the score.

'What did I do wrong?' his daughter asked.

'Nothing.' He couldn't bring himself to reprimand her for telling the truth, or at least her slant on it.

'When is she going?'

'Next week, Puppy.'

'Will you come back then?'

'Sure. Of course. I told you that.' He reached across and wiggled one of the tight little braids Nguyet had woven for her. 'Where else would I go, silly?'

'I dunno.' Shawna ducked her eyes. 'Are you still mad at Mary Ann?'

'No. I'm just . . . I've never been really mad at her, Puppy. We had a misunderstanding. It makes me sad to be around her now, so I'm gonna stay with Michael and Thack until she leaves.'

'Will you be sad when she's gone?'

He hesitated. 'Some. Yes.'

'I don't want you to be.'

He looked at her. 'I'll give it a shot.'

She was distracted by a passing station wagon. A black Lab was in the back seat, poking his rubbery nose through a crack in the window. She waved at it briefly before turning back to him. 'Does Michael have AIDS now?' she asked.

'No, Puppy. Michael is just HIV positive. Remember when he explained that to you?'

'Yes.'

'Why'd you ask, then?'

The child shrugged. 'Mary Ann said he was sick. She said you were taking care of him.'

'Oh.' So that was the excuse she'd used. 'He had an upset stomach for a while, but he's fine now.'

'Oh.'

'It was just a regular ol' upset stomach. Just like you have sometimes.'

211

She looked out the window again.

'Michael would tell you if he was really sick. Don't worry about that.'

'OK,' she said.

That afternoon, as they clipped the brown spikes off the yucas, he told Michael about Shawna's distress. 'She was so confused, poor kid.'

'I'm not surprised,' said Michael.

'What do you mean?'

'Well . . . she's pretty much in the dark about this, isn't she?'

There was the suggestion of negligence to this, which annoyed Brian. 'Look . . . I've been perfectly straight with her. I wasn't the one who fed her some cock-and-bull story about taking care of you.'

'I realize that.'

'Well . . . you sounded pretty judgemental.'

'Sorry.'

'It's typical of her not to level with the kid, to make it even worse by . . .'

'She's got to tell her something, Brian.'

'Tell her the truth, then. Tell her I'm hurt and pissed. What's so difficult about that?'

'Is that what you told her?'

'No . . . not exactly . . .'

'OK, then. She's just trying to spare Shawna's feelings.'

'And I'm not, huh?'

'Brian . . .'

'It's my fault her mother's running off to join the goddamn circus. I get it.'

'I'm not talking about fault, Brian. If you would just sit down and hash this out with her . . .'

'Have you talked to her or something? Did she tell you to say this?'

'No.'

'She's been giving you grief, hasn't she? What did she do? Accuse you of defecting?'

Michael rolled his eyes. 'I haven't talked to her once since you left.'

'Well . . .'

'I do think it's time you grew up a little and talked to her. You're only making things worse.'

'Is that right?'

'The longer you put if off . . .'

'Thanks, Michael. I get the point. Just what I needed – another nagging wife.'

Michael stuck his clippers in his belt and began to walk away.

'Wait,' said Brian. 'I'm sorry, man. Don't listen to me. I don't mean this shit.'

'I can't handle it, Brian. I don't know what to tell you any more.'

'You don't have to. I don't expect you to.'

'You haven't stopped pumping me all week. I can't keep playing middleman like this.'

'When have I ever . . . ?'

'Oh, Jesus, Brian, for years and years. I'd like to have a nickel for every time you've asked me what she really thinks about something.'

'Because she talks to you, man. She never tells me shit. You know stuff about my life that I don't even know.'

Michael gave him a long, steely glance. 'It helps to get her trust first.'

'What's that supposed to mean?'

'Oh, Brian . . .'

'No. Tell me. I wanna know.'

Michael gave him a weary little smile. 'You fucked around on her so much.'

'If you mean Geordie . . .'

'No. Not just Geordie. What about that woman from Philadelphia?'

'What woman from Philadelphia?'

213

'You know. Brigid Something. With the tits and the saddle shoes. You said she was your cousin. Give me a big break.'

Brian remembered. He had brought her by the nursery one day years ago, long before he'd become a partner here. He had just come off an incredible no-oner and wanted to show her off a little. Michael had still been a bachelor, still a trusted co-conspirator in matters of lust.

'Did you tell Mary Ann about that?' he asked.

'Hell, no,' said Michael. 'She told me. I had no idea. I thought the cousin bit sounded too obvious to be an out-and-out lie.'

'Then how could she have possibly . . . ?'

'She's got eyes, Brian. You're not as subtle as you think you are.'

Brian took this in, smarting a little. 'Did she just tell you this?'

'No. Years ago.'

'Then why are you bringing it up now?'

His partner heaved a sigh. 'Because you keep acting so wronged.'

'I am wronged.'

'Fine.'

'When did you get to be such a little Calvinist, anyway?'

'I'm not talking about sex; I'm talking about lying.'

'I haven't fucked around for years, and you know it.'

'Since Geordie, right? Since you got scared shitless. Sorry, but no cigar.'

Brian's face was aflame. 'This is really ironic coming from you.'

'From me? Why is that?'

'You were the Whore of Babylon, Michael.'

'Maybe so, but I wasn't married.'

'Only because you couldn't be. You and Jon were a couple. If he were still alive . . .' He cut himself off, horrified by the careless ease with which he'd waded into these waters.

'If he were still alive, what?'

'Nothing. I'm sorry. I shouldn't have said that.'

Michael regarded him with cow-eyed melancholy, then walked back to the office without a word.

They avoided each other for the rest of the day.

Remembering's Different

'I wouldn't count on him,' Michael told Thack that evening. 'Not for dinner, anyway.'

Thack looked up from the chicken breasts he was breading. Behind him, beyond the big window, the fog tumbled into the valley like white lava. 'What happened?'

'We had a fight.'

'Over what?'

'Nothing much. We called each other sluts.'

Thack arranged the breasts on a baking dish. 'How tired.'

'I'm well aware.'

'Was it over Mary Ann?'

Michael paused. 'Somewhat.'

'Thought so.'

'Well . . . he was getting so sanctimonious. He hasn't exactly been a saint. She's had plenty of reason to . . .'

The phone rang.

Michael picked it up, pulling out the antenna. 'Hello.'

'It's me, Mouse.' It was Mary Ann.

'Hi.'

'Is he there?'

'No.'

'Is that her?' asked Thack, not exactly *sotto voce*.

Michael gave him an annoyed nod and turned away. 'I'll tell him you called, OK?'

'No. Don't. You're the one I wanted.'

'What for?'

'She's gonna suck you in.' Thack was being a real pain. Michael gave him a dirty look and walked out of the kitchen. The cordless model came in handy sometimes.

'How 'bout a date, Mouse?'

In the living room, he collapsed on the sofa and kicked off his shoes. 'Come again?'

'Don't make this hard on me,' she said.

'Well, what are you talking about?'

'I've got tickets to this open house tonight.' She paused dramatically. 'Would you like to go with me?'

'Babycakes . . . look . . .'

'I feel so ganged up on, Mouse.' Her voice was small and plaintive.

'Well, you shouldn't,' he said, melting fast.

'How can I not?' She sounded almost on the verge of tears. 'Come with me, Mouse. Just so we can talk. We don't have to stay long.'

'If you just wanna talk, can't we just . . . ?'

'I have to be there. I'm committed. I thought Brian would be here when I told them . . .'

'Oh . . . so you need a walker.'

Her response was grave and wounded. 'You know that's not true. I just thought we could . . .'

'Kill two birds with one stone?'

The silence was so long he wondered if she'd hung up. 'Why am I so awful?' she said at last. 'What did he tell you?'

'Nothing.'

'Well, why are you acting like this?'

He heaved a sigh of resignation.

'I thought you'd enjoy it,' she said. 'It's black tie, and it's in this beautiful house out at Sea Cliff.'

Thack, of course, saw his acquiescence as something just short of betrayal.

'Give me a break,' Michael argued. 'I can't stop seeing her just because they're . . .'

217

'Why not? She dumped him, didn't she? That's clear enough.'

'And we men have got to stick together. Is that it?'

Thack frowned. 'What do our dicks have to do with it?'

'A lot, if you ask me.'

'You think I'm being sexist?'

Michael shrugged. 'Maybe unconsciously.'

'Well, you're full of shit, then.'

'I didn't say . . .'

'Is that what she told you? That this was the men versus one poor little woman?'

'No.'

'She's jerking you around, Michael. Just the way she does him. She'll say anything to get what she wants.'

'And women aren't supposed to do that.'

'Nobody's supposed to do that! It's got nothing to do with sexism. You know I'm not a sexist. Why are you so blind about this? I don't get it.'

Michael let him calm down for a moment. 'You haven't known her as long as I have.'

'Well, maybe I can see her more clearly, then.'

'Maybe you can.' He sighed. 'You want me to cancel?'

'Do what you want to do.'

'Oh, right.'

'I'm not gonna lie to Brian about it.'

'I don't expect you to.' Michael's tone was glacial as he left the room. 'I hadn't planned to myself.'

His tux was spotted in several places and required major sponging. His dress shirt was clean, but he ended up stapling the cuffs, since he couldn't find his cuff links and he wasn't about to ask Thack for his. His beeper went off in the middle of this procedure, causing him to fling down the stapler and skulk off in search of water.

Back in the bedroom, he sat on the bed and finished dressing. As he put on his socks, he spotted something on his ankle – his lower calf, really – that he hadn't noticed before. He leaned over to look at it.

'Hey,' said Thack, walking into the room, 'if you wanna wear my red cummerbund, go ahead.'

Michael didn't answer.

'What is it?'

'Come here a second. Look at this.'

His lover came to the bed. 'Where?'

'There.'

Thack studied the purplish inflammation, touching it lightly with his forefinger.

'Does that look like it?'

No answer.

'It does to me.'

'I don't think so,' said Thack. 'It looks like a zit or something. Something healing. Look at the edges of it.'

When had he ever seen a zit down there? 'The color seems right, though.'

'Go see August, then, if it worries you. Isn't tomorrow your day for pentamidine?'

'Yeah.'

'It'll put your mind at ease, anyway.'

'Yeah.'

'I'm sure it's nothing,' said Thack, shaking Michael's knee. 'I'll get the cummerbund.'

Mary Ann had done a show that morning on baby evangelists, so that was what they talked about on the long drive to Sea Cliff. His guess was that the heavier stuff would come later, when they were both feeling a little more sure of each other.

The fog in Sea Cliff was as dense as he had ever seen it. The house was seventies modern, a cluster of multi-leveled metallic boxes with thick glass walls overlooking the ocean. Flashcubes of the Gods, he thought, as Mary Ann turned the Mercedes over to a valet parker.

'What's the deal here?' he asked. The lights along the

path glowed soft and spongy in the fog. Out on the dark-ling plain of the Golden Gate there were horns bleating like lost sheep.

'We just walk through and look at it,' she said. 'It's a benefit for the ballet.'

'Whose house is it?'

'I don't know, really. Some guy who died. He left a provision in his will that they could let people see it after he died.'

'How odd.'

'Well . . . he was a realtor.' She shrugged as if this explained it.

Suddenly it hit him. 'Arch Gidde. Was that his name?'

'Yeah,' she said. 'That's it.'

'Christ.'

'You knew him?'

'Not very well. Jon did. He used to come here all the time.'

'This Gidde guy was gay?'

'What did you think he died of?'

'Prue said it was liver cancer or something.'

'Right,' said Michael.

'Well . . . I guess he has a right to his privacy.'

Michael knew what Thack would have said to that.

The house was nicer than he'd imagined, but this was hardly the night to show off its view. The fog pressed against the windows like a fat lady in ermine. While Mary Ann sought out 'somebody in charge,' he loitered in the living room and gave the place an embarrassed once-over. It seemed a little callous to be checking out the digs of a dead man, even with the blessing of the deceased.

He remembered the day the realtor had propositioned him at the nursery – back when it was still God's Green Earth. Arch had come in for primroses and recognized Michael as an ex-lover of Jon's. Moving in for the kill, he had stuffed a business card into Michael's overalls and made an overt and clumsy reference to owning a Betamax.

Now 'Betamax' had the ring of 'Gramophone,' and the travertine reaches of Arch Gidde's living room, circa 1976, seemed as quaintly archival as a Victorian parlor preserved in a museum. The focal point was a gleaming chrome fireplace (with a matching chrome bin for the logs). Facing the hearth was a pair of enormous Italian sofas – pale arcs of buttery leather, burnished over the years by the endless buffing of gym-toned asses. The only thing missing was a lone anthurium in a crystal vase.

He could picture Jon here easily, sprawled in the golden light like some surly sweater spread out of *GQ*. He had been a mess in those days, but he had changed dramatically toward the end, and that freer, more forgiving person was the one Michael chose to remember.

'Wait till you see the bedroom.'

Mary Ann was back, taking his arm at the bar as he ordered a Calistoga.

'Is it nice?'

'The walls are brown suede. And padded. It's such a *womb.*'

'What are you drinking?'

'Nothing. No, fuck that. A white wine.'

'Hey,' said Michael. 'Wild woman.'

She smiled at him. 'I'm so glad you're with me.'

When their drinks came, he lifted his to hers. 'To things getting better.'

She took a sip, then said: 'Why am I no good at this, Mouse?'

'At what?'

'Ending things.'

'Oh.'

'I wanted so much not to hurt him . . . to do it the right way . . .'

'You think there is one?'

'One what?'

'A right way.'

'I don't know.' She took a sip of her wine. 'I guess if I'd told him earlier . . .'

'Yeah.'

'I know I'm doing what has to be done. But even so . . . I feel like such a piece of shit, you know?' She looked at him almost reverently, as if she was expecting absolution.

'Well, c'mon . . . you're not a piece of shit.'

The room was beginning to fill up. It seemed to make her uneasy. 'Why don't we get away from the bar?' she said.

'Fine.'

They found a quieter spot – a den of sorts – on a lower level. 'The thing is,' she said, continuing where she'd left off, 'I can't ever remember what it was like when I did feel something toward him. I wake up some mornings, and I look at him, and I think: How did this happen?'

What did she expect him to say to that?

'I mean . . . I remember feeling it, but I don't remember how it felt. Like that time at the candlelight vigil . . .'

'Harvey Milk's?'

'John Lennon's.'

'Oh, yeah.' He smiled, remembering it too. Brian had bought strawberry-scented candles to invoke 'Strawberry Fields.' He and Mary Ann had spent hours on the Marina Green, paying homage to the world's most celebrated househusband, then returned to Barbary Lane bleary-eyed and exultant.

'He was so sweet,' said Mary Ann. 'And afterwards he left this note on my door that said: "Help me if you can, I'm feeling down, and I do appreciate your being 'round." '

Michael nodded.

'It was so completely him. So overblown and corny and really nice.' She smiled wanly. 'I wish to hell I could feel that now.'

'You must. You're telling me about it.'

'Only what I remember. Remembering's different.'

'But you must at least feel . . .'

'Not a thing, really.' She paused and gazed bleakly out at the fog. 'Just a little sorry for him sometimes.' Turning, she looked directly at him, her eyes brimming with tears. 'If that makes me a bitch, I can't help it.'

He took her hand. 'It doesn't make you a bitch.'

She began to weep quietly. When he tried to take her in his arms, she pulled away. 'No, Mouse, I can't. I'll come unglued.'

'Be my guest.'

'No. Not here.'

A clubby-looking woman appeared in the doorway. 'Oh, isn't this nice? Is this the study?'

'The orgy room,' said Michael.

The woman tittered briefly, nervously, before her face fell like a soufflé and she retreated.

'You're terrible.' Mary Ann wiped her eyes.

'Well . . . it probably was.'

'Let's get out of here.'

'Fine by me,' he said. 'You wanna get some coffee in the Avenues?'

'Oh, that sounds wonderful.'

'I know a perfect place.'

'I knew you would,' she said, squeezing his arm.

They were nearly out the door when Mary Ann spotted the shining, sculpted faces of Russell and Chloe Rand, floating through the crowd like a pair of beacons. She stopped in her tracks. 'Mouse, look . . .'

'Yeah.'

'We should say hello, don't you think?'

'I thought we were . . .'

223

'They must be back from LA.'

'Must be.'

He followed dutifully as she plowed through the throng. For a fleeting moment, when she reached back to take his hand, he thought he knew how it felt to be her husband.

Nickel-Dime Stuff

It was a generic valley, a dark bowl twinkling with porch lights and undistinguished by landmarks. There was neither bridge nor bay nor pyramid to tip you off that this was San Francisco, but – to Brian, at least – it couldn't have been anywhere else in the world.

Thack joined him on the deck, gazing out at the fleecy fog. 'They must be socked in out at Sea Cliff.'

'I guess so.'

'There's some Häagen-Dazs in the freezer.'

'Maybe later.'

'Don't worry about it, Brian. He wasn't upset.'

'Are you sure? I know I shouldn't've brought up Jon like that.'

'Why not?'

'Well . . . you know . . . a dead guy.'

Thack smiled at him. 'We talk about dead guys all the time.'

Brian nodded absently.

'It's just the way it is.'

'I guess so.'

'He was defending Mary Ann, right? And it got out of hand.'

'More or less,' said Brian.

'Well . . . serves him right. He shouldn't walk the fence so much.'

Brian was surprised by this cavalier reaction. 'He's known her a long time,' he said in Michael's defense.

'Yeah.'

'I don't expect him to take my side, just because . . .'

'He knows that,' said Thack. 'He also knows you're getting a bum deal. The trouble is he wants everyone to like him. He works at it way too hard. He's spent so much time being a good little boy that he's never figured out which people aren't worth it.'

Brian figured this was said for his benefit. To convince him that what he was about to lose was nothing of value, nothing worth crying over. He didn't buy it.

Thack kept his eyes on the fog bank. 'Where'd you go after work? We were worried about you.'

'Just out for some brews.'

'You holding up OK?'

'Yeah.' He looked at Thack sideways. 'You must be tired of hearing me piss and moan.'

'Nah.'

'It's nickel-dime stuff, though, compared to what you and Michael have to deal with.'

Thack shrugged. 'We've all gotta deal with something.'

'Maybe, but . . .'

'If Michael were leaving, I wouldn't consider it nickel-dime.' He gave Brian a sleepy smile. 'You're entitled to be miserable.'

There was another long silence.

Brian asked: 'Doesn't it scare you?'

'What? Michael?'

'Yeah.'

Thack seemed to sort something out for a moment. 'Sometimes I watch him when he's playing with Harry or digging in the yard. And I think: This is it, this is the guy I've waited for all my life. Then this other voice tells me not to get used to it, that it'll only hurt more later. It's funny. You're feeling this enormous good fortune and waiting for it to be over at the same time.'

'You seem happy,' Brian ventured.

'I am.'

'Well . . . that's a lot. I envy you that.'

Thack shrugged. 'All we've got is now, I guess. But that's all anybody gets. If we wasted that time being scared . . .'

'Absolutely.'

'You ready for that ice cream?' said Thack.

In the Loo

The Rands, bless their hearts, had greeted her like an old friend, obviously tickled to see a familiar face at yet another alien benefit. They were a little slow in coming up with Michael's name, so she let them off the hook right away.

'. . . and you remember Michael.'

'Of course,' said Chloe.

Russell extended his hand. 'Sure thing. How's it going?'

'Great,' Michael told him.

'Were you on the way out?' Chloe asked.

'Well . . .'

'Oh, don't be. I'm sure we don't know a soul.'

'Yeah,' said Russell, addressing Michael. 'Stay and keep us company.'

'Well, OK,' said Mary Ann. 'Sure.'

'Fabulous.'

'How was the benefit?'

Chloe's high ivory forehead furrowed.

'Didn't you go to some AIDS benefit in LA?'

'Oh, sure,' said Russell. 'It was very nice. Very moving.'

'Right,' said Chloe. 'I spaced out for a second.' She perused the crowded foyer. 'Is it this packed everywhere?'

Michael replied: 'It's better once you get past the bar.'

'Actually,' said Chloe, 'I have to pee like crazy. Know where the loo is?'

'C'mon, I'll show you.' Mary Ann took her hand, feeling

sisterly and conspiratorial all of a sudden.

Chloe looked back at her husband. 'Can you boys play on your own for a while?'

'Sure,' said Russell.

Michael shot a glance at Mary Ann. One of those stranded-puppy-dog looks that Brian was so fond of giving her.

'We won't be long,' she told him.

The bathroom designated for women was gleaming black onyx, huge.

'So,' said Chloe, 'I'm dying to know. I didn't wanna ask in front of your husband.'

This threw her for a moment. 'Oh . . . Michael's not my husband.'

'Oh. Shit. The other guy . . .'

'Right.'

'I'm sorry.'

'It's OK,' she said. 'Really.'

'So . . . what's the verdict on the show?'

Mary Ann gave a sheepish shrug. 'I'm gonna do it.'

Chloe squealed and hugged her. Though she had never actually experienced it, Mary Ann felt like a freshman at a sorority rush night. 'Tell me I won't be sorry,' she said.

'You won't be sorry. How's that?'

Mary Ann smiled at her gamely.

'Is . . . what's your husband's name?'

'Brian.'

'Is he OK about it?'

She faltered for a moment, then decided to come clean. Chloe had felt like an ally from the moment she met her. 'He's not going with me,' she said. 'We're getting a divorce.'

Chloe nodded slowly. 'Uh-huh.'

'It's been coming on for a long time.'

'Was this your idea or his?'

'Both, really.'

'Well, that's good.'

'I'm kind of freaked out about it. I mean, I know it's the right thing to do, but . . . it's a lot of new stuff all at once.'

'You'll be OK. Look at you. You'll land on your feet like a cat.'

'Think so?'

'Absolutely.'

'It's not just him I'm leaving, though. It's my whole life here, my friends . . . Michael out there . . .'

'They can come see you. This isn't Zanzibar you're moving to.'

'Oh, yes it is.'

'Look, you're talking to an Akron girl, remember? If I can do it . . .'

'But you did it with somebody you care about . . .'

'Yeah . . . well . . .'

'I am so envious of that. Having somebody on your own wavelength. Who loves the same things you love, laughs at the same jokes. Goes to things with you.'

Chloe looked as if she didn't quite understand.

'It's never been that way with me and Brian.'

'What has it been?'

'I don't know. Sex, mostly.'

Chloe fixed her lips in the mirror. 'Poor baby.'

Mary Ann laughed uncomfortably. 'I don't mean we did it all the time. I mean that's what . . . you know, kept us together.'

'Is that what you married him for?'

'No, not completely.'

'Then what?'

'He was also . . . very gentle.' Mary Ann paused. 'Plus he didn't have a name for his dick.'

'Excuse me?'

She rolled her eyes. 'For the longest time every guy I dated had a name for his dick.'

'You're not serious?'

'Yes.'

'Like what?'

'I dunno. Ol' Henry or something.'

Chloe snorted. 'Ol' Henry? Was this here or in Ohio?'

'Here! It was so depressing!'

They laughed together raucously.

'So,' said Chloe, recovering. 'Ol' Brian came along with this nameless wonder between his legs . . .'

Someone knocked on the door.

Muffling their giggles, they composed themselves. 'Come in,' said Chloe with exaggerated mellifluousness.

The door swung open slowly and a face appeared. Mary Ann recognized her as one of the pillars of the ballet board. 'Oh, I'm sorry,' the woman blurted. 'I thought . . .'

'No problem,' said Chloe. 'It's all yours.'

She recognizes us both, thought Mary Ann. Won't she have something to tell the girls?

They were in a sort of glass gazebo now, high above the water.

'Shouldn't we look for the guys?' Mary Ann asked.

'Fuck, no. Let 'em look for us.'

Mary Ann chuckled. She felt a little guilty about deserting Michael, but she knew he could handle himself. Besides, he was probably thrilled to death to be hobnobbing with Russell Rand.

'This house is weird,' said Chloe. 'So seventies.'

Mary Ann nodded, though she wasn't quite sure what Chloe meant.

'This looks like one of those elevators at the Hyatt Regency. You know?'

'It does, doesn't it?'

'I guess it was pretty hot shit once upon a time. Russell said it was, anyway.'

'This house?' said Mary Ann. 'He knows it?'
'He knew the guy who lived here.'
'Oh.'
'Not well, but he came to a few parties.'
Mary Ann nodded.
'If you know what I mean,' said Chloe.

That Eternity Crap

'Isn't this where we started?' asked Russell Rand, grinning boyishly.

They had wandered from one crowded level to another in search of Mary Ann and Chloe. So far, all they'd come up against were slack-jawed fashion victims, people who simply stopped what they were doing and gawked when the famous New Yorker appeared.

'I think you're right,' said Michael.

'I know I've seen that one before.' Rand nodded toward a champagne-blond matron in gold lamé knickers.

'You're right. Maybe she moved, though.'

'No. She's been there the whole time. A veritable beacon. I'm sure of it.'

'Well . . .'

'Oh, Christ.' The designer spun on his heels, ducking his head in the process.

'Who is it?'

Rand seized Michael's elbow and steered him away from the advancing menace, all the while pantomiming a surprised, jovial greeting to an imaginary person in the other room. Michael played along, waving vaguely to the same phantom.

When they had made their way to a lower, less populated level, Michael laughed and said: 'Who was that?'

'Prue Giroux.'

'Oh.'

233

'You know her?'

'No. I know of her.'

'Don't *ever* know her. You'll regret it deeply.'

Michael laughed. 'She likes to talk, I hear.'

'Oh, Christ. I thought we could get through here without seeing her this time.' He gazed imploringly at Michael. 'Let's get some air. This is too much for me.'

Without waiting for a response, the designer opened a door leading out to a cliffside rock garden. A pink spotlight beamed through the fog at a bank of succulents. At the end of the path was a stone bench, where Rand sat down with a sigh of relief. 'The people in this town are carnivores,' he said.

Michael joined him on the bench. 'Not everybody.'

'Well, everybody here.'

He couldn't argue with that.

'What do you do?' asked Rand.

'I'm a nurseryman.'

'Oh, yeah?'

'Uh-huh.'

'That's a nice solid profession.'

'Well . . .' Michael shrugged, not sure what to say about that.

'Have you known Mary Ann long?'

'Years.'

'Has she told you about her new show?'

'Oh, yeah.'

'Why isn't her husband here tonight?'

Michael decided not to elaborate. 'He doesn't like this kind of stuff.'

Rand nodded ruefully. 'But you do.'

'Not really. She asked me as a special favor.' He hoped he hadn't come off as her walker.

After a pause Rand said: 'You're not married, then?'

Michael smiled. 'To a woman?'

His interrogator obviously hadn't expected this.

234

'I have a lover.' It was hardly necessary to specify the gender.

Rand nodded.

'Three years.'

'That's nice.'

'Yeah . . . it is.'

The silence breathed heavy with suggestion.

'Is it an open relationship?'

'Oh, sure.' Michael smiled at him. 'Everybody knows about it.'

Rand shook his head. 'That's not what I meant.'

'Oh . . .'

'I've got a suite at the Meridien. You could be home by midnight.'

Well, well, thought Michael. How do you like this? 'What about your wife?'

Rand's lip curled handsomely. 'She's got her own suite.'

'Right.'

'Ours is open.'

'Your suite?'

'Our marriage.'

'Oh.'

'How 'bout it?'

'No, thanks.'

'Sure?'

'Yeah.'

'We'd play safe,' said Rand. 'I believe in that.'

'It's cold out here,' said Michael. 'I'm gonna look for Mary Ann.'

'C'mon, sport. Stay for a minute.'

Michael stared at the ground for a while, then said: 'You're really amazing, you know.'

The designer's brow furrowed.

'How can you live with yourself?'

'Look, if you mean Chloe . . .'

'No. I mean your own self-worth. What do your friends

think when you start spouting that crap?'

'What crap?'

'You know. About the love of a good woman. The joys of being straight. I saw you on the *Today* show last week. I've never heard such a line of shit in my life. You're not fooling half as many people as you think.'

Even in the fog, and under a pink light, Rand colored noticeably. 'Look, you don't know me . . .'

'I know you're a hypocrite.'

Rand took a long time to react. 'You run a nursery, for Christ's sake. Nobody expects you to be straight.'

'You think they expect dress designers to be?'

Rand nodded dolefully. 'The world doesn't want to know. Trust me.'

'Who cares?'

'I do. I have to.'

'No you don't. You're just greedy. Keeping up a front while your friends drop dead.'

Rand gave him a flinty glare. 'I've raised more money for AIDS than you'll ever see.'

'And that lets you off the hook? Entitles you to lie?'

'I think it entitles me to . . .'

'You had a chance to make a real difference, you know. You could've shown people that gay people are everywhere, that we're no different from . . .'

'Oh, get real!'

'Why not? Are you that disgusted by yourself?'

'Why should the public know about my private life?'

'We sure as hell know about Chloe, don't we?'

Rand grunted and stood up, obviously beating a retreat.

'You're a dinosaur,' Michael said. 'The world has moved on, and you don't even know it.'

Rand glowered back at him as he headed for the house. 'What do you know about the world? You live in San Francisco.'

'Thank God for that,' yelled Michael. 'And good luck getting laid.'

When Rand was gone, Michael remained there in the rose-tinted fog, filling his lungs with the stuff as he collected his thoughts. Then, remembering suddenly, he leaned over, lifted his pants leg, and examined the purple spot again.

When he found Mary Ann, she was in the act of autographing a cocktail napkin for an ecstatic fan.

'Are you about ready to go?' he asked.

She handed the napkin to the fan, who looked at it disbelievingly, then backed off, bobbing like a court servant. 'I guess so,' she answered. 'Are you bored?'

'No. I've just sort of . . . done it.'

'Right.' She perused the crowd. 'We should say goodbye to Russell and Chloe.'

'No,' he said. 'We shouldn't.'

She frowned. 'What's the matter? What happened?'

'We had sort of a scene. I'll tell you about it later.'

'Mouse . . .'

'I'll get the car.'

She followed him up the path to the valet parker. 'What sort of a scene?'

'He made a move on me.'

'What do you mean?'

'He invited me back to his hotel.'

'Well, that may not have been . . .'

'I think I would know,' he said.

In the car, after a weighty silence, she asked: 'What did you tell him?'

'Not much. That he was a closet case and should go fuck himself.'

'You didn't.'

'In so many words, yes.'

'Mouse . . .'

'What was I supposed to say?'

'It isn't what you say, it's how. Were you rude to him?'

'Does it matter?'

'It does to me, yes.'

'Why?'

'Because they've been very nice to me. Chloe's helping me with my move, and . . .'

He laughed as bitterly as he could.

'I mean this,' she said.

'What was I supposed to do? Suck him off to show your gratitude?'

'Don't put words in my mouth.'

'The guy is a slimeball.'

'You've been hit on before,' she said. 'You know how to turn somebody down in a pleasant way.'

'I can't believe this.'

'Where do you get off being so sanctimonious, anyway? You picked up plenty of guys before you met Thack.'

As usual, she had missed the point entirely. 'This has nothing to do with picking up guys,' he said.

'Then . . . what?'

'He's a liar, Mary Ann.'

'He's a public figure.'

'Oh, I see. Can't have Amurrica knowing he's queer. Anything but that, God knows.'

'There are practical considerations,' she said. 'You're not being at all reasonable.'

'I haven't got time for people who don't like themselves.'

He peered sullenly out the window. Pale stucco facades slid past in the darkness. It made him sad to realize that she hadn't grasped this fundamental concept in all their years of knowing each other. If she, of all people, didn't get it, was there any hope for the serious bigots?

She turned and looked at him. 'You sound so strident. It isn't very becoming.'

He kept quiet.

'You liked Russell the other night. Did Thack bad-mouth him or something?'

'No.'

'Then what's gotten into you?'

His beeper went off, answering her question more eloquently than anything he might have said.

She looked flustered for a moment. 'Do you want me to stop for water?'

'No.'

'Are you sure?'

'Yes. I'll take it when I get home.'

'I can always . . .'

'I'm fine, all right?'

They were silent for a while, staring out of different windows. As they dipped into Cow Hollow, he turned to her and said: 'You're the one who's changed, you know.'

'Have I?' Her voice was surprisingly gentle.

'Yes.'

'I'm sorry if my leaving . . .'

'It isn't that. It happened some time ago.'

'Oh.'

'I wish there was some way to convince you I'm not dead yet.'

She gazed at him, blinking.

'That's the way you've acted,' he added. 'Ever since I told you I was positive.'

She pretended not to understand. 'What do you mean? Acted how?'

'I don't know. Careful and distant and overpolite. It's not the same between us any more. You talk to me now like I'm Shawna or something.'

'Mouse . . .'

'I don't blame you,' he said. 'You don't wanna go through Jon again.'

'What do you think tonight was about? And that day at the Wave Organ?'

He shrugged. 'Insecurity.'

'C'mon.'

'You needed somebody to hold your hand. Somebody to listen. Nothing more.'

'That's not very kind.'

'Maybe not,' he said. 'But it's true.'

'If I can't count on you, Mouse . . .'

'Hey, it works the other way too.'

She looked wounded. 'I know that.'

'You're leaving more than one man, you know.'

She seemed to be composing her words. 'Mouse . . . you and I will always . . .'

'Horseshit. You scrapped our plans tonight as soon as that closet case walked through the door. Don't gimme that eternity crap. You've got your new friends now. The rest of us are just an interim measure.'

'I know you don't mean that.'

'I do mean it. I wish to hell I didn't, but I do. You don't give a shit about anybody.' He looked away from her, out the window. 'I'm amazed it took me this long to figure it out.'

'I don't believe this,' she said.

'Believe it.'

'Mouse, if I've said something . . .'

'Jesus, why are you always so innocent?'

'Look, if you'd tell me where this coffee place is . . .'

'Fuck that. Stop at the next corner. I'm getting out.'

'Oh, for heaven's sake.'

He turned and gave her a look to signal his seriousness. 'I said stop, please.'

'How will you get home?'

'A bus, a cab. I don't care.'

She pulled next to the curb at Union and Octavia.

'This is so unnecessary,' she said.

He opened the door and left the car without looking back. As the Mercedes sped away into the fog-fuzzed corridor, he stood on the curb and wondered bleakly if she even cared, if she was feeling anything at all.

Love on the Machine

He woke at dawn the next morning. The only dream he could remember had been a real doozie, a full Dolby extravaganza involving dead turtles, vintage biplanes, and a brief, heart-stopping walk-on by the Princess of Wales. Out of old habit, he lay there for a while reconstructing this epic, honouring it with his stillness, like a moviegoer who remains in his seat until the credits are over.

Leaving Thack in bed, he slipped into jeans and a corduroy shirt and took Harry on his morning walk – the abbreviated version – before sorting the laundry and fixing a breakfast of apples and yogurt. His pentamidine appointment was at nine, but the office opened at eight. He knew from experience that August wouldn't mind squeezing in an unscheduled examination.

As he left, Thack was lurching toward the shower in his morning muddle. 'Want me to come with you?'

Michael told him no.

'Are you coming home afterwards?'

This was a hard one to call. 'I dunno.'

His lover pecked him on the shoulder. 'Call me, then. Or I'll call you at work.'

'OK.'

'And don't worry,' said Thack.

August's office was in a black glass building on Parnassus opposite UC Med Center. Michael parked in the basement garage, then rode an elevator smelling of disinfectant and the hot dogs in the fourth-floor snack bar. On the fifth floor he was joined by a bulky Samoan lady who smiled pathetically and held up a splinted forefinger. He offered his condolences, then got off at the seventh floor.

In August's waiting room the receptionist behind the glass restrained her smile enough to hide the braces he'd seen many times before. 'Morning, Michael.'

'Hi, Lacey.'

'You're early, aren't you?'

'I've got pentamidine at nine, but I was hoping August could take a look at something.'

She nodded. 'He's out till noon.'

'Oh.'

'He's testifying in Sacramento.'

'Oh, yeah.'

'You know, funding . . . something like that. Joy is here. You wanna see her?'

Joy was a nurse practitioner. 'Sure. I guess. It's just a place on my leg.'

'OK.' Another camouflaging smile. 'Have a seat. She'll be free in a little while.'

He sat down, grabbed a copy of *HG*, and thumbed through it mechanically. One of the featured homes was Arch Gidde's house at Sea Cliff, almost unrecognizable amid the jungle of exotic flora imported for the photograph. He checked the date of the magazine – two months back. The realtor must have been close to death when it hit the stands.

'Hey,' said Lacey, 'did you see where Jessica Hahn is making a video?'

Michael managed a chuckle.

'Is that disgusting or what?'

'That's pretty bad.'

'They say she's had a boob job.'

'Chances are,' he said.

243

He returned to his magazine and, feeling his palms begin to sweat, studied the lucite-framed cavalry uniforms in Arch Gidde's bedroom.

Five minutes later, Joy met him at the door and led him down a sunny hall lined with August's collection of Broadway show posters.

'By the way,' she said, 'that was me who honked at you yesterday.'

He drew a blank.

'On Clement,' she explained. 'You were leaving your nursery, I think.'

'Oh, yeah.' He pretended to remember. At the moment he couldn't focus on anything. Certainly not on yesterday.

'I hate it when people honk at me and I can't see who they are. It fucks up my whole day.'

'I know what you mean,' he said.

When they reached the examining room, she said: 'What can I do for you?'

He sat on the table and rolled up his pants leg. 'Is that what I think it is?'

She studied it in silence for a moment, then straightened up. 'How long has it been there?'

'I don't know. I haven't noticed it before.'

'When did you find it?'

'Last night.'

She nodded.

'Is it?'

'It looks like it,' she said.

He made himself take a deep breath.

'I'm not a hundred percent certain.'

He nodded.

'August'll be back at noon. He should look at it. We can take a biopsy.'

'Whatever.'

'Are you feeling OK otherwise?'

'Fine.'

'I'm not completely sure,' she said.

'I understand.' He smiled faintly to show that he wouldn't hold her to it.

He loitered in the waiting room until nine, then went to the third-floor lab for his pentamidine. While he sucked away on the phallic plastic mouthpiece, the nurse who attended him carried on his usual monologue.

'. . . so George went to this big, fancy gay and lesbian banquet in Washington, only the airlines lost his luggage with all his leather in it, and . . . well, you can imagine . . . he had to get up in front of everybody in wool pants and a white button-down shirt . . .'

Michael smiled feebly under the mouthpiece.

'He was totally upstaged by this S-and-M dyke, who made her entrance in a merry widow . . . with *visible lash marks* on her back. Is that a fashion statement or what?'

Michael chuckled.

'Are you OK, guy?'

'Yeah, fine.'

'Am I talking too much? Just tell me, if I am.'

'Not at all.'

The vapor, as usual, left a bitter, tinfoilish taste in his mouth.

He left the building just before ten and walked down the hill to the park, where he wandered amid people frolicking with Frisbees and dogs. Three years of daily fretting had left him overrehearsed for this moment, but it still seemed completely unreal. He had vowed not to rail against the universe when his time came. Too many people had died, too many he had loved, for 'Why me?' to be a reasonable response. 'Why not?' was more to the point.

And there were lots worse things than KS.

245

Pneumocystis, for one, which could finish you off in a matter of days. August had assured him the pentamidine would prevent that, if he did it faithfully. And KS had been known to disappear completely with the proper treatment. Unless it spread, unless it got inside you.

He remembered Charlie Rubin when the lesions moved to his face, how he'd joked about the one on his nose that made him look like Pluto. They had covered him eventually, forming great purple continents. Charlie was blind by that time, of course, so at least he was spared the sight of them.

He sat on a bench and began to cry. It wasn't major grief at all, just another pit stop in the Grand Prix of HIV. He still felt fine, didn't he? He still had Thack and a home. And Brian and Shawna. And Harry. And Mrs Madrigal, wherever she might be.

He tilted his head and let the sun dry his tears. The air smelled of new-mown grass, while what he could see of the sky seemed ridiculously blue. The birds in the trees were as fat and chirpy as the ones in cartoons.

As soon as he returned to August's office, Lacey's face grew soft with concern. She had obviously gotten the word.

'August is back,' she said. 'He's expecting you.'

He found the doctor in the first examining room, washing his hands. 'Young man,' he said, smiling. 'Sorry we missed each other.'

August was in his late forties, not that much older than most of his patients, but he called them all 'young man.' Over the years he had watched his peaceful little dermatology practice grow into something that seemed more like a fraternity than a medical venture.

'How's that handsome husband of yours?'

'Fine,' said Michael.

246

'Good, good. Sit on the table for me.' He tore off a paper towel and dried his hands.

Michael sat.

'Where is it?'

He held out his leg and pointed.

August leaned over the place and squinted at it. 'Does it hurt?'

'Not really.'

'Yeah.' August shook his head. 'I wouldn't say so.'

'What?'

'I don't think that's a lesion.' He let go of Michael's leg and left the room, returning moments later with his nurse practitioner.

'Hi again,' said Joy.

'Hi.' Michael was sure he could feel his heart beating.

'There's a sort of ring around it,' Joy said, looking at the spot again. 'That's why it seemed to me . . .' She didn't try to finish this.

'I can see why you'd think that,' August said evenly, 'but there's only one of them.'

She nodded.

'They almost never come singly.'

'Yeah . . . I see.' She gave Michael an apologetic glance.

'It doesn't really warrant a biopsy,' the doctor told him. 'If it's not gone in a week, we can talk again, but I'll be surprised if it doesn't clear up on its own.'

Michael nodded. 'There's nothing I need to do, then?'

'You might try a little Clearasil,' said August.

Like the other false alarms he'd experienced over the years, this one sent him on his way with a noticeable spring in his step. He felt an irresistible urge to buy something. Clothes, maybe, or furniture. Or maybe he'd just go ride the circular escalator at the new

Nordstrom store and see what occurred to him. Nothing extravagant; just something useful and commemorative.

He knew this feeling well. When his T-cells soared to six hundred following his first six weeks of AZT, the orgy of consuming that ensued had not been a pretty sight. Limiting himself to the bare essentials, he had pushed his Visa card to the limit in the linen department at Macy's before going berserk with his pocket cash at the Fair Oaks Street garage sale.

He phoned Thack at home from the garage of the medical building. 'It's me, sweetie.'

'Oh, hi.'

'August says it's just a zit.'

'Well . . . great.' He could hear the relief in Thack's voice. 'Told you.'

'You working today?' Michael asked.

'No.'

'I thought I might call Brian and tell him I'm taking the day off.'

'Good idea. Do it.'

'You wanna have lunch somewhere?'

'Sure. You pick.'

'It doesn't matter. Someplace cozy and lesbian.'

His lover laughed. 'Sounds like you're on the verge of buying things?'

Michael chuckled. 'I might be.'

'Can we do it together?'

'Sure.'

'What's it gonna be?'

'I dunno,' said Michael. 'I thought maybe chairs.'

'Chairs?'

'You know . . . for the kitchen table. Like we decided.'

'Oh, yeah.'

'We could go down to the Mission, check out the junk stores.'

'OK.'

'Mrs Madrigal swears by that one at Twentieth next to the organic food . . .'

'Oh,' said Thack. 'She called.'

'Mrs Madrigal?'

'Yes.'

'What did she say?'

'Nothing. Just sent her love. It was on the machine. She was in Athens, apparently.'

'She must be on the way home.'

'Yeah,' said Thack. 'I guess so.'

D'orothea's Grille was a little short on celebrities that day, so their people-watching centered around the bubble-butted boy who brought them their Chinese chicken salads. DeDe emerged from the kitchen when they were almost done, kissing Michael's cheek, then Thack's. 'Hi, boys. Like the new decor?'

'Not bad,' Michael told her.

'Not finished either. We've still gotta knock out that back wall, open the whole thing up. God, it makes me tired just thinking about it. How were the salads?'

'Great,' said Thack.

'You should've come earlier. Chloe Rand was here.'

Thack grunted.

'You know her?'

'No,' said Thack. 'But her husband tried to fuck my husband last night.'

DeDe turned to Michael and let her jaw drop comically. 'No!'

Michael chuckled.

'Did you do it?' asked DeDe.

He smiled cryptically.

DeDe glanced at Thack. 'I think he did, don't you?'

Thack laughed.

'Where was this?' asked DeDe.

'Out at Arch Gidde's.'

She nodded. 'We were invited to some brunch thing

at Prue Giroux's, but D'or didn't think she could stomach it. She used to model for him, you know, back when he was still gay.'

This got a hoot out of Thack.

An hour later they scored big in a junk store on Valencia Street: two matching wooden dinette chairs, covered in cruddy white vinyl but displaying an unmistakably Deco silhouette. They paid an old man ten bucks for the pair and tied them on to the VW, fussing like nuns with a fresh busload of orphans.

Back at the house, they set to work with hammers and crowbars, ripping away two, three, four layers of plastic and stuffing, until the original chairs were revealed. Their peaked backs and oval handholds conveyed a sort of Seven Dwarfsish feeling, which Michael thought suited the house perfectly.

At dusk, as the fog rolled in, they lay on the deck completely spent, staring at their treasures.

'What should we paint them?' asked Michael. 'A Fiesta color, maybe?'

'How about turquoise?'

'Perfect. God, look how many tacks there were!'

'Yeah.'

'They must feel better,' said Michael.

'Who must?'

'The chairs. To have all those tacks out.'

'Right.'

'Well, think about it. It was like a crucifixion or something.'

Thack gave him a sleepy smile. 'You're such a weird guy,' he said.

Michael reached over and took hold of Thack's cock. It felt fat and warm through the padding of his sweat pants. Holding on, he slid closer and kissed Thack softly on the lips.

'Feeling better?' asked Thack.

'Much.'

'I want you to stick around, OK?'

'OK,' said Michael.

They heard the hiss of a pop-top in the kitchen and realized without looking that Brian had come home.

Inheritance

On her way back to New York the morning after, Chloe
had left a chirpy see-you-soon on Mary Ann's machine,
so whatever nastiness had transpired between Michael
and Russell must not have made its way back to his wife.
Thank God for that, anyway. Four days after the
debacle in Sea Cliff, Mary Ann still hadn't heard from
Michael, and knowing him, he wasn't likely to relent
anytime soon. His tantrums had a way of lasting.

Ditto Brian. Yesterday she'd left a message on
Michael's machine, telling her husband that she'd be
gone by the end of the week, that Shawna should not be
deprived of her father any longer than necessary. He
hadn't called back. She'd begun to wonder if he was
deliberately trying to screw up her departure, knowing
she couldn't leave in good conscience without turning
over Shawna to his care.

Shawna, thankfully, had taken all this grownup child-
ishness in stride. (If anything, she seemed more distressed by her father's current absence than by Mary
Ann's impending one.) The same could not be said for
Mary Ann's bosses at the station. Their ill-disguised
resentment over her new position had been gratifying
only to the degree that it confirmed – or betrayed,
rather, since they'd always kept it a secret – her real
value to the station.

As she'd sat there outlining her new duties and

252

watching a vein throb in Larry Kenan's temple, it was all she could do not to pull a Sally Field and blurt out the revelation that had finally come to her after all these years:

You like me . . . you really like me.

She had endured *Mary Ann in the Morning* for one last program—'The Truth About Breast Implants'. Now she was home in her walk-in closet, dragging out a trunk, which had been there unopened for ages. It was crammed with things from Connie's apartment in the Marina. Connie's little brother, Wally, had brought it by Barbary Lane only days after he'd shown up with the newborn Shawna. 'She might want this someday,' he'd told them somberly, bestowing a sort of heirloom status on stuff he'd simply been too softhearted to throw out.

When Mary Ann pushed back the lid, Shawna all but dove into the musty interior.

'Hey, Puppy. Take it easy.'

'What's this?'

It was a filthy terry-cloth python with plastic eyes that rolled. She remembered it all too well. Connie had kept it on her bed, next to her giant Snoopy. 'It's a snake, see?' She made the eyes role for Shawna.

'Was that hers?'

'Sure. All of this stuff was.'

'Gah!' Obviously impressed, the kid lunged into the trunk again and pulled out a little cardboard crate that Mary Ann recognized immediately.

'What's this?'

'Open it.'

Shawna did so and frowned. 'It's just a dumb rock.'

'No, it's a Pet Rock.'

'What's that?'

'Well . . . people used to have these.'

'What does it do?'

'It's kind of hard to explain, Puppy. Look at this, though.' She removed a satin pillow, maroon faded to rose, and read the inscription: 'School Spirit Day, Central High, 1967.'

'What is it?'

'Well, that's where your . . . birth mommy and I went to high school in Cleveland. She was head majorette. You know what that is?'

Shawna shook her head.

'She marched in front of the band. With a baton and this really neat uniform. It was a big deal. Everybody saw her. You know, I think maybe . . .' She foraged through the trunk, hoping that Wally had rescued Connie's *Buccaneer*.

Sure enough, there it was, tucked behind an atrocious painting of a bullfighter on black velvet. The raised medallion on the front cover had been rendered medieval by mildew. 'I'll show you a picture,' she said.

It was a full-page photo at the front of the sports section: Connie strutting her stuff, buttons gleaming, teeth and tits to the wind. At the time, Mary Ann had written it off as slutty looking, but she had probably just been envious. It seemed almost virginal now.

Sitting Indian style on the floor, Shawna took the yearbook on her lap and studied the page. 'She was pretty,' she said at last.

'She was,' said Mary Ann. 'Very. I think she looks a lot like you. Don't you?'

Shawna shrugged. 'Did you move out here with her?'

'No. She was here a long time before I was. But I stayed with her when I came out here from Cleveland.'

'How long?'

'Oh . . . a week.' It had been a long week too, what with Connie dragging home guys from Thomas Lord's and Dance Your Ass Off. She had moved out with a sense of profound relief, putting all that tackiness behind her. Or so she thought at the time. Who would have dreamed she would end up as the custodian of Connie's memory?

'Didn't you like her?' asked Shawna.

This caught her off guard. 'Of course, Puppy. Sure I liked her. Why would you say a thing like that?'

The child shrugged. 'You left her.'

'I didn't leave her.'

'But you said . . .'

'I found a place at Anna's house. I wanted my own apartment. I was only at your birth mommy's place for the time being. She knew that.'

Shawna seemed to weigh this, her blue eyes narrowing. She looked down at the yearbook again. 'Are you in this?' she asked.

Mary Ann found her ridiculous class picture with the ironed hair and showed it to the child, wincing privately at the meager credits and the condescending epigram: 'Still Waters Run Deep.'

'Is that all?'

'That's it.' What could she say? She'd been a nerd.

Shawna closed the book and laid it aside. 'Can I play with this stuff?'

'Sure. It's yours, Puppy. That's why . . . your mommy left it for you.' She had almost said 'birth mommy' again, but it sounded a little stingy somehow.

For a moment, remembering, she felt a rush of unfettered affection for Connie, something she'd never been able to manage while her old classmate was still alive. She flashed on Connie looking radiant in her BABY T-shirt – the one with the arrow pointing to her bulbous belly – and it struck her again how much single parenthood would have suited Connie.

When Shawna had repaired to her room with Connie's python, Mary Ann dragged out her suitcases and made a few decisions about the stuff she would take to New York. Burke had reserved her a suite at the Plaza, and Lillie Rubin was furnishing her wardrobe, so

255

she resolved to pack light and ship the rest of her things later. Anyway, Chloe had promised to take her shopping as soon as she arrived.

It would be cold, of course, so she went mostly for the tweed and cashmere. She made choices that were businesslike and neutral, so they would see she was an empty canvas, not the finished product. She would work on her look later, after she'd been able to analyze the setting they had planned for it.

Shawna seemed to sense that this was a good time to ask for the moon. It was by her decree that they drove to Mel's Drive-In for chocolate shakes that night, following a roller coaster of a route, which included the steepest slope of Leavenworth.

'Look!' said Shawna, pointing, as they passed the Barbary Steps. 'There's Daddy and Michael.'

'Sit down, Puppy.'

'Look, there . . . see?'

'I see.' They were trudging up the steps, their backs to the street. She saw Thack's pale, feathery head under the streetlight at the top. She decided that Mrs Madrigal must be back from Greece.

She felt a brief pang of paranoia, knowing they would talk about her tonight – distorting the facts, no doubt – making her seem like an unfeeling monster. It wasn't a bit fair.

Shawna made a lunge for the wheel. 'Honk,' she ordered.

She held the kid back with an arm. 'Sit down, Puppy. That's very dangerous.'

'Honk the horn.'

'No. This isn't the time. Put your seat belt on.'

The child threw herself back against the seat and pushed out her lower lip.

'We'll call them when we get back.'

Silence.

256

'OK.?'

'When is he coming home?'

'Soon.'

Shawna turned and looked out the window. 'I want extra malt,' she said.

Not That

'She sounded funny,' said Michael, as they picked their
way along the ballast stones at the head of the lane.
'Didn't you notice it?'

'Not particularly,' said Thack.

'Well, she did to me.'

'It's probably jet lag,' said Brian. 'Unless you mean
funny about . . . ?'

'No,' said Michael, knowing he meant Mary Ann. 'Not
that. Something else.'

As they passed through the lych-gate at Number 28, a
cat leapt from the mossy roof, clambering for safety up
an ivywrapped tree. The windows of the old shingled
house seemed to glow with gratitude for their mistress's
return.

There was music – a pleasant sort of new age ragtime
– coming from Michael's old apartment on the second
floor. He had never met his successors and really didn't
want to now. Tonight he hoped it would just be family.
He didn't want to share Mrs Madrigal with people he
didn't know.

When the landlady opened the door, the first thing
that struck him was her tan. Her Wedgwood eyes went
wide and actressy as she hugged them one at a time, in
order of their appearance: Michael, Thack, Brian.

'You all look gorgeous!' she said, leading them into her
parlor. 'Sit down. There are joints on the table there.
Some sherry if you like. I have a few adjustments to

make in the kitchen. I'll be back in two shakes of a lamb's tail.'

Brian and Thack took the sofa. Michael remained standing, unconvinced and a little unsettled by this flurry of ferocious hostessing. 'Can I give you a hand?' he asked.

The landlady seemed to hesitate. 'If you like.'

In the kitchen, after slipping several cottage pies into the oven, she gave him another hug and said: 'That was from Mona. She made me promise.'

'How is she?'

'Lovely. A very charming, grown-up person.'

'*Mona?*'

The landlady smiled and closed the oven door. 'I tried to get her to visit us, but, as usual, she's completely wrapped up in that house of hers.'

'Can't imagine where she gets that.'

Her smile turned a little wan. 'I've missed you, dear.'

'I'm sorry I didn't call before you left.'

'Don't be silly.'

'No,' he said. 'I promised.'

'Well, you had so much on your mind. Oh . . . here, before I forget.' She dashed off to the bedroom and returned with a small cardboard box. 'Lady Roughton said to tell you this is the last trace of Sappho on the island.'

It was a key ring with a green enamel medallion bearing the poet's likeness. He smiled and enjoyed the smooth feel of it beneath his thumb. 'Did she fall in love?'

'She wouldn't tell me,' said Mrs Madrigal.

'I'll bet.'

'I don't blame her, really.'

'How about you?'

'What do you mean?'

He shrugged.

She batted her eyes at him in a way that suggested he

was being impertinent. 'I had lovely walks in the hills.'

He chuckled. 'Good.'

She turned away and began rinsing spinach leaves under the tap. 'I've some pictures to show you later.'

'Great.'

After a silence, she asked: 'Is she leaving for good?'

'Looks like it.'

She gave a little murmur and continued rinsing.

'It's a big break, really.'

'Is he all right?'

'No,' he answered. 'Not particularly.'

'When does she leave?'

'Day after tomorrow, I think.'

The landlady dried her hands on an Acropolis dish towel. She had about her such an air of quiet competence that he imagined for a moment she would set to work fixing things. Like a doctor who'd been given all the symptoms and was ready to prescribe the cure.

Instead, she opened her ancient refrigerator and removed a tray of stuffed grape leaves. 'Take these in for me, would you, dear?'

Snaps

'... And in petra, which is the next village over, there is something they call a tourist collective, which is made up solely of women. They sell crafts and rent out their homes and such. And it's the first time the women of that village have ever made a penny – or a drachma or what have you – independent of their husbands. They just sit there with their little trays of lace, with these enormous grins on their faces ...'

After several joints and a long dinner, Brian's mind had begun to wander, but this part of the landlady's travelogue, drifting toward him out of nowhere, seemed somehow pertinent to his pain. He wondered if she'd intended it to be.

'I thought you had snapshots,' said Michael.

'Now, dear ... are you sure you want ... ?'

'Absolutely,' said Thack, flicking his worry beads vigorously. The landlady had given them each a string, marking their places at the table with them. Blue ceramic for Brian, orange for Thack, olive wood for Michael. Somewhere, undoubtedly, there was a string for Mary Ann.

Mrs Madrigal left the room, apparently in search of her snapshots.

Across the table Michael smiled drowsily. 'She looks good, doesn't she?'

Brian nodded.

'Something agreed with her,' said Thack.

Mrs Madrigal returned with the photographs, fanning them out like playing cards on her velvet-draped sideboard. 'I'll let everyone look for himself. You can do without my narration for a while.'

Brian joined the others at the sideboard.

'I didn't know you owned a camera,' said Michael.

'I don't, actually,' said the landlady. 'Someone else took these.'

The shots were largely what Brian had expected, except maybe for the absence of whitewash. Parched hills above vibrant blue water. Random donkeys. Brightly painted fishing boats. Anna and Mona squinting into the sun, the family resemblance more evident than ever as they held up middle age from either end.

'The villa looks wonderful,' said Thack. 'This is it, isn't it? With the terrace?'

'That's it.'

'This is Mona.' Michael showed one of the snaps to Thack.

'Yeah. I recognized her.'

'How?' Michael asked.

'That shot she sent us last Christmas.'

'Oh, yeah.'

Brian was drifting again, dwelling morosely on the consolation of 'us' and how it was about to vanish from his own vocabulary. Mrs Madrigal locked eyes with him and smiled with excruciating kindness.

Michael held up another snap. 'Is this the one who took the pictures?'

'Which?' said the landlady.

'This guy who looks like Cesar Romero.'

Brian was sure he saw the color rise in the landlady's cheeks.

'Yes,' she replied demurely. 'That's Stratos. He showed us around.'

Michael nodded, giving her a sly look.

262

'Who needs sherry?' asked Mrs Madrigal, holding out the bottle and looking everywhere but at Michael.

'Here,' called Thack, reaching toward her with his glass. He had noticed Michael's teasing, apparently, and was helping her change the subject. 'This stuff is great, by the way. So nutty.'

'Isn't it?'

'Mmm.'

'It was new down at Molinari's ...'

'I'll take some,' Brian put in.

'Lovely.' As she poured she looked directly at him and spoke in a low, even voice. 'Let's take ours to the court-yard, shall we?'

Somehow, he felt as if he'd just been summoned to the principal's office.

'You boys will excuse us, won't you?'

Michael and Thack answered 'Sure' in unison.

The bench where they sat was usually referred to as 'Jon's bench,' since his ashes had been buried in the flower bed just beyond it. The soil there was bare now, but by the end of winter, the air would be narcotic with the scent of hyacinths.

'Michael told me,' the landlady began.

'I know.' He smiled at her a little. 'He told me he told you.'

'Are you all right?'

He shrugged.

She paused awhile, then said: 'I won't tell you it'll get better ...'

He finished it for her. '... because you know I know that.'

She chuckled ruefully. 'Oh, dear. Am I that easy to read?'

'No. Not really.'

'I hate old ladies who have homilies for everything.'

'Don't worry,' he said. 'You're not like that.'

263

'I hope and pray not.'

He smiled at her wearily.

'Have you spoken to her?' she asked.

'Not lately.'

She took this in silently.

'You think I should, huh?'

Mrs Madrigal arranged her long fingers in her lap. 'I think there are some scenes . . . we're simply required to play. If we don't, we rob ourselves of ever feeling anything at all.'

'Oh, I feel something.'

'I know.'

He snatched a little pine cone from the ground and flung it into the shrubs. 'She's leaving day after tomorrow. I was planning to be back then.'

'What about Shawna?'

'I'm still taking her to school every day.'

'I meant afterwards.'

'Oh. I'll manage. That's no problem.'

'If you need help during the day, you know how glad I'd be to keep an eye on her.'

'Thanks.'

The landlady cast her eyes around the courtyard. 'She loves it down here, you know.'

He nodded. 'Yes.'

'She's a smart little girl.' Mrs Madrigal looked at him. 'She'll know how to deal with this.'

Another nod. 'She's already doing better than I am.' His embarrassment finally got the best of him. 'I'm sorry we stopped bringing her by.'

'Don't be silly.'

'No . . . I mean it.'

She reached over and took his hand.

They sat there in silence, staring into the shadows. Finally he said: 'You think I oughta do it, huh?'

'What's that?'

'Go up there and say goodbye like a man.'

She nodded.

'Bummer.'

'I know.' She sighed a little. 'I just had to do it myself.'

He was thrown. 'With Mary Ann?'

'No. In Lesbos.'

He thought about it for a moment. 'The man in the picture?'

She nodded.

'So you had a little . . . ?'

'Yes.'

'And you miss him.'

'Like a sonofabitch,' she said.

Stay, Then

No show tomorrow meant no homework, she realized. With Shawna in bed and her bags packed, she felt oddly like a sixth grader on Saturday morning. Determined to enjoy it, she had taken a long bath, then curled up in her bathrobe on the sofa with the Linda Ellerbee book. She'd been trying to finish the damned thing for almost a year.

When a key rattled in the front door, she knew that Brian was home.

'Hi,' he said.

'Hi.' She laid the book on her stomach and yawned so unexpectedly that 'Excuse me' followed as a reflex. It must have sounded idiotic to him.

He walked past her and down the hall to the bathroom. She heard him taking a leak, then splashing water on his face. She sat up on the sofa but didn't rise. If he wanted to talk to her, he'd be back.

He was, and he took the chair across from her. 'I was down at Mrs Madrigal's.'

'She's back, then.'

'Yeah.'

'Did she feed you? There's some turkey salad if . . .'

'No, thanks. I'm full.'

She nodded.

'I'm not staying.'

After a pause she said: 'I wish you would.'

He shook his head.

'I hate that it's happening like this.'

He shrugged.

She gave him the gentlest look she could manage. 'Please don't be mad.'

'I'm not mad.'

'Stay, then.'

'It's not a good idea, OK?'

He was obviously hurting, so she didn't pursue it. 'I picked up the laundry,' she said instead.

'Thanks.'

'I thought you might be low on shirts.'

He nodded. 'Is Shawna OK?'

'Fine. Did she tell you she got a part in the Presidio Hill Christmas play?'

'Uh-huh.'

'I have a feeling it's not the lead, *but* . . .' She widened her eyes as winningly as possible.

'It's an atom.'

'Adam?' She frowned. 'A girl plays Adam?'

'No. *An* atom. Like . . . a nuclear particle.'

That school, she thought. 'Doesn't sound very Christmasy.'

'It's about . . . you know, saving the planet.' He smiled at her, sort of.

'When can I tell her you'll be back?'

'Friday.'

After she was gone, in other words.

'She knows that already,' he added.

'Oh . . . OK.'

'She won't be alone, will she?'

'No,' she answered. 'Nguyet'll be here. I've explained everything to Shawna. She's OK about it.'

He nodded.

'The logistics have all been worked out.'

'I'm sure,' he said. 'What time are you leaving?'

'There's a limousine coming at six.'

'P.m.?'

'A.m.'

He winced, apparently empathizing. 'You have to get up early for this job too.'

She smiled. 'I guess I'm in the habit.'

Their eyes met for a moment, then sought safer places to rest.

'I'm really sorry,' she said.

He held up his palm. 'Hey.'

'I think you're such a great guy . . .'

'Mary Ann.'

'I don't know what to say. I feel so awful.'

'Fuck it,' he said quietly. 'I'm over it.'

He didn't look a bit over it.

'Michael's the one you should talk to,' he added.

'What do you mean?'

'Well . . . this is kind of it for you guys.'

'What?'

'I mean, if he got sick . . . You've thought about this, haven't you?'

'What is this? What are you saying? I shouldn't be going, because he might get sick and I should be here to . . . ?'

'Did I say that? I didn't say that.'

'Well, good, because Mouse would never . . .'

'I know that.'

'Let me finish. He would never, ever, accuse me of . . .' She felt close to tears, so she collected herself. 'He knows what I'm doing and why I'm doing it, and he wishes me well. I'm glad he's going to miss me, if that's what he told you, because I'm going to miss him too. But that's what happens, Brian. Life just sort of does this sometimes.'

He looked at her blankly and said: 'Your life.'

'Yes. OK. My life. Whatever. Just don't accuse me of running away from . . . his illness.'

'I didn't.'

'I would be back in a second if . . .'

'You can't. How could you?'

She hated thinking about this. He knew it too. Michael was his last card, and he was determined to play it. 'This is the lowest, Brian. If Michael knew you were using him to . . .'

'Talk to him. That's all I'm saying.'

'No it isn't. You're laying this big guilt trip on me.'

'I can't help how you take it.'

'You don't know what goes on between me and Mouse. You don't know how much we understand each other.'

He gave her a dim, mournful smile. 'No,' he said, 'I guess not.'

She could see the effect this had and tried to undo it. 'I didn't mean it that way.'

'Just call him, OK?'

'Sure.'

He rose.

'Don't go yet,' she said.

He smiled faintly. 'I'm getting my shirts.'

She stood by the window and stared out at the bay. He was back in less than a minute, his laundry flung over his shoulder like a cavalier's cape.

'You could sleep on the couch,' she said, 'if the bed bothers you.'

He leaned over and pecked her on the top of her head. 'That's OK.'

At the door, for some stupid reason, she touched his arm and said, 'Drive carefully.'

Another Letter to Mama

Dear Mama,

When you were talking about Papa's headstone the other day I noticed you mentioned there was room at the plot for the entire family.

No. Awkward. Start again.

Dear Mama,

It was wonderful talking to you the other day. Thack says you and I should talk more, and I guess he's right, since it always makes me feel better.

Stop lying and get to the point.

Dear Mama,

I'm glad we talked the other day. There was something you mentioned, though, that concerned me. You seemed to think that someday the whole family would be buried at the cemetery there. I know how you meant this, but frankly, the idea of Christian burial strikes me as unnecessary and a little ghoulish.

Real subtle, Tolliver.
Keep writing. You can change it later.

I don't know how much time I have left – whether it's two years or five or fifty – but I don't want to be taken

270

back to Orlando when it's over. This is my home now, and I've asked Thack to make arrangements for my cremation here in San Francisco.

This wouldn't be so important to me if I didn't believe in families just as much as you do. I have one of my own, and it means the world to me. If there are goodbyes to be said, I want them to be here, and I want Thack to be in charge. I hope you can understand.

If you still want to do a memorial service in Orlando (assuming you can't come here), Thack can send you part of the ashes. I think you know I'd prefer not to have a preacher involved, but do whatever makes you comfortable. Just make sure he doesn't pray for my soul or ask the Lord's forgiveness or anything like that.

Please don't get the wrong idea. I'm fine right now. I just wanted this out of the way, so we don't have to think about it again. I'm not too worried about how you'll take it, since I know how much you like Thack. He sends his love, by the way, and promises to send pix of the new chairs as soon as we get them painted.

I'll try to call more often.

All my love,
MICHAEL

PS My friend Mary Ann Singleton (you met her once years ago) has a new syndicated morning talk show. It starts in March, so watch for it. She's a good friend of mine, and we're all really happy for her.

Relief

With winter came precipitation, but not nearly enough. The puny mists and drizzles drifting in from the ocean barely dented the parched reservoirs of the East Bay. Michael watched the nightly forecasts with a sense of mounting dread for the nursery. By the end of February the weatherman was leading off the news again, speaking darkly of the stringent water rationing to come.

Then, on the day after Saint Patrick's Day, huge flannel-gray clouds appeared over the city like dirigibles, hovering there forever, it seemed, before dumping their cargo on a grateful population. The rain came with sweet vengeance, making things clean again, sluicing down the hills to whisk away the dog shit like logs in a flume.

It kept up like this all week, until Harry's running meadow in Dolores Park had become a bog, impenetrable to man or beast. When the skies cleared temporarily on Saturday morning, Michael stuck to the concrete route along Cumberland as he gave Harry his first real exercise in twenty-four hours. The blue rip in the clouds was about to be mended again, so they would have to make it quick – a fact that even Harry seemed to grasp.

At the top of the Cumberland stairs, while the dog squatted ingloriously in the wet weeds, Michael sat on the rail and looked out over the rain-varnished valley. There were lakes beginning to form on the flat roofs of the non-Victorians.

A tall, thin man with a little blue backpack came toward him up the stairs, taking his time. When he reached the landing, Michael recognized him as the guy from the Rawhide II. Eula's son. With the six T-cells. 'How's it going?' he asked, recognizing Michael.

'Pretty good. Isn't this air great?'

The man stopped next to him and filled his lungs. 'Beats pentamidine.'

'Doesn't it?' Michael smiled. 'How's your mother?'

'Fabulous. They asked her to judge the Bare Chest Contest.'

He chuckled. 'She must be in hog heaven.'

'She is.'

'You live around here?'

The man shook his head. 'I was just down at the Buyer's Club.'

'The one on Church?'

'Yeah.'

'What did you get?'

'Dextran. Some freeze-dried herbs.'

Michael nodded. 'I did Dextran for a while.'

'No good?'

'Well, I heard your body can't absorb enough to make any difference.'

'I heard that too.' The man shrugged. 'Can't hurt. The Japanese take it like aspirin.'

'Yeah.'

'Have you heard about this new thing? Compound Q?'

Michael hadn't.

'It's been killing the virus in lab tests. Without damaging the other cells.'

'Oh, yeah?'

'They haven't tried it on people yet, but there's a lot of . . . you know.'

'Cautious optimism.'

'Right.'

Michael nodded. 'Wouldn't that be something?'

'Yeah.'

'What is it? A chemical?'

'That's the amazing part. It comes from the root of some Chinese cucumber.'

'No shit.'

'It's a natural thing. It's right here on earth.' The man gazed out over the valley for a while, then looked back at Michael. 'I try not to get too hopeful.'

'Why the hell not?'

'I guess you're right,' said the man.

They swapped names again. His was Larry DeTreaux, and he was on the way to Metro Video. 'My lover told me to get *Mother Teresa* and *Humongous II*. Does that tell you about my life or what?'

Michael smiled. 'Which do you watch first?'

'Good question.'

'*Humongous II* is pretty good.'

Larry nodded. 'We just keep the sound off and use it as background.'

'Yeah. Same here.'

'The voices are the worst.'

Harry pawed impatiently at Michael's leg.

Larry smiled. 'This is yours, huh?'

'Yeah. It's hard finding time to walk him in this rain. Mellow out, Harry.'

'Poodles don't know the meaning of the word.'

Michael clipped on the leash, peering up at him. 'You're not a poodlephobe, are you?'

'No. But I know these dogs. Eula's had a few in her time.'

I'll bet she has, thought Michael. 'I'll walk with you,' he said. 'My house is just over there.'

Thack was in the garden when they arrived. He was bent over his trellis, examining the new growth. He did this at hourly intervals, it seemed.

'You remember Larry from the Rawhide II.'

'Oh, yeah.' Thack smiled and shook hands with him. 'Thack Sweeney.'

'New trellis?' asked Larry.

'Fairly.'

'Interesting shape.'

'We're growing clematis on it,' said Michael, 'so it'll be a pink triangle this summer.' He was certain more than ever that it wouldn't read, but he was trying to be supportive.

'What a great idea! Who thought of that?'

Thack puffed visibly. 'Me.'

Larry glanced up at the clouds, which had turned threatening again. 'Better haul ass.'

'Need an umbrella?' Michael asked.

'Got one here.' He patted his backpack. 'You guys take care.'

'You too,' said Thack.

Michael added: 'Say hi to Eula for us.'

'Sure thing.'

'Eula,' said Thack, as soon as Larry was out of earshot. '*That* was her name.'

Michael let Harry into the house and closed the door. 'How could you forget?'

'We should fix her up with your mom when she visits.'

'Don't you dare.'

'She could take her to all the piano bars . . .'

'Look, if you know what's good for you . . .'

His lover laughed. 'You're just afraid it'll agree with her.'

'Damn right.'

'She'll move here and we'll have to drag her out of the Galleon every Sunday afternoon.'

Michael opened the mailbox. 'Hasn't the mail come yet?'

'I took it inside.'

'Anything good?'

'A postcard from Mona.'

'Oh, yeah?'

'She wants us to visit this summer.'

'Really? At Easley House?'

'Yep.'

Michael caught his breath at the thought of it.

'Should we do it?'

'Sure! You won't believe this place, Thack!'

'What about you know who?'

He felt a sudden pang of guilt, vaguely parental. 'Oh, yeah.'

'Dogs have to be quarantined for six months before they'll let them in.'

'Forget it,' said Michael.

'Elizabeth Taylor used to keep hers on a barge in the middle of the Thames. That way it was only subject to maritime law.'

Michael rolled his eyes. 'Now there's a travel tip I'll be sure to remember.'

'What about Polly?'

'What about her?'

'Hasn't she offered to house-sit?'

'You're right,' said Michael. 'And Harry loves her.'

'You don't think she'd mind?'

'Are you kidding? She can drag babes home from Francine's.'

'Good point,' said Thack, grinning.

The rain drove them indoors. They made tea and watched the downpour from the kitchen table. Michael thought of his rainy spring at Easley House, over five years before. It was there, at the folly on the hill above the house, that he had finally told Mona about Jon's death. Now, more than anything, he wanted her to meet the man who had made him happy.

He picked up her postcard and studied it again. It was a garden view of the great house. A ballpoint-penned arrow on one of the gables was labeled: 'Your Room, Gentlemen.'

'We should really do this.'

'Then we will,' said Thack.

'I know you'll love her. She doesn't take shit from any-body.'

Thack smiled and poured more tea for him.

That Much in Love

'Now roll it up really tight...like so...then take one of those rubber bands and put it on the end there . . . that's right, lovely...'

It was a sunny May Sunday in Mrs Madrigal's court-yard. Stretched out on the bricks in his Speedos, Brian listened while the landlady taught Shawna how to tie-dye. To his amazement, his daughter had actually requested this; tie-dyed stuff was cool again, she said. It made him tired just thinking about it.

'OK, now put some more rubber bands on.'

'Where?'

'Anywhere.'

'Point, OK?'

'No, dear. I mean put them anywhere you like. That's what makes them beautiful. The designs are all different.'

'But I want one like you just did.'

'Well, what good would that be? Then it wouldn't be yours, would it?'

Silence.

'Go on, now. You'll see.'

Sitting up, Brian shielded his eyes from the sun as he watched the child coax the rubber bands on to the rolled T-shirt. 'How's it going?' he asked the landlady.

'Beautifully.'

Shawna rolled her eyes like the great Drew Barrymore. 'I haven't done anything yet.'

'Well, go to it, then.'

His daughter donned rubber gloves that were much too big for her, then dunked the trussed T-shirt into Mrs Madrigal's big porcelain tub.

'These are for Michael and Thack,' Shawna volunteered.

'That's a good idea.'

'They can wear them to the May Festival.'

'Hey . . . there you go.'

'Are they both mediums?'

'Think so, yeah.'

Shawna turned to Anna. 'Told you.'

'Yes, you did,' said the landlady, turning back to Brian. 'How is Michael, by the way?'

'Fine.'

'He had strep throat the last time I talked to him.'

'It's gone now.'

'I'm making the green one for Thack and the blue one for Michael.' Shawna raised her voice to get back their attention.

'Yeah,' said Brian. 'I think green looks better on Thack.'

'Can we take them by there tonight?'

'If you want to, sure.'

'Michael says he'll show me the parrot tree.'

'Don't count on it,' Brian warned her. 'You can't be sure of them.'

'I know.'

'Anyway, it's more special when it's a surprise. When they just swoop down out of nowhere.'

The child turned back to Mrs Madrigal. 'If we add more salt it makes it brighter?'

'Yes, indeed.'

'Let's add some more, then.'

'All right, dear. Now watch very closely . . .'

Shawna gazed at her mentor with a look of such adoration that Brian felt a brief stab of jealousy.

*

Later, while his daughter was inside napping, Mrs Madrigal sat on the bench and talked to him as he sunned. 'How is her new place?' she asked.

'Didn't you see *People* this week?'

'What people?'

'The magazine.'

'Oh. No.'

'She's in it. There's a picture of the apartment.'

'Ah.'

'It looks good. Old-fashioned, with high windows.'

'That does sound nice.'

'Not much furniture, of course . . .'

'No.'

'They call her the new Mary Hart.'

'The who?'

'Just this woman on *Entertainment Tonight*.'

'Oh.'

'I'll bring you the article.'

'Don't go to any trouble, dear.'

He smiled a little.

'You've lost weight,' she remarked. 'Your tummy looks so flat.'

'I've been working out again.'

'Where?'

'At home. I made her old closet into a weight room.'

She chuckled. 'There's a clever boy.'

'I thought so,' he said.

His goal was to be back in shape by the end of summer.

When Brian arrived at the nursery the next morning, Michael was in the office, watching television in the tie-dyed T-shirt.

'Hey,' said Brian. 'Looks good.'

'Doesn't it?' Michael swiveled his chest for an instant, then turned his gaze back to the set. 'Guess who she's got on.'

Brian looked up and saw a very tanned Russell Rand,

280

arranged with studied elegance on the near end of Mary Ann's couch. He had just said something funny, apparently, because Mary Ann was laughing merrily.

'But it was such a natural idea,' she said, composing herself. 'Designer wedding rings. You wonder why no-one thought of it before.'

The designer's expression was appropriately modest.

'And you and Chloe, of course, are your own best ad.'

Rand ducked his head. 'Well . . .'

'I mean it. It's just so damned nice to see two people that much in love.' There was scattered applause from the studio audience, so she egged them on a little. 'Isn't it? Isn't it nice for a change?'

'Gag me,' said Michael.

Brian smiled. 'You think she's got Chloe behind the curtains?'

'Probably. So Russell can kiss her on camera.'

'And let me tell you . . .' Mary Ann was on a roll now, developing her theme. 'Those of us who haven't had such good luck in matters of the heart . . .'

'Fuck me,' Brian said.

'. . . can't help but feel a little envious.'

'Fuck me fuck me fuck me.'

Michael gave him a rueful look.

'She can't do one goddamn show without talking about it. Not one. She's a professional divorcée.'

'Yeah . . . seems like it.'

Brian swatted off the set. It felt curiously satisfying. 'You'd think she'd at least wait until the divorce was final.'

His partner gave him a half-lidded smile. 'I think she wanted to start with a new persona.'

Brian grunted. 'Have you talked to her lately?'

'Not lately, really. Last week.'

'That's lately.' He glanced guiltily toward the blank screen. 'I'm sorry, man. If you wanna . . .'

281

'No. Who cares? I just thought she might do a Lucy tribute.'

'Well, here . . .' He reached toward the set. 'Let's turn it back on.'

'No. Really. I'm Lucyed out.'

How could he not be? thought Brian. Only yesterday his partner had passed an impromptu memorial at Eighteenth and Castro and been so moved by the sight that he'd bought a small box of chocolates ('for my favorite episode') and laid it ceremonially among the flowers.

'Are you sure?' asked Brian.

'Yeah. All they ever show is the grape-stomping scene.'

He leaned against the counter. 'So what did she say?'

'Who?'

'Mary Ann.'

'Not much. Just stuff about the show.'

'Nothing about me?'

Michael looked annoyed.

'Sorry . . . I promised I wouldn't do that.'

'That's right. You did.'

'OK.' Brian nodded. 'Point taken.'

'Life goes on, sport.'

'I know.'

'You wanna do a movie tonight?'

'Sure.'

'Thack wants to see *Scandal*.'

'What's that?'

'You know. The Christine Keeler thing.'

He shrugged. 'Sure. Whatever.'

'Can you find a sitter?'

'Yeah. I think Mrs M. is probably . . .'

'Well, well, well.' Michael was suddenly distracted by something out the window. 'Look at that, would you?'

He looked.

'Jessica Rabbit is back.'

Sure enough, she was. This time in a pink cotton

blouse and khaki short shorts. Brian moved to the window and watched as she strode down a sun-dappled aisle, her rust-colored hair swinging like draped satin. He could practically smell her.

Then, out of nowhere, Polly bounded on to the scene, taking a shortcut through the Burmese honeysuckle to head off her quarry at the pass. He couldn't hear what was said, but both women smiled a lot, and Polly reached out at one point to touch Jessica's arm.

'I knew it,' he said with quiet resignation.

Michael regarded him with sympathetic spaniel eyes.

'I had her spotted the minute she laid eyes on Polly.'

'Oh, well.'

Brian turned his gaze from the women and tried to be a good sport about it. 'What the hell. More power to 'em.'

'I dunno,' said his partner, still watching.

'C'mon. That's a pickup if I've ever seen one.'

'Then what's she doing now?'

Jessica, in fact, was walking away from Polly, a purposeful glint in her slanting cat's eyes. When she reached the end of the aisle, her creamy legs pivoted and scissored smartly up the path to the office.

'I'm outa here,' said Michael.

'Where are you going?'

'Just in back. I've got some reorganizing to do.'

'Michael . . .'

But his partner had already ducked into the storeroom and closed the door. By the time Brian had turned around again, Jessica Rabbit was at the door of the office. 'Hi,' she breathed, gliding in.

'Hi.'

She came to the counter and gave him a languid smile. 'Remember me?'

'Sure.'

'The bushes are doing great,' she said.

'Well . . . good. Glad to hear it.'

283

She studied him for the longest time, looking wryly amused.

'Is something the matter?' he asked.

'Oh, no.' She wet her lips. 'Not a thing in the world.'

He did his damnedest not to squirm.

'Your friend out there'—she jerked her head toward the window, but didn't take her eyes off him—'says you're a free man again.'

He gazed uneasily out the window. Polly stood by the door of the greenhouse, watching them. She grinned at him for a moment, then thrust out her thumb triumphantly. He was certain he was blushing when he turned back to Jessica.

'Yeah,' he told her. 'Looks like it.'

THE END

The Night Listener
Armistead Maupin

'HIS MOST MATURE, MELLOW AND MOVING NOVEL YET'
Independent

Gabriel Noone is a writer whose late-night radio stories have
brought him into the homes of millions. Noone is in the midst
of a painful separation from his lover of ten years, when a
publisher sends him the memoir of a thirteen-year-old boy who
suffered horrific abuse at the hands of his parents.

Pete Lomax is not only a brave and gifted diarist but a devoted
listener to Noone's show. When Noone phones the boy to offer
encouragement, it soon becomes clear that Pete sees in this
heartsick, middle-aged storyteller the loving father he's always
wanted. Thus begins an extraordinary friendship that only
grows deeper as the boy's health deteriorates, freeing Noone to
unlock his innermost feelings.

Then, out of the blue, troubling new questions arise, exploding
Noone's comfortable assumptions and causing his ordered
existence to spin wildly out of control. As he walks the
tightrope between truth and illusion, he is finally forced to
confront all his relationships – familial, romantic and erotic.

'ELEGANTLY CONCEIVED AND EXECUTED, *THE NIGHT
LISTENER* MARKS A LONG OVERDUE RETURN TO FICTION
BY ONE OF AMERICA'S BEST-LOVED WRITERS . . . A REAL
PAGE-TURNER'
Sunday Telegraph

'*A MYSTERY STUDDED WITH ELEGANT TWISTS AND
TURNS*'
New Tork Times Book Review

'*A COMPLEX MEDITATION ON THE FRAILTY OF FACT AND
PERSPECTIVE*'
The Australian

'*A TREMENDOUS, HUGELY SATISFYING READ*'
Time Out

'*ABSORBING, SOPHISTICATED, FUNNY AND TOUCHING*'
Sunday Times

0 552 14240 9

BLACK SWAN

'THE "TALES OF THE CITY" SEQUENCE HAS BEEN ONE
OF THE LITERARY *MENUS PLAISIRS* OF THE LAST
DECADE . . . MAUPIN, WITH ALL HIS ELEGANCE AND
CHARM, HAS FOUND A PLACE AMONG THE CLASSICS'
Jonathan Keates, *Observer*

TALES OF THE CITY
'San Francisco is fortunate in having a chronicler as witty
and likeable as Armistead Maupin'
Independent
0 552 99876 1

MORE TALES OF THE CITY
'Charming and compelling'
Literary Review
0 552 99877 X

FURTHER TALES OF THE CITY
'(Maupin) is the perfect chronicler of the moral, political,
sexual and social fluxes of the world'
City Limits
0 552 99878 8

BABYCAKES
'I love Maupin's books for very much the same qualities that
make me love the novels of Dickens'
Christopher Isherwood
0 552 99879 6

SIGNIFICANT OTHERS
'A book of enormous humanity. It is funny, wise,
melancholy, topical and a terrific read'
Simon Brett, *Punch*
0 552 99880 X

SURE OF YOU
'I know I was not the only one who was up until two in the
morning, promising myself to stop after just one more
chapter'
David Feinberg, *New York Times Book Review*
0 552 99881 8

BLACK SWAN

Maybe the Moon
Armistead Maupin

'WONDERFUL, FUNNY, POIGNANT AND GUTSY . . . YOU
CAN FEEL THE AUTHOR'S HUGE AND HURT AND
LOVING HEART BEAT ON EVERY PAGE'
Anne Lamott, *Mademoiselle*

All of thirty-one inches tall, Cadence (Cady) Roth is a true
survivor in a town where – as she says – 'you can die of
encouragement'. Her early leading role as a lovable elf in a
smash-hit American film proved a major disappointment
since moviegoers never saw the face behind the rubber mask
she had to wear. After a decade of hollow promises from the
Industry, she is still waiting for the miracle that will make
her a star.

Through a series of bracingly frank journal entries,
Armistead Maupin tracks his spunky heroine across the
saffron-hazed wasteland of Los Angeles – from her
infrequent meetings with agents and studio moguls to her
regular, harrowing encounters with small children, large
dogs and human ignorance. Then one day a lanky piano
player saunters into Cady's life, unleashing heady new
emotions, and she finds herself going for broke, shooting the
moon with a scheme so hare-brained and daring that it
might just succeed . . .

Maybe the Moon, Armistead Maupin's first novel since his
bestselling *Tales of the City* sextet, is the tale of an outsider
told from the inside. It is a work that speaks to the resilience
of the human spirit.

'DELIGHTS, AMUSES, MOVES AND ANGERS YOU WITH
THE LIGHTEST OF TOUCHES. IT IS, AS MIGHT BE SAID
OF CADENCE HERSELF, A SMALL MASTERPIECE'
Simon Callow, *Vogue*

'*MAYBE THE MOON* WILL DISAPPOINT ONLY THE
ENVIOUS. RICH, MOVING, SEXY AND FUNNY, IT ALSO
HAS A PLEASINGLY ANGRY STREAK'
Patrick Gale, *Daily Telegraph*

0 552 99875 3

BLACK SWAN

A LIST OF ARMISTEAD MAUPIN TITLES AVAILABLE FROM BLACK SWAN

THE PRICES SHOWN BELOW WERE CORRECT AT THE TIME OF GOING TO PRESS. HOWEVER TRANSWORLD PUBLISHERS RESERVE THE RIGHT TO SHOW NEW PRICES ON COVERS WHICH MAY DIFFER FROM THOSE PREVIOUSLY ADVERTISED IN THE TEXT OR ELSEWHERE.

All Transworld titles are available by post from:

Bookpost, PO Box 29, Douglas, Isle of Man IM99 1BQ

Credit cards accepted. Please telephone 01624 836000, fax 01624 837033 or Internet http://www.bookpost.co.uk or e-mail: bookshop@enterprise.net for details.

Free postage and packing in the UK. Overseas customers allow £1 per book (paperbacks) and £3 per book (hardbacks).